PROMISE ME

Colin fastened his gaze on hers. "You must swear to me you won't go out alone."

"But—"

"Swear." Colin grabbed her shoulders. Her green eyes stared into his, and he knew he was lost. He might have believed her a thief, but he no longer cared if she was. "I don't want to see you die. I can't let you die."

In the next moment, he pulled her to him. He kissed her as if he were trying to solder her to him. Her heat burned his lips, tantalized him, left him aching for more. She trembled in his arms, giving rise to every protective emotion in his breast. He would save her . . . No, she would save him.

She pulled free. "We mustn't."

The ragged desire in her voice fanned his desire into a raging conflagration. "Yes, I must."

<u>BOOK YOUR PLACE ON OUR WEBSITE</u> <u>AND MAKE THE</u> <u>READING CONNECTION!</u>

We've created a customized website just for our very special readers, where you can get the inside scoop on everything that's going on with Zebra, Pinnacle and Kensington books.

When you come online, you'll have the exciting opportunity to:

- View covers of upcoming books
- Read sample chapters
- Learn about our future publishing schedule (listed by publication month *and author*)
- Find out when your favorite authors will be visiting a city near you
- Search for and order backlist books from our online catalog
- Check out author bios and background information
- Send e-mail to your favorite authors
- Meet the Kensington staff online
- Join us in weekly chats with authors, readers and other guests
- Get writing guidelines
- AND MUCH MORE!

Visit our website at
http://www.kensingtonbooks.com

YOURS ALWAYS

Gabriella Anderson

ZEBRA BOOKS
Kensington Publishing Corp.
http://www.kensingtonbooks.com

ZEBRA BOOKS are published by

Kensington Publishing Corp.
850 Third Avenue
New York, NY 10022

All Kensington titles, imprints and distributed lines are available at special quantity discounts for bulk purchases for sales promotion, premiums, fund-raising, educational or institutional use.

Special book excerpts or customized printings can also be created to fit specific needs. For details, write or phone the office of the Kensington Special Sales Manager: Kensington Publishing Corp., 850 Third Avenue, New York, NY 10022. Attn. Special Sales Department. Phone: 1-800-221-2647.

First Printing: February 2004
10 9 8 7 6 5 4 3 2 1

Printed in the United States of America

To Joe Raschke
You asked for this one, so here it is. And now for the mushy part . . . If one's wealth were based on one's friends, we'd be filthy, stinking rich with just you.

Chapter 1

London, July, 1854

Colin Savernake glanced at the pile of correspondence on his desk and let out a puff of air in disgust. Most were requests from spoiled society matrons for his help in finding their lost lap dogs. A few were slightly more intriguing—cheating spouses, untrustworthy servants, checking the circumstances of potential suitors—but even these didn't hold much interest for him. The rest were demands for money—the price of success.

He flipped through the letters with growing disdain. The last noteworthy case he'd taken on had involved an attempt on the life of the Earl of Tamberlake, but that affair had resolved itself before he could present his evidence to his lordship. Didn't matter. He had received his pay and proven his ability with that one.

A sheet of parchment caught his attention. *Maxwell Jenkins, Solicitor.* The name wasn't familiar. He opened the letter and scanned the contents. Lord Stanhope was dead and had left him a bequest. A bequest? From Lord Stanhope? Odd. He hadn't known the man really. Only that Lord Stanhope and his father had been close friends. And Savernake didn't have much to do with his father. Still, an unexpected bequest was enough to hold his attention.

He glanced at the day's schedule. His afternoon could be free if he shifted his appointments. He scribbled a note to the solicitor, sealed it, and set it to the side for the moment. Folding his hands behind his head, he leaned back. Perhaps the morning's correspondence had brought him something intriguing after all.

A few hours later, Savernake sat in a spoon-backed chair in the solicitor's office. The burgundy-striped wallpaper with the walnut wainscoting was impressive. Stuffy, perhaps, but impressive. He should consider it for his own office. Perhaps it would discourage the people who tried to hire him for the more frivolous cases.

"Mr. Savernake," said Mr. Jenkins. Mr. Jenkins wasn't an imposing man, but his eyes looked keen with intelligence. He polished the lenses of his spectacles and placed them on the bridge of his nose. "I trust you are here about the bequest."

"I *am* curious. Lord Stanhope died several months ago."

"Lord Stanhope was very particular about his bequests." The solicitor pushed an envelope across the desktop. "His will specified when I could contact you."

Colin raised an eyebrow. He reached for the envelope.

"Before you read that, I am to tell you Lord Stanhope left you a small farm in Cheshire near Chester. But there is a stipulation."

"A stipulation?"

"Yes. A task you are to perform. I believe Lord Stanhope explained everything in the letter."

"And if I refuse?"

"The farm will revert to the present earl. You have one week to decide." Mr. Jenkins gathered his papers.

Colin recognized the gesture of dismissal. He took the envelope and stood. "Thank you for your time, Mr. Jenkins. I shall let you know." He left the office.

After climbing into his carriage, he tapped on the roof. "Home."

"Yes, sir."

The coach lurched into motion. Colin broke the seal on the envelope and pulled out three pages.

Dear Colin,

I reserve the right to call you by your first name. I've known you since you were a boy, after all. Besides, there's very little you can do about it now.

Strange sense of humor, thought Colin. He read on.

I imagine you are surprised to receive this. And knowing you, you won't relax until you know why. Now that question is easy to answer.

I need your help.

Colin stopped reading in surprise. Stanhope was dead. How could he possibly help him?

Your abilities as a man of affairs are renowned. Then again, I always knew you were bright. And you have made the best use of the education your father gave you. You can thank him for that, if nothing else. Your father and I never did agree on how he raised you. I believed keeping you in his house and subjecting you to the disdain of his wife and your half siblings a mistake. But you turned out a fine gentleman, so perhaps I was wrong.

He wasn't. Colin wondered how the man had gained such an accurate picture of his childhood.

But back to your question. (Assuming, of course, you had one.) Not long ago, I met a gentleman with a problem. Mr. William Hobblesby, Esquire, of York has been plagued with petty theft on his estate. When I heard of his troubles, I at once thought of you. Perhaps you deem this task beneath you, especially after the work you did for the PM. (Don't ask me how I know. I can't tell you now in any case. Besides, it's too late for repercussions.) But consider it a favor for an old friend.

Colin ran his fingers through his hair. Unless the Prime Minister himself told Stanhope, Colin didn't know how Stanhope could have discovered he had worked for the man. But Stanhope was right. It didn't matter now.

I have arranged for my former butler and housekeeper, Fletcher and Mrs. Pennyfeather, to be employed by Mr. Hobblesby. They are aware of Mr. Hobblesby's problem and are ready to help you. You will find them useful in many ways. Fletcher and Pennyfeather had another task to complete for me before they could work for the squire, but since you are reading this letter, that task is done, and my solicitor has been allowed to contact you.

Which explained the delay between Stanhope's death and news of the bequest. Colin frowned in concentration. If he wasn't mistaken, he had met Fletcher when he worked for Lord Tamberlake. Obviously, the first task had had something to do with the earl.

Think of the farm in Cheshire as payment for your services. (I trust Jenkins has informed you of your bequest.) It includes a house and one hundred acres of land. At present there is a caretaker and farmer who watch the property, and you may keep them on at your discretion should you choose to accept my offer.

Colin paused for a moment. He would have to look into this farm before he answered. If it was a derelict, it wouldn't cover his expenses. Another consequence of success—he could set his rates where he wanted. He resumed his reading.

I have a final reason for singling you out for this bequest. You have enjoyed making your living off the problems of the ton. *You most likely see it as some sort of ironic justice.*

Lord Stanhope was full of surprises. Colin had to admit he did take a sort of perverse pride in out-thinking his social superiors.

I'm not hoping to change your mind about the aristocracy, but I hope you will think more kindly about this particular member of the ton. *Not all of us are self-centered and spoiled. There are actually members of aristocratic families who are noble not only in name. Don't let your father and his family sour you on everybody. Don't let your bitterness toward your father blind you to the goodness and beauty you might find.*

Jenkins has the rest of the information should you decide to accept the bequest. Good luck to you, Colin. I would have been proud to call you son.

Yours,

Lord Stanhope

Colin folded the sheets and tucked them back into the envelope. What a strange man Lord Stanhope must have been. And what a pity he hadn't had the chance to know the man better. Stanhope was correct. The resentment he felt toward his father did color his view of the world, but he wasn't about to change now. He enjoyed his cynicism, and his jaded view of the *ton* had served him well in his line of work. He had no qualms in charging the spoiled members of society dearly for their petty problems.

Still, he wasn't sure he wanted to embark upon this little adventure. His business had brought him all the money he could want and more than enough repute. He lived well, and could afford to be choosy. On the other hand, he had nothing to keep him in London either. Perhaps a stay in York would be just the thing.

Before his coach reached home, he had decided. Even if the farm wasn't worth twopence, he would take on Squire Hobblesby's problem.

Two weeks later, Colin stood on the platform of Middle Hutton in Yorkshire. His two trunks stood beside him. He looked around at the near empty platform.

"Mr. Savernake?"

Colin turned to see a tall man with thick arms gazing at him. "Yes."

The man snatched his cap from his head. An unruly thatch of red hair sprung out of his scalp. "I'm Joe. The squire sent me to fetch you. These your things?"

"They are."

"Right." Joe lifted one of the trunks and hefted it over his shoulder as if it were no more than a sack of potatoes. "This way to the wagon."

Lifting his satchel, Colin followed the burly man to a simple wooden wagon.

"Seat up front's the most comfortable." Joe dropped the trunk into the back. "You can climb up whilst I get t'other."

Arching an eyebrow, Colin climbed onto the bench up front. The plank was hard, but he supposed it would suffice until they reached the manor. The horses attached to the front of the wagon looked more capable of strength than speed. He thought of the carriage and horses he kept in London and wondered what sort of reaction they would garner here. Settling his satchel at his feet, he shifted on the wooden plank. The new spot was no more comfortable than the last.

Joe returned carrying the other trunk with as much ease as the first. He placed it next to the other, then climbed up beside Colin. The wagon rocked as he settled himself onto the wooden plank.

"Git up, now." Joe clicked his tongue and shook the reins. The two horses stepped forward.

"How far to the manor?" asked Colin.

"'Bout two miles," said Joe, his gaze never wavering from the road.

"What do you do for Mr. Hobblesby?" Couldn't hurt to begin his questioning now.

"Who's Mr. Hobbles—ohhh, you mean the squire?" Joe sucked in air between his teeth. It whistled. "I do whatever needs to be done."

"How long have you worked for the squire?"

"Always. I was born at the Grange. Me and me brother, Bob. My pa worked for the squire's father and me grandpa afore that."

The man was loyal to the Hobblesby family, that much was clear. Colin looked at the corded muscle on the man's forearm. He wasn't a small man himself, but he wouldn't like to tangle with strength born of years of hard labor. He decided not to pursue his questions until later.

The wagon turned off the main road. Colin gazed down the long drive to the sprawling manor house owned by William Hobblesby. The house had all the charm of a man trying to appear more important than he was. Its two-story facade jutted up between two single-story wings as if it were throwing out its chest. The gray stone of the wings contrasted with the red brick of the main house. A row of gables under the roof gave evidence to a third story, and a castle turret on one end tried to give the impression of age. Colin was sure it was built at the same time as the rest of the house.

A series of outbuildings lay beyond the main house. He recognized the horse stables, but he was hopeless at guessing the reason for the rest of the buildings. A sheep shed, perhaps, or a cow byre. Or both. He would find out soon enough.

"I'll drop you at the front door, then drive your things around back," said Joe.

"Thank you," said Colin. In the next moment, Colin grabbed on to the seat as the wagon descended into the small valley that held Heatherstone Grange. Deep ruts ran through the dirt road, sometimes catching the wheels and tilting the wagon. The trunks shifted in the back, but neither Joe nor the horses seemed aware of the precarious condition. When they reached the front door, Colin leaped from his seat, clutching his satchel to him.

"Eager to get here, are you? Aye, 'tis a fine place indeed." Joe nodded his big head, then clicked his tongue. At the familiar command, the horses moved again, pulling the wagon around the house.

Colin stared after the wagon. Thank goodness his business didn't require many trips up that drive. He turned to the house and found the knocker.

A few moments later the door opened. Fletcher stood in the doorway. "Mr. Savernake. How very good to see you again, sir. Welcome to Heatherstone Grange."

The man looked no different than the last time Colin saw him. Fletcher's graying hair was cut in uneven tufts, giving him the look of a hedgehog. The thick spectacles hid the butler's expression well, and a definite hump protruded from his back. Fletcher must have been an extraordinary butler. Colin couldn't see such a man serving the nobility. Lord Stanhope must have trusted him indeed. "Good day, Mr. Fletcher."

Fletcher took the satchel from him. "I'll have this put in your room. The rest of your things . . . ?"

"Joe took them to the back of the house."

"Excellent. I'll see they are unpacked for you. Now if you would follow me. The squire has been expecting you. He is quite excited about your stay. But at the moment his gout is troubling him, so he cannot walk." Fletcher left the satchel in the front hall as he led Colin to the parlor. Opening the door, Fletcher said, "Mr. Savernake is here, sir."

"Come in, come in," boomed a hearty voice.

Colin walked into the room as Fletcher closed the door behind him. A white-haired man occupied a chair in front of the fire. His heavily bandaged foot was propped up on a stool. His round face showed the years of exposure to the sun and elements of his holdings. Although his clothes were fashionable, his great belly stuck out over his trousers. "Forgive me for not rising. Damned gout has struck me down at the moment."

"I quite understand, sir."

"So you're going to help me with my little problem, are you? Lord Stanhope was good to remember me. Sorry to hear about the poor fellow. Just goes to show you, a title doesn't guarantee you long life. Give me the healthy outdoor existence anytime."

Colin wasn't about to point out that Hobblesby was suffering from gout, which had little to do with a healthy outdoor existence and everything to do with a rich diet. "Have you told anyone why I am here?"

"No. Your letter said not to. Though I don't like keeping secrets from my family."

"I understand, sir, but I think it would be best to present me as your secretary. That way I can have access to people and things without arousing the suspicion of the person or persons stealing from you."

Hobblesby nodded. "Smart man. I never would have thought of it. But surely I can tell my son and daughter."

"It would be better not to."

"My betrothed, then?"

That information surprised Colin. "No, not her, either. You're engaged?"

"Yes," said Hobblesby, and he let out a robust laugh. "To a sweet young thing. Daughter of an earl, you know. If you can't take advantage of being the richest man in the county, why bother to have money?" He laughed again.

Colin smiled in return, but found little humor in the situation. She was probably the spoiled daughter of some impoverished nobleman, and unable to snag someone in the *ton,* she had to settle on an older rich farmer.

The door to the salon opened. "There you are, my dear," said Hobblesby. "We were just speaking of you."

"Nothing bad I hope," said the woman.

Colin turned and felt his stomach drop. The tall, graceful figure of the woman filled his gaze. She was younger—much younger—than he'd expected. Maybe twenty-two, twenty-three. He glanced at the squire. The old man had to be nearing sixty. Colin looked back. She was beautiful. Her blond hair was coiled around her head, and her cheeks reminded him of ripe peaches. But her eyes fascinated him. They were a green he had once seen in an emerald.

Hobblesby waved her over. "Mr. Colin Savernake, this is my betrothed, Lady Anthea Fortesque, the daughter of the late earl."

Chapter 2

Anthea turned to the visitor and almost dropped the cup of tea she carried. His dark good looks startled her. His hair, nearly black, framed a strong visage, and he stood a good head above her. She looked up at him and nearly gasped. His eyes were a dark gray-green, like that of the sea on a stormy day.

The man stared at her for a moment, then looked away, but not before she noticed a hint of distaste in his mien. She couldn't imagine how she had earned such disgust.

She cleared her throat before she spoke. "How do you do, Mr. Savernake?"

"Very well, thank you, Lady Anthea." He bowed to her.

"To what do we owe this visit?" she asked.

"Didn't I tell you, my dear? Savernake is my new secretary," said Hobblesby.

Her eyes widened. "A secretary? I didn't know you had need of one, William. Have you been displeased with the way I've handled your correspondence?"

"Not at all, my dear, but soon you shall have too much to do with the planning of the wedding to worry about my petty concerns. Savernake is here to help. Besides, a man of my position should have a secretary, don't you think?" Hobblesby smiled at her as if he were awaiting her approval.

Hobblesby had no need of a secretary. She almost winced at the thought of the money that would go for the man's salary, but she bit back any negative reply. "Then he is most welcome, I'm sure. I've brought you your tea." She handed him the cup.

Hobblesby twisted his lips, but took the cup. "Bah. I'd prefer a good whiskey."

"You know you aren't allowed," she said, drawing on her patience.

Facing Savernake, Hobblesby said, "They treat me like an invalid. They don't realize I've looked after myself for over fifty years."

"Yes, that's why your gout is troubling you now," said Anthea in an even tone. She turned to the younger man. "May I bring you some tea, Mr. Savernake?"

"Offer the boy something stronger. Just because I can't enjoy myself doesn't mean he shouldn't."

"Tea would be fine, thank you," said Savernake.

Anthea nodded and left the room. She paused outside the door and leaned against the wall. Drawing in several deep breaths, she reached for the medallion that hung from a ribbon around her neck. The familiar feel of the cool metal in her fingers calmed her. Mr. Savernake disturbed her more than she cared to admit, and he didn't seem to like her for some reason.

She pushed herself off the wall and headed for the kitchen. How odd that the squire never mentioned he was hiring a secretary. Mr. Hobblesby wasn't known for acting without getting advice first, or at least boasting about his latest acquisition.

Anthea opened the door into the kitchen. "I need another cup."

"Did he break the first?" asked Violet. Her sister set aside the pen and rose from the large wooden table. She retrieved a cup and saucer from a shelf.

"No. He has a guest." Anthea pulled a tray from a cupboard and set it on the table. "Hobblesby has hired himself a secretary."

Violet laughed. "My, my, the squire is becoming important."

"Stop, Vi. He is an important man here in the county." Anthea filled the creamer and the sugar bowl.

"I'm sorry." Her sister said nothing else, but gave her a small smile.

Anthea hated the pity she saw in her sister's look. She laid a cloth on the tray and placed the cup and saucer on it. "I just wonder why he thinks he needs a secretary. It isn't as if the squire has such a busy schedule."

"Perhaps he plans to after you're wed."

"Where? Here in the thriving social climate of Middle Hutton? Hobblesby hasn't ever traveled more than ten miles from Heatherstone Grange." Anthea filled the cup with tea and placed a spoon beside it. "How's your story coming?"

"I'm stuck. The characters haven't told me what happens next."

Anthea lifted the tray. "They haven't told you?"

"I know you don't believe me when I say things like that." Violet shrugged. "I don't think they liked it when I forced them to go into the woods."

Anthea shook her head. "I hope they tell you what's wrong soon." She took the tray back to the parlor.

As she entered the room, both men looked up at her. Once again she noticed the disdain in Mr. Savernake's gaze before he rose to his feet.

"Sorry I can't get up, my dear," said Hobblesby.

"I would be angry if you did." She placed the tray on a side table and turned to Savernake. "Your tea."

"Thank you, Lady Anthea."

"Cream or sugar?"

"Just a little cream please."

She splashed a few drops into the tea and handed him the cup. His fingers brushed hers, and for a moment she found his touch tickled her all the way to her stomach. An urge to snatch her hand away overwhelmed her, but she chided herself instead. She had no room for imagination in her life, and she wouldn't act on some foolish impulse. Her father had had impulses enough to last her entire life.

"Where's my son?" asked Hobblesby. "I want Savernake to meet Dougal."

"I believe he is in the byre," she said. "One of your cows is calving, and she's having a difficult time."

"Damn this gout. It's keeping me from my work. I should be there, not he. Heatherstone Grange is *my* farm."

"Your son is only helping you while you're indisposed. He's not planning a coup," she said in the tone of a mother scolding a child.

"He's a good lad to help, but the Grange will be his soon enough." Hobblesby frowned, then he winked at her. "But not too soon, eh, my dear?"

She smiled, but said nothing.

"When is the wedding?" asked Savernake.

"In September. My wife died fifteen years ago, so it's high time I remarry. Not that my children need a mother now." Hobblesby chuckled at his own joke. "My sons are men, and my daughter is married off and awaiting a child of her own. But I've got a few good years left in me. No need to spend them alone."

"No. No need at all," said Savernake.

She didn't know why he glanced at her. Nobody would mistake her marriage as a love match. Hobblesby was twice her age. More, actually. But he was a kind and generous man, and she would wed him.

"Well, don't disturb Dougal then. Savernake can meet him after the calf is born. But I want him to meet everyone soon. Tell that new housekeeper . . . Blast, what is her name? Something to do with money. Poundworthy? Shillingfree?"

"Pennyfeather," said Anthea.

"Right. Too hard to remember. I may have her change it if she wants to stay. Tell that Pennyfeather woman that I want my children to dine with me tomorrow, so she's to prepare a grand meal. Will you write the invitation to my daughter?"

"Of course. What time do you want her here?" Anthea crossed to a small writing table.

"If you will excuse me, Squire Hobblesby, you did hire me as your secretary. Perhaps I should write the invitation?" suggested Savernake.

Hobblesby stared at him for a moment, then barked out a laugh. He gave the man a broad wink. "Of course. I quite forgot. Didn't think you'd actually want to work on your first day. Anthea, my dear, you handle the more important things now. My *secretary* will write the invitation."

She didn't understand the squire's amusement. "If you have nothing else for me to do today, I think I'll go home. May I take some of our lunch to Mother?"

"Certainly. I'll see you tomorrow. And bring your sister again. Now that Savernake is here, she'll help balance out the table."

"I've left strict orders with Mrs. Pennyfeather,

William. You're not to step on your foot while I'm gone." She crossed to her betrothed and kissed him on his bald pate. "I'll give Pennyfeather your message before I leave."

"There's my good girl."

As she left the parlor, she heard Hobblesby say, "You must admit I am a lucky man, Savernake. The prettiest girl in the county, and she's to be my bride."

"But have you ever asked yourself why?" came Savernake's response.

Hobblesby laughed. "Because I'm the richest man in the county."

Anthea didn't want to hear more. She hurried to the kitchen. Her sister was bent over her pages, writing with great speed. "I take it your characters are no longer silent."

"What? Oh, no. Now they won't shut up. Wait a moment until I finish this sentence." Violet wrote on the paper, drew a line through something she had scribbled above, then finished the line. She put her pen down next to the ink well. "There."

"I'm glad you had some success today." Anthea picked up a basket and started to fill it with food.

"Are we going home now?" asked Violet with disappointment in her voice.

"Yes. I have nothing left to do here, and I'm sure Mother needs help with the twins."

Violet glanced at her pages with longing. "I suppose Leticia and the earl can wait. I can't get anything done with all the noise at home."

"You've changed her name again." Anthea covered the now-full basket with a towel.

"Gertrude was not the right name for a long lost

heiress." Violet grabbed an apple from a dish and bit into it.

"Well, you can return with me tomorrow. The squire has invited his children for dinner, and he wants you to complete the table."

"He's never needed me before."

"He's never had a secretary at his table before." She hooked the basket over her arm. "Have you seen Mrs. Pennyfeather?"

"I'm right here, my lady." Mrs. Pennyfeather entered the kitchen. She was a striking woman, no longer young, but Anthea couldn't call her old either. The housekeeper was younger than the squire. "Did you need something, my lady?"

"Mr. Hobblesby asked me to tell you his family is coming for dinner tomorrow. My sister and I will also be in attendance, as well as the squire's new secretary."

"Leave it to me," said Mrs. Pennyfeather. "Are you and your sister going home now?"

"Yes."

"Please wait a moment." The housekeeper disappeared into the pantry and returned a moment later holding a large fruit tart. She laid it atop the covered basket. "I made an extra one. I'm sure the twins will enjoy this."

Anthea saw her sister's face grow red, but Anthea was beyond embarrassment at the gift. No sense in refusing a treat her family would enjoy because of some misplaced pride. "Thank you, Mrs. Pennyfeather."

Anthea led her sister outside, and they started the walk home.

"Did you have to accept the tart?" asked Violet.

"Would you rather the twins complain of hunger again?"

Violet cast down her gaze. "No, of course not. It's just so humbling."

"Mrs. Pennyfeather made us a gift, that's all." Anthea shifted the basket to her other arm so she could hook arms with her sister.

"Yes, but have you noticed how many gifts Mrs. Pennyfeather has made us in the past weeks?"

"I have." Anthea sighed. "She's been very kind."

Violet frowned. "I do so hate being poor."

She allowed herself a chuckle. "It's not as if we have a choice in the matter."

"I know, but I hate it all the same. Our clothes are in tatters, we go hungry at times, and our house is cold." Violet let out a loud puff of air. "If I could only sell one of my books, then you wouldn't have to marry the squire."

"Yes, I would. One book isn't going to keep us clothed, fed, and warm for long. When I marry, Mother will have one less mouth to feed, and I shall be able to help you all as well."

"You can't tell me you want to marry that old man." Violet shot her sister a look of disbelief.

"Enough, Violet. The squire is a good man, and I am quite happy to be marrying him."

A stubborn expression covered Violet's face.

"Not another word. Squire Hobblesby will be my husband, and I won't have you speaking ill of him."

Violet unhooked her arm from hers and fell silent. Anthea was grateful for the peace. In truth, she wasn't as eager to wed the squire as she told her sister, and she was afraid if she thought too much about it, she might become too nervous to carry through with the marriage. Her family needed her help, and the squire was their only hope.

If only she hadn't seen a man as young and handsome as that Mr. Savernake.

From where had that thought sprung? She hadn't exchanged more than a few words with the secretary, and the man hadn't exactly warmed to her either. For all she knew, he was a beast with manners worse than any farmer.

But she did wish he wasn't so handsome.

They continued their walk in silence. Anthea had no desire to ease Violet's anger, but neither did she have the desire to weaken her sister's dreams. Someone in their family should be allowed to dream. They turned down the small lane that led to Skettle Cottage. The shabby stone house looked better than when they moved in last summer, but it needed many more repairs before it was truly habitable. She supposed she should be grateful to the new Earl Fortesque for providing them with a home at all, but her generosity didn't extend that far.

She could hear the twins' shouts from here. She looked around, hesitated, then looked up. Sure enough. They were in a tree. "Come down, at once. I just mended those pinafores."

"But, Thea," said Daisy, "we're just having a little fun."

"And we've finished our chores," said Rose.

"Doesn't matter. There's precious little left to mend in your clothes, and I'll not have you tearing them again. If you won't climb down, I shan't give you any of the fruit tart Mrs. Pennyfeather sent."

"Fruit tart?" asked Rose.

"Strawberry?" asked Daisy.

"You'll just have to come down and see." Anthea held the basket at her side so the girls couldn't peek into it from their perch.

The twins scrambled out of the tree and rushed to their sister's side. "It *is* strawberry," said Daisy.

"We'll carry it for you, Thea," said Rose.

"I think not. You'd carry it off and eat it all before supper." Anthea looked at their pinafores and shook her head. The aprons were streaked with dirt. "At least you didn't rip them this time."

The girls scurried up the path toward the cottage. "Mother, Thea's home," yelled Daisy.

"And she's brought us a strawberry tart," shouted Rose.

"What? Did you forget me because I didn't bring you something to eat?" asked Violet with her hands on her hips.

"Violet's here, too, Mother," said Rose, and ducked away from the playful swipe her sister sent her way.

Her mother appeared in the doorway. Anthea waved. Mother looked so tired, and lines of worry and fatigue that had only appeared in the last year etched her face. But Mother smiled at her two eldest daughters, then turned to the eight-year-olds. "Unless you wash up, you won't have any supper, much less strawberry tart."

The girls scampered away to the pump. Anthea reached her mother and handed her the basket. "I brought some leftovers."

Her mother sighed. "Thank you, Anthea."

"Any word today?"

"No. It seems no one wants an elderly teacher with five daughters, even if she can speak fluent French." Lady Fortesque took the basket to the small kitchen.

"Perhaps I should apply for the job of a companion," said Violet.

"Being at the beck and call of some cranky old woman wouldn't suit someone of your temperament,

Violet." Her mother placed the basket on the table and began to unload it.

"My temperament? There's nothing wrong with my temperament," said Violet with a scowl.

"Don't worry, Mother. I'll be wed soon," said Anthea.

"You know how I feel about that." Lady Fortesque pursed her lips. "That man should be marrying someone my age, not yours."

"Please, Mother, we've already discussed this. Hobblesby is a good man, and it was my decision."

"Yes, but—"

"Mo-ther."

"Very well, I won't say another word." Her mother hugged her. "You'll have a family yourself someday, and then you'll know just how much I love you all."

"Where's Iris?"

Lady Fortesque smiled. "I believe she's hiding in the attic with a book. Fetch her, would you, Anthea? Then we'll eat."

"If the twins are clean."

"There is that of course." Her mother handed plates to Violet. "Set the table, Violet."

"Yes, Mother. See, my temperament is fine." Violet wrinkled her nose at her mother.

Anthea stifled her chuckle as she climbed the stairs to find the last member of their female household.

Chapter 3

Colin looked over the list of items missing from Heatherstone Grange, but he could see no pattern to the thefts. "Anything else?"

"No, although I did misplace my pipe one day." Hobblesby laughed and slapped his thigh. "Not that Thea will let me smoke now. Damn gout."

With a forced smile, Colin nodded his acknowledgment of the squire's humor. Hobblesby seemed to treat the thefts with annoyance more than anger. Colin shuddered to think how little he might have accomplished if he hadn't cornered the squire this morning and started to ask questions. Hobblesby probably would have paraded him about the town, showing him off as his new secretary.

Colin returned to his notes. The first item, a diamond bracelet, had disappeared a little over six months ago. The bracelet had belonged to Hobblesby's deceased wife, and Hobblesby had intended to give it to his new wife when they married. The local constable discovered nothing, but Colin didn't fault the man. A bracelet was too easy to dispose of, especially if one pried the diamonds from their settings and sold them one by one. Colin had to assume the article of jewelry was long gone.

But the next item puzzled him. How did one steal an entire wagonload of woolen fabric? Better said, why? The wool had come from Hobblesby's own textile mill and wasn't of the finest quality either. Simple stammel. Then one of a draught pair of oxen. Then a silver set from the era of George II.

He required little reasoning to deduce the thief had to come from within Heatherstone Grange or at least had to be familiar with the squire and his house. Colin hadn't met most of the household yet. He tapped his pen against the paper. "Who are the members of your household?"

"Myself, of course. My son, Dougal, moved into a field hand's cottage just after I announced my betrothal about eight months ago. I imagine he didn't want to see the newlyweds." Hobblesby chuckled again. "But the house is his as well."

"And your daughter?"

"Jane? She and her husband have a house in town, but they are always welcome here. I have rooms for them." Hobblesby pointed at him with his cane. "You don't think they're doing this, do you?"

"I don't know." Colin paused. "So your daughter doesn't live here."

"No. "

"What's her husband's name?"

"Hubert Fanning. He runs one of my mills."

Colin copied the names onto his notes. "Dougal's not married?"

"Hasn't had time to find a girl. My boy works too hard. But I wouldn't be surprised if I have a grandchild or two roaming the village that I know nothing about." The squire grinned, as if enjoying the thought of his son's bastards.

Colin steeled his expression.

Hobblesby continued. "Besides, I found the most eligible woman for miles. We have to be careful of our position in the county. There aren't many suitable women available, and I wouldn't let him marry beneath him. There is the reverend's daughter, but a greater mouse has never existed. And her mother is enough to put one off women for eternity. Thea has sisters, but it would be damned awkward if he wed one of those girls. That would make him my brother-in-law. No, he'll just have to wait for the right girl."

"And your other son is in the army?"

A look of sadness crossed the squire's features. "Not any longer. He was in Burma, fought in the war there, but he was injured. Not before he proved himself a hero, mind you. Saved his captain. The man was an idiot, but that's beside the point. My son has sold his commission and is on his way home now."

"What of your servants and hands?"

"The butler, Fletcher, and the housekeeper, Poundsworth . . . No, damn, what is that woman's name?"

"Pennyfeather?"

"Yes, Pennyfeather. Terrible name. Don't like it." Hobblesby shook his head. "Only they are new. The others have served me for years. In some cases, for generations."

"Ah, yes. I met Joe yesterday."

"Right. He and his brother, Bob, grew up beside my own Dougal and Brody. My wife was Scottish, you know."

"I didn't know." Colin made a few more notations on the paper. Fletcher and Pennyfeather he could exclude from his list of possible thieves, but he couldn't narrow his list further. He added one more name, then looked at the squire. "When did you meet Lady Anthea?"

"She moved here with her family about last July. Her father had died, and the new earl sent them to Skettle Cottage to live. I started inviting the two older girls and their mother to my soirees. Of course, I couldn't help noticing Thea's beauty. Imagine my surprise when she was amenable to my suit." Hobblesby nodded. "Not so surprising actually. There are few good families around here, and none better than mine."

"When did you become betrothed?"

"Must have been in November."

Colin wrote down the dates and looked at his notes. The thefts didn't occur at regular intervals, nor were the squire's losses devastating. It was as if the thief just wanted some extra pocket money rather than to bring harm to the squire. He looked at Hobblesby. "And you haven't told anyone the real reason I'm here?"

"No, although I don't see why—"

"Mr. Hobblesby, the thief is from Heatherstone Grange. If we want to catch him, no one must think I am anything but your secretary. Don't be afraid to give me assignments." Colin stood.

Hobblesby sighed. "Very well. Then perhaps you could fetch Thea for me. I want her to be my hostess tonight, but I can't drive the gig myself." He pointed at his foot.

"My pleasure, Squire." And the drive back would give him the chance to ask her some questions.

He spent the rest of the morning familiarizing himself with the grounds and the house. After eating a light lunch, he made the short drive to the cottage. As he pulled up, his gaze fell over the dwelling. Two of the shutters hung crooked from their hinges, and one window was covered with a board. The disrepair of the small dwelling surprised him, as did the size. He didn't expect the daughter of an earl to live in little more than a hovel. He stopped the rig and tied the reins to a post.

Before he could wonder if he came to the wrong house, two little girls dashed out of the door. They looked alike from the color of their hair to the color of their eyes. Their dresses had seen many days of hard play, and today their pinafores had streaks of dust and mud. These must be Lady Anthea's sisters. He hadn't realized they were twins. In fact, the only difference Colin could see was the smear of what he believed was strawberry jelly at the corner of one girl's mouth. The other had her smear on the tip of her nose.

"Who are you?" asked the one with the strawberry on her nose.

"I'm Colin Savernake. And who are you?"

"I'm Rose, and this is Daisy," said the girl with the jam on her lips.

"Daisy, we're not supposed to speak with strangers," said Rose in a hiss.

"Quite right you are," said Colin, hiding a smile. "Do you know where I may find Lady Anthea?"

Rose pointed up, but Daisy cupped her hands around her mouth and yelled, "Thea, someone's here to see you."

"Daisy, you know better than to shout." A lovely young woman strolled from the doorway. "Do forgive my sisters. They sometimes forget they have manners."

Colin smiled. This woman must be another sister. The resemblance was clear. "They're charming."

"Yes, unless you have to live with them." She held out her hand. "I'm Violet Fortesque."

He took her hand and bowed over it. "Colin Savernake. I'm here to fetch Lady Anthea for the squire."

"But I thought the squire was expecting us for dinner."

"He wants Lady Anthea to serve as his hostess and would like her to come early."

"That means I shall have to walk over by myself." Violet frowned.

"I shall be happy to return for you later."

"Thank you, Mr. Savernake. I do hate walking in my dress shoes."

An older woman came to the doorway. "Violet, would you please find Iris for me? I need her help."

"Yes, Mother," said Violet.

"Who is Iris?" he asked.

"My other sister. Will you excuse me, Mr. Savernake?" Violet returned to the house, passing her mother.

Lady Anthea had four sisters? As he pondered that information, he crossed to the woman. "How do you do, Lady Fortesque?"

The woman smiled at him. "Do I know you?"

"No, my lady, but my employer sent me to fetch Lady Anthea. I am Colin Savernake."

"Oh, you must be the new secretary."

"Yes, my lady. Is Lady Anthea here?"

"Yes. She's on the roof."

"What?" His gaze darted to the shingles. Sure enough, the tip of her head was just visible from this side of the house. A panic gripped him, and without a thought to the dowager countess, he ran around the side to the ladder. "Lady Anthea?"

A few moments later, her face poked over the edge of the roof. "Oh, good day, Mr. Savernake. What brings you here?"

"What are you doing on the roof?" He grasped the edge of the ladder and stepped on the first rung.

"We had a leak. I'm trying to fix it."

He climbed higher. "You shouldn't be up there. It's dangerous."

She let out a sigh. "Well, someone had to fix it. The rain drips right onto the twins' bed."

"You should have called someone." He climbed another rung.

"Do be careful, Mr. Savernake. The ladder is old, and I'm not sure it will hold you."

"You're worried about my safety?" He looked up at her in disbelief and climbed higher.

Crack. The wood split beneath his sole. He grabbed the sides of the ladder and kicked his feet about for purchase. He found another rung. For an instant, he believed he had averted disaster, until he realized the ladder now swung a good foot away from the house, leaning on nothing, standing in mid-air with him at the top. The wood creaked, sounding all too much like ominous laughter.

In the next moment, the ladder tilted toward the earth and splintered around him. He fell, hitting the ground with a loud thump.

"Mr. Savernake," shouted Anthea from the roof.

"Oh, dear," said her mother as she rushed forward.

Colin lay on the ground for a moment, taking a mental inventory of his parts. They all seemed to be there, intact. He couldn't feel this much pain if parts were missing, could he?

Lady Fortesque knelt beside him. "Are you hurt?"

He wanted to give flight to the sarcastic answer that rose in his throat, but he tethered it. With a groan he sat up, wincing with every movement, but at least he had movement. He would have bruises, but nothing was broken.

The woman put her arm around him. "Let me help you into the house. I'm afraid I have no spirits to help you revive, but I could give you a cold glass of water, or perhaps some tea?"

"Water would be fine." He tried to rise. He failed on the first attempt. On the second, he leaned against the older woman and used her strength. This time he succeeded, but he stood on wobbly legs.

"What's happened?" asked Daisy, who ran outside with her twin. Or was it Rose? The girls seemed to have washed their faces.

"Mr. Savernake fell, Daisy," said her mother. "Will you and Rose please go inside and fetch a glass of water for him? I'll take him to the parlor."

"Yes, Mother," the girls said in chorus.

"Do you think you can walk?" asked Lady Fortesque with concern in her voice.

"I believe so." He hoped so, as he *didn't* believe she could carry him. He took a step and stopped. His gaze flew to the roof where he witnessed Anthea swing off the edge and onto a windowsill. "Are you mad?" he shouted as she disappeared through the open glass and into the house.

Lady Fortesque sighed. "I do so hate it when the girls climb that way, but without the ladder . . ."

He glanced at the splinters of wood on the ground.

Lady Fortesque patted his arm. "It doesn't matter now."

Anthea rushed outside in the next moment. "Oh, dear." She ran right past them and straight to the ladder. "Our poor ladder."

She was concerned for the ladder? He wondered if perhaps he hadn't hit his head on the way down.

"Anthea, where is your sympathy for poor Mr. Savernake?" asked her mother in a chiding tone.

"Yes, of course, Mother, but he is standing, isn't he? Whereas our poor ladder . . . isn't." Anthea took a place at his other side and draped his arm across her shoulders. "Come, Mr. Savernake. Let's get you into the house."

After a few steps, Colin was grateful for the help, but he knew his injuries weren't severe. He let himself be led inside by the two women. They placed him on a worn armchair in a small parlor. Lady Fortesque hurried to bring him a cushion, and the twins appeared in the next instant. One of them held a glass of water. As he drank it, he took in the room. The hearth looked as if it hadn't been used in months—too clean. A lopsided sofa stood against one wall. Books replaced a missing leg. No paintings of any sort adorned the walls, and the shelves held only a few books in addition to the ones holding up the end of the sofa.

"Why are you here, Mr. Savernake?" asked Anthea.

"The squire wants you to come over early and take on the duties of hostess tonight," he said.

"But I can't possibly go dressed like this." Anthea glanced down at her dull gray skirt in dismay. Her garb suited a farmer's daughter more than an earl's. "I thought I'd have time to change before Violet and I left for the party."

He eyed her with disdain. "I'm sure Mr. Hobblesby didn't know I'd find you climbing the roof."

"I wasn't climbing the roof; I was fixing it." Ire stirred in her voice.

"You should have called someone to do the work for you."

"Now, why didn't we think of that? Oh, yes, I remember now. It's because I enjoy climbing the roof."

"There's no need for sarcasm, Anthea," said her mother. "Go upstairs now and change your clothes. I will wait with Mr. Savernake."

Anthea opened her mouth as if to protest, but changed her mind, leaving the room without saying another word.

"You must forgive my daughter, Mr. Savernake. She didn't mean to be rude." Lady Fortesque straightened her skirt, which also looked as if it had seen much wear. "The truth is that we couldn't afford to have anyone come to fix the roof, so Anthea volunteered."

Colin scratched his head. The dowager countess's answer created several more questions in his mind, but he didn't know how to phrase them without sounding rude or bringing too much attention to his curiosity.

Violet burst into the room followed at a more sedate pace by a younger girl. *This one must be Iris,* he thought. The middle sister was paler than her siblings, but her girlish face held the promise of the striking beauty of her older sisters.

"Good heavens, Mr. Savernake. Are you hurt?" said Violet.

"Only my pride."

Lady Fortesque smiled at him and took the glass from him. "Don't trouble yourself over Anthea's words. She likes to protect us. Would you care for more water?"

"No, thank you, Lady Fortesque." Colin stretched out his legs and winced.

"Will you be able to return to the Grange, or shall I send Anthea for a wagon?"

"I should be fine. A few bruises and sore muscles is all. I'm quite capable of driving the gig."

Violet glanced at him and sighed. "I can walk tonight. You needn't come to fetch me as you promised."

"And I am quite capable of returning to fetch you, Lady Violet."

"Excellent." Violet smiled.

"Violet, you mustn't impose on Mr. Savernake," said Lady Fortesque.

"No imposition, I assure you, my lady. In fact, I feel quite fit now." He stood and walked a few steps to prove his words, hiding his grimaces with a broad smile.

Anthea returned to the room. She had changed out of the gray skirt into a bright dress with a floral print. The crinoline made the skirt swish as if it were a bell. "I'm ready."

"Then we should leave. The squire is waiting for you." Colin bowed to Lady Fortesque. "Thank you for your help, my lady."

"I did little to earn your thanks," said Anthea's mother. She crossed to her daughter and kissed her forehead. "Don't be too late, my dear."

"Yes, Mother." Anthea shot a quick glance at him, then said in a low voice, "I'll see if I can bring some food . . ."

Colin didn't react, but wondered at her words.

"That would be nice." Her mother patted her arm and turned to her other daughters. "Iris, would you help the girls with their letters while I prepare dinner?"

"Mo-ther," came the protest in chorus from the twins.

Lady Fortesque silenced them with a look. "Violet, you may start dressing for the party."

Violet nodded and left the room.

"But we want to go to the party, too," said Rose. Or was it Daisy?

"When you are old enough, and only if you can write with a legible hand."

"But, Mother . . ." The protest faded as the girls followed their mother from the room.

Colin looked at Anthea. "Shall we?"

"Do you need any help?" she asked.

"No. I'm fine."

Anthea nodded. She walked from the room without waiting for him.

He followed, matching her pace and gritting his teeth against the painfulness of every step.

Chapter 4

"Are you sure you're well enough to drive, Mr. Savernake?" asked Anthea as he handed her into the gig.

Colin climbed in behind her. He picked up the reins. "I won't lie and tell you I'm not in pain, but I think I can handle a gig." He clicked his tongue, and the conveyance rolled into motion.

He waited until they reached the road to begin his questioning. "Have you no brothers?"

"Not a one." Anthea smiled. "Father used to tell us he wouldn't know what to do with one of those dirty smelly boys. 'Wouldn't have one in my house,' he'd say."

"You're the oldest of your sisters?"

"Yes." She turned to him. "What of you?"

"I?" The question surprised him. "I have . . . siblings."

"How many?"

"Three."

"And your parents?"

"My mother died several years ago."

Anthea sighed. "I'm sorry. To lose a parent is terrible. And your father?"

"He lives still." A wave of frustration washed over him. *He* was supposed to ask the questions, not she. "Your father was an earl."

"Yes, Earl Fortesque. The title and our name are the same."

"When did he die?"

"Two years ago. But he was ill for a while before that."

"Why did you move to Middle Hutton? Wouldn't London have been a better choice?"

"Middle Hutton is a nice town."

"I'm sure it is. Forgive me, but with five daughters, two of whom are of marriageable age, your mother should have chosen London to live in. You would have had better prospects there."

"I've found a husband here." Anthea frowned. "Why all this interest in my family?"

"Just curiosity. My greatest flaw, I'm afraid." He fell silent for a moment. She was hiding something, or at least not telling him the entire story. Why would a woman of the *ton* with five daughters move to Middle Hutton? It made no sense unless there was something Anthea wasn't saying.

"What of your father?" she asked suddenly.

"My father?" he repeated, startled by the sudden change of topic.

"What does your father do?"

Colin hesitated. "He does nothing. He's the Earl of Warksbooth."

"But—"

"My mother was not the countess."

"I see." She fell silent.

Heatherstone Grange lay before them. Colin turned the gig down the road leading to the farm and tried not to grimace as the ruts grabbed the wheels and bounced the rig. He didn't ask any further questions. He would have to find someone else willing to talk to him.

They pulled up to the door. "Thank you for the lift, Mr. Savernake," said Anthea. She started to climb out.

He jumped from his seat and winced as his feet hit the ground. Despite the pain, he rushed to her side to help her from the conveyance, but she was on the ground before he reached her.

"Good day, my lady." He gave her a curt bow. When he rose, she had already entered the house.

He stared after her. She hadn't been entirely forthright with him, and the knowledge troubled him. He wondered what she was hiding.

Colin smiled. He turned back to the gig and climbed in, ignoring the pain of his actions. He wasn't known as the most efficient man of affairs for nothing. He knew how and where to make inquiries, and in this case, he would use his abilities to ferret out the answers to his questions.

Anthea set to work with a feeling of annoyance. The torrent of questions from Savernake had left her in a state of disquiet. She wasn't ashamed of her family, but she resented the questions. Why was he so interested in her family and their circumstances anyway?

She had spent the hours until dinner with Mrs. Pennyfeather planning the seating arrangement, then helping to set the table until it looked enough like the parties her mother had thrown caused her to sigh. She didn't like to admit even to herself that she missed their life at Mansfield when Papa was alive.

Anthea took one final look at the table. Nothing was out of place. She had no excuse to delay any longer. Anthea plastered a smile on her face and entered the parlor to greet the guests. The squire was not yet present, but his son and daughter presided over the room. As she expected, they frowned at her arrival. The Reverend Ulster stood by the bookshelf reading the titles. His mother, seated at the center of the sofa like a gray-haired queen, watched the occupants of the room with interest. The reverend's wife hovered near Hobblesby's children. Violet stood beside the hearth. Her look of impatience didn't bode well for the evening. Anthea didn't see Mr. Savernake yet. She straightened her shoulders and crossed to Hobblesby's daughter. "Good evening, Jane."

"Anthea, don't you look charming?" Jane turned to the man beside her. "Hubert, you remember I had a dress like that about five years ago." She turned back to Anthea. "It looks lovely on you."

"Thank you, Jane," said Anthea. Her smile didn't slip a fraction. "How are you feeling?"

"Unwieldy at best." Jane patted her stomach. "Our little heir is eager to come out. I'm sure Father can't wait to meet his first grandchild. Just think, Anthea, you'll be a grandmother before you're a mother."

Hubert laughed behind his hand.

A slow heh-heh-heh came from her left. Anthea turned. Hobblesby's son didn't bother to hide his amusement. "Anthea a grandmother. There's something to think about," the man said. His eyes squinted with his grin until he looked like a prize pig. His beefy fingers played with the signet ring on his right hand. With little difficulty, Anthea could picture him struck by gout in a few years.

"Good evening, Dougal. I didn't have a chance yesterday to ask you how the calf fared."

The big man shrugged. "The calf is fine. You needn't worry. Father's wealth is intact and growing."

"That's not what she meant, and you know it, you big oaf," said Violet. She stepped up beside Anthea and placed her hands on her hips.

Anthea glanced at her sister. Mr. Savernake had arrived and stood behind them. From the expression on his face, he was amused.

As Dougal gazed at Violet, his lips curled into a sneer. "Gad, why are you here?"

"Perhaps he wanted a little class at his table," said Violet.

"Hush, Violet," said Anthea. From the corner of her eye she saw Mrs. Ulster, the vicar's wife, step closer. Anthea fought the urge to sigh in exasperation. This little argument would be all over the village tomorrow. Anthea leaned to her sister. "Take care. Mrs. Ulster is listening."

"That harpy," whispered Violet in return.

Dougal walked past them to Savernake. "You must be the secretary."

"I am," said Savernake.

"One more mouth to feed," said Dougal. "Father is far too generous with his wealth. He doesn't need a wife or a secretary."

"A man of my position has a reputation to uphold." Hobblesby entered the room and limped to his son. "You'll understand when you are in my position. I'll not have you questioning my decisions."

"Sorry, Father. But I don't see why she can't eat at home." He jerked his thumb in Violet's direction.

"Because I need her to complete my table."

"As long as she's not here for me," said Dougal. He moved to the sideboard and poured himself a large brandy.

"Get me one of those, boy," said Hobblesby.

"No, you mustn't," said Anthea. "Remember your gout."

The squire smiled and patted her arm. "You take such good care of me, my dear."

"Of course she does," said Jane. "She doesn't want anything to happen to you before the wedding when she can get her hands on your money."

"Now, now, Jane. You needn't be jealous of Anthea. She's a help to me, and she'll be one to you as well when she's your mother."

"Mother? I'm older than she." Jane's voice squeaked.

Reverend Ulster's mother laughed. "Age doesn't matter. Men can make fools of themselves at any age."

The Reverend Ulster turned red. "Mother, please."

"What? The man is twice her age. Everyone can see that," said Mother Ulster.

"Mother Ulster, I can understand your objection." Hobblesby gave the old woman a grin. "But have you ever seen me as happy? You can thank my Anthea for that."

Anthea's face burned. She shot a glance at Mr. Savernake. He watched her with an intensity she could almost feel, and his scowl marked his disapproval.

Fletcher entered the room on his uneven gait. "Dinner is served."

Hobblesby held out his arm to Anthea. She took it, grateful for the diversion. Dougal took Mrs. Ulster's arm, and Hubert escorted his wife. The Reverend Ulster offered his arm to his mother, leaving Savernake to escort Violet.

As Fletcher served the hare soup, Mrs. Ulster said, "Have you heard Mrs. Paxton's boy is moving to London?"

"What would a nice boy like that want in a dirty place like London?" asked Hobblesby.

"It seems he has developed an affinity for a factory girl. Mrs. Paxton thinks distance should cure him." Mrs. Ulster lifted the spoon to her mouth.

"Now, my dear, it isn't as if the girl is a disease," said the reverend.

"Of course not, but the Paxtons have a nice farm. They must be careful with whom they associate."

Violet opened her mouth, but Anthea shook her head at her sister. Violet ate a spoonful of soup with a frown. Anthea knew her sister was about to protest such blatant discrimination. In truth, Anthea thought her sister was correct, but she had learned that small society held to such distinctions even more strictly than the *ton* in some ways. Frivolity reigned in the *ton* when compared with the rigid class rules of the rural areas.

"Listen carefully, Dougal," said Hobblesby. "Haven't I told you how important the right match is?"

"Yes, Father," said Dougal, but his lips thinned as he sipped his soup.

Fletcher removed the dishes and brought the second course. Over the roast pheasant, the company held forth on the problems of a loose morality. Mrs. Ulster happily provided the names of girls who had married with undue haste. Anthea's gaze sought Savernake's expression at the condemnation of these women. No reaction sat upon his visage. His face was as calm as if he wore a mask.

The meal continued through three more courses. Fletcher served with impeccable manners, even if his appearance was odd. Anthea wondered how the squire had acquired such a capable, if unusual, butler. And without her help. Fletcher and Mrs. Pennyfeather were excellent servants. And now Hobblesby had hired himself a secretary. Perhaps the squire wasn't as primitive as she believed.

Stop it, Anthea. The man is to be your husband. She pushed the food around on her plate, but didn't eat another bite. She couldn't allow herself such thoughts. Hobblesby was a good man. He would make a good husband.

Against her will, her gaze shot to Savernake. Violet laughed at something he said, and a spark of jealousy flared within her. Savernake was a secretary, certainly not a candidate for marriage. But they weren't in circumstances to be choosy any longer. If Violet could find happiness with him . . .

Frowning, she speared a chunk of meat with her fork.

"Is the meat not to your liking, my lady?" asked Fletcher near her elbow.

Anthea drew in a deep breath. "No, everything is delicious. Perhaps it is time for dessert."

"As you wish, my lady." Fletcher took her plate, then cleared the rest from the table. The butler brought a strawberry custard to the table, followed by a variety of fruit tartlets.

Hobblesby reached for two of the tarts, then spooned the custard on top of the pastries. He bit into the rich combination. "Delicious. I swear that Mrs. Birdsworth has done wonders with Cook."

Anthea didn't bother to correct him.

The desserts did look scrumptious, but Anthea had no appetite for the sweets. She watched the others consume the food, but ate no more herself.

At last, the squire pushed himself back from the table. He patted his stomach. "Excellent meal, my dear. I'd say you're ready for the responsibility of running my household."

Anthea nodded her acknowledgment, although she had done little more than choose the dishes.

"I daresay if I ate this way every night, I should soon not fit into my robes," said Reverend Ulster. The rail-thin man patted his belly in a poor imitation of the squire.

"I don't see why Anthea let you eat so much rich food," said Jane. "Such a meal can't help your gout."

"Yes, Anthea, where is your concern now?" added Dougal.

"Leave it alone, you two. I'll not have my eating habits be the subject of discussion." Hobblesby took Anthea's hand and kissed the back of it. "I am allowed to indulge every now and again, eh, my dear?"

She smiled at him, but said nothing.

"Fletcher, let's have that port I ordered." Hobblesby turned to his guests. "A fitting way to welcome Savernake to my house, don't you think?"

Fletcher bowed his head. "Shall I serve tea for the ladies in the parlor, sir?"

"Of course. They won't be interested in our gentleman's discussion."

Fletcher disappeared into the pantry as the assembly finished their final bites. The men rose from their seats to help the women from their chairs.

"Dougal, help Anthea," said Hobblesby. "I don't think my foot can stand standing." He laughed. "Stand standing. Did you hear me?"

Two of the three Ulsters chuckled, but Mother Ulster sent him a look of impatience.

Jane let out a shrill giggle. "Oh, Father, you're so witty."

Anthea released a sigh. Thank goodness the meal had ended. She just had to endure tea with the ladies;

then she could go home. She wanted nothing more than to crawl into her bed. By morning her foul mood should have vanished.

Fletcher returned to the dining room empty-handed. "Sir, there is a problem."

"Well, speak up, man. What is it?"

"The port, sir. It's gone."

"Well, fetch another. I bought a whole case of the stuff."

"No, sir, you don't understand." Fletcher gave his employer a serious look. "I have already been to the cellar for a new bottle. It seems the entire case is missing."

Chapter 5

"Missing? Preposterous," said Hobblesby. "This is impossible."

"I'm afraid not, sir." Fletcher inclined his head.

"Show me. Take me to the cellar and show me." Hobblesby pushed up onto his cane to stand.

"Allow me, Squire." Colin leaped to his feet and hurried to Fletcher's side. "I believe I can be of service in this matter."

"Why, yes. Yes, of course." Hobblesby settled back into his chair. He let out a chuckle. "Savernake will take care of everything. That's what I hired him for."

"Forgive me, ladies." Colin bowed his head and followed Fletcher from the room.

In the cellar, Fletcher led him to a corner. A variety of wines lay on racks, and a thin layer of dust covered the bottles. Colin stopped in front of the racks. On the floor was a rectangle of disturbed dirt.

"This was where the case was?" asked Colin.

"Yes, sir. We hadn't the time yet to unpack it, so it stood on the floor."

Around the marks of the crate, Colin saw several footprints, but none of them distinct enough to identify the thief. Besides, Fletcher's and his now mingled with the other smudges.

"When did you last see the wine?" asked Colin.

"This afternoon. I came down earlier to loosen the lid because I knew we'd need a bottle tonight."

Just a few hours, then. "Who was here this afternoon?"

Fletcher thought for a moment. "The regular staff, of course."

"Yourself, Mrs. Pennyfeather and the cook."

"Yes, Mr. Savernake, and don't forget the two chambermaids. Then the gardener stopped by for lunch, as well as the two boys, Joe and Bob." Fletcher laughed. "Why everyone insists on calling them boys, I'll never understand."

"Who else?"

"Let's see. The members of the house. The squire, his son, and Mrs. Fanning came early with her husband. The squire keeps a room for her."

Mrs. Fanning? Ah, yes, Jane and her husband. "Were any deliveries made today?"

"I know the butcher came, and one of the mill workers. I shall ask Mrs. Pennyfeather if she can recall anyone else."

"Is that everyone you can think of?"

"Well . . ." Fletcher hesitated.

"What is it, man?"

"You brought Lady Anthea this afternoon."

He hadn't forgotten. He couldn't imagine Anthea carrying a case of wine, but if she had employed help . . . The port would fetch a good price.

"Mr. Savernake?"

He whirled around. Anthea stood at the bottom of the stairs.

"Do you need anything?" said Anthea.

Her beauty was as out of place in the dim, dank cellar as it was beside Squire Hobblesby. He remembered his most recent thoughts and eyed her with suspicion. "What are you doing here?"

"Mr. Hobblesby wanted to know if you needed anything. He sent me."

Colin didn't know whether to believe her. Was she here for the reason she claimed, or to see if he had uncovered proof against her? He had seen the circumstances of her family and knew money from the sale of the port would be welcome.

Anthea turned to the butler. "The squire would like you to serve tea in the parlor if you are finished here, Fletcher."

"May I leave, sir?" Fletcher asked Colin.

"Yes. If you think of anything else out of the ordinary, let me know."

"Of course, sir." Fletcher made a neat bow and ascended the stairs to the main house.

"Did you learn anything?" asked Anthea.

"Not enough." Colin paused. "Has the squire told you about his other losses?"

"You mean the thefts? Yes, but he doesn't seem overly concerned."

"Why do you suppose that is?"

Anthea shrugged. "It hasn't really hurt him much, has it?"

"And how do you feel about it?"

"I haven't thought about it much."

"Doesn't it trouble you that someone is stealing from you?"

"No one is stealing from me."

"In a sense, they are. You are to marry Mr. Hobblesby, and as his wife, the thief is stealing from you as well."

"But I'm not married yet."

Colin paused. "Yet you've been betrothed since November."

"Yes, but this time the squire asked for the postponement."

"This time?"

"Well, I . . ." Her cheeks pink, Anthea looked at the floor. Her fingers toyed with the medallion at her neck. "We were to marry in March, but the twins fell ill, so Mother asked me to postpone the wedding until summer."

"It's July now."

"Yes, and the squire postponed it this month because of his gout. He said, 'I can't stand up to be married if I can't stand up.'" Anthea smiled and waited for his reaction. He gave her none. She sighed. "Now he wants to wait for the birth of his grandchild."

"You must be disappointed."

"No . . . I mean . . . Of course, I'm disappointed, but I understand."

"Could it be you're not eager to wed the squire?"

"I am looking forward to being Mrs. Hobblesby."

"That's not what I asked." Colin took a step nearer to her. The flicker of panic in her eyes amused him. He didn't enjoy tormenting women, but this one aggravated him. She was marrying the man for some reason of her own, and it certainly wasn't love.

He took another step toward her, and this time she stepped back. Her heel hit the back of the bottom stair, and her arms shot out to control her balance. He grabbed her by the wrist to steady her. When she regained her footing, he drew her toward him. "Would any rich man have done, or did you need to find an old one?"

Anthea gasped and tried to pull her wrist from his grasp. "Unhand me at once, Mr. Savernake." She pushed against his chest.

He captured her other wrist in his free hand. "Not until you've answered my question. Would any rich man do you? What price did you sell yourself for?"

He felt her struggle, but Anthea couldn't loosen his hold. Her eyes glittered with unshed tears, yet he didn't feel the slightest urge to release her. She lifted her head and looked him in the eye. Her features took on their haughtiest expression. He almost grinned at this sudden show of her aristocratic roots. "I shall scream, Mr. Savernake."

No fear flashed in her eyes. Dear God, she was magnificent, and he wanted to kiss her. That thought shook him more than his aberrant behavior. Disgusted with himself, he gave her a look of condemnation. "And who shall hear you from the cellar?" He released her then.

Anthea rubbed her wrists. "I shall see that the squire dismisses you."

"I don't think so. He enjoys parading me around too much. Just think, he's marrying an earl's daughter and has a secretary. He's more pompous now than before." He leaned closer. "Besides, what could you tell him? That I grabbed your hands when you were about to fall?"

"You are a hateful man."

"You don't know the half of it, *my lady*." His tone made the words sound like an insult. "You should leave before I do give you a reason for your scorn."

"A—a reason?"

"Yes, a reason to have me dismissed, a reason to look down at me, a reason to dislike me." Before he could question his own actions, he pulled her into his arms and kissed her.

She tasted better than he'd expected. Her lips reminded him of a fine cognac, warm and smooth. He must have surprised her, for she still did not try to escape. He lifted one hand to touch her cheek, to trace the lines of her jaw, to hold her neck and deepen the kiss. His fingertips brushed against the pulse point in her throat. Her heart hammered and raced.

He didn't know why such a small vibration would capture his attention, but he pushed himself away from her. He held her at arm's length. Her eyes wide, she stared at him like a doe in the crosshairs. Colin didn't like the sensation running through him. Shame was an emotion of his youth, something he had suffered before he realized the shame was not his, but his father's. But the shame he felt tonight was of his own making.

"There. Now you have a reason," he said.

She pressed her fingers to her lips, but didn't move away yet.

"Go."

She turned and fled up the stairs.

"Damn." What possessed him to act against his own nature when she was around? He drew his hand over his face. How *would* he explain his behavior to Hobblesby?

"Damn."

The party had moved to the salon when he returned upstairs. The squire had ensconced himself in the large armchair. A puffy ottoman elevated his bandaged foot. The other guests stood or sat around the room. Colin searched the room for Anthea. She stood beside her sister. She lifted her gaze, and her cheeks filled with a hint of pink when she saw him. He turned away first.

"Well, Savernake? What news?" Hobblesby's voice boomed.

"Give me time, Squire," he said.

"Waste of effort if you ask me," said Dougal. "Anyone could have taken that wine."

"Not I, certainly," said Reverend Ulster with a laugh.

Hobblesby barked out a chuckle. "I think I can safely rule you out, Reverend."

Mrs. Ulster clapped her hands together. "This is rather exciting. To be witness to a theft."

"What is exciting about seeing Father stolen from?" asked Jane in a sour voice.

"It was only a few bottles of wine, my dear. Easily replaced," said Hobblesby.

"But you'll have to spend more money," Jane said in a whine.

"Just a pittance. Nothing to fret about," Hobblesby said.

"It's as if the thief is stealing from your grandchild. It's his inheritance they're stealing." Jane pouted and rubbed her extended stomach.

"There's plenty left for my grandchild, and any other children I may yet have," said Hobblesby, flashing a broad grin to Anthea.

Colin turned away. He didn't want to see her reaction.

"Don't be disgusting, Father," said Jane. "Remember my delicate condition."

"Delicate? You've never been delicate a day in your life," said Hobblesby. "If you're at all like your mother, you'll give birth and be up the same day ready to make dinner for your husband."

"Please, Father. We have a cook," said Jane.

"I don't expect Jane to do domestic work, especially now," said Hubert. "What's the point of having money if one can't hire people to do the work for us?"

"Weak," muttered Hobblesby.

Colin glanced at the squire.

"Anthea isn't afraid of a little work, and she's the daughter of an earl," said Hobblesby.

"Well, she has to work, doesn't she?" said Dougal. "Her father didn't leave her anything."

"But she was quick enough to find the richest man in the county to wed so she'd never have to work again," said Jane.

"Thea isn't afraid of hard work," said Violet. "And if you think she'd marry anyone just to get out of it, you're mistaken."

Anthea took her sister's arm. "It doesn't matter, Violet."

"Yes, it does. They act as if your feelings don't exist."

"It doesn't matter." Anthea glanced at Mrs. Ulster.

Colin followed her gaze. Mrs. Ulster's eyes glittered with excitement. She watched the exchange with more interest than befitted the wife of a clergyman.

Mother Ulster banged her cane on the ground. "Seems to me, Anthea shows more sense than the lot of you. Peter, I'm tired. I want to go home."

"Yes, Mother." The reverend crossed to his mother and helped the old woman to her feet.

"We've had a lovely evening," said Mrs. Ulster to the squire.

"Do forgive me for not rising. My gout, you know. Anthea, will you see the reverend and his wife out?"

"Of course." Anthea left her sister's side and crossed to Mrs. Ulster. "It was such a pleasure to see you again."

"I hope we shall have many such evenings when you and the squire are wed," said Mrs. Ulster.

"Come along, Rowena," said Mother Ulster. "Stop your simpering. I want to get home."

Mrs. Ulster giggled. "Mother Ulster is such a love. I care for her as if she were my own dear mother."

"Rowena, I said I'm tired." Mother Ulster left the room.

"Good night, all," said Mrs. Ulster, following her mother-in-law and husband. Anthea trailed behind them.

Hobblesby nodded. "Excellent. They might be idiots, the lot of them, but they served their purpose."

"What purpose is that, Squire?" asked Colin.

"Spreading the news of your arrival. You've been launched in Middle Hutton."

Chapter 6

"You're quiet," said Violet. The sisters stood in front of the washbasin in the cottage kitchen. Two buckets of water, one sudsy, one clear, stood in the basin. Violet dipped the plate into the rinse water and handed it to Anthea.

"I'm not quiet." She dried the dish and placed it into the cupboard.

"You haven't said anything since last night. You said nothing in the wagon on the way home, you said nothing when we went to bed, and you've said nothing all morning."

"Don't be ridiculous, Violet."

Violet dropped the plate she held into the sudsy water and crossed her arms. The water sloshed up over the side of the basin and splashed on Violet's skirt. "You haven't said a word to anyone all morning."

"Watch out. You'll get everything wet."

"Oh, no, no, no. Don't try to distract me. What happened last night?"

Anthea sighed. The truth was she *knew* she had been preoccupied. She couldn't stop thinking about Mr. Savernake's kiss.

"Something *did* happen, didn't it?" Excitement tinged Violet's words.

"You mustn't tell anyone."

"How can I tell anyone anything if you won't talk?" Violet threw her hands in the air.

Anthea nearly laughed. It was too easy to bait her sister. "I'm getting to it."

Exasperation filled Violet's mien. "If I were smart, I'd tell you I'm no longer interested, but I'm too curious."

"Mr. Savernake kissed me."

Violet stared at her; then a broad grin stretched her lips. "Brilliant."

Anthea shot her sister a surprised look. "Excuse me?"

"That's exactly what my characters need to do." Violet wiped her hands on the dish cloth. "Do you mind finishing up for me? I need to write this down."

"What do you need to write down?"

"The kiss. My characters needed something to shake them up. This will do it. You're a dear." Violet kissed her on the cheek and left before Anthea could protest.

"You're welcome." Anthea plunged her hand into the sudsy water with ill-disguised impatience.

In a minute or two, she finished two more plates and set them aside to dry. She didn't mind helping out, but Violet's excitement over the kiss wasn't the reaction she had expected. Lost in her thoughts, Anthea scrubbed another plate.

"Anthea, you have a visitor."

She jumped at the sound of her mother's voice. Her mother laughed. "I had no idea you were so engrossed in your work. I'll take over here. You go see your guest."

"Who is it?"

"Mr. Savernake."

"I only have a few more dishes. Let me finish first—"

"Nonsense. Go out to your young man."

"He's not my young man, Mother."

"I didn't mean it that way. Now go."

Anthea dried her hands and left the kitchen. She didn't want him to be here. She didn't want to see him.

As she entered the parlor, he turned from the window. Her heart started to pound as she remembered his lips against hers. And how much she had enjoyed his kiss. She drew in a deep breath and steeled herself. "Mr. Savernake."

"Lady Anthea. I can understand your coolness."

She said nothing.

"It's the reason for my visit. I came to apologize for my intolerable behavior last evening."

"Oh, do you fear for your job, after all?"

He gave her a crooked smile. "No, but I do owe you an apology nevertheless. And my thanks. You didn't tell him."

She didn't have to ask who "he" was. "I didn't want to trouble him. He has enough to worry him."

"Indeed?" He raised an eyebrow.

Anthea nodded and folded her hands in front of her. "I accept your apology, Mr. Savernake. Please don't make me regret it."

He laughed then. "You aren't afraid to put me in my place."

"Only if you need it." She kept her answering smile from her expression.

An awkward silence followed, although Anthea had the notion that the quiet didn't bother Mr. Savernake at all. Well, she could play that game, too. Smiling at him, she faced him without timidity. He smiled back. She didn't look away from him despite the discomfiture she felt. She could outlast him. Even if the sight of his lips brought back the memory of the kiss they had shared.

She tugged on her lower lip with her teeth. The kiss meant nothing to her. Why couldn't she stop thinking about it? Why couldn't she stop staring at his lips? Why wouldn't he say anything?

With an inward groan, she acknowledged her defeat. "Do you have any idea who might be stealing from the squire?"

"I have an idea, but I need more information before I can be sure. I wouldn't want to accuse someone of something he's not guilty of."

"I should think not." Another silence overtook the room. Anthea held her breath for a moment, then nodded. "If there is nothing else, Mr. Savernake, I have several chores to attend to." Anything, even the laundry, to escape his presence.

"Of course. I'm relieved you have forgiven my behavior so easily."

"I expect we shall see each other regularly. I'm pleased there shall be no awkwardness between us."

"None at all." He looked at her with an expression she couldn't fathom, then smiled again. With a bow he said, "Good day, Lady Anthea."

"Good day, Mr. Savernake."

Savernake left the room. Anthea let out a loud sigh. Just why had he looked at her that way? And why couldn't she control the butterflies in her stomach when he was near?

Colin let himself out of the house and started down the lane. The visit hadn't told him anything new, except that his fascination with Anthea hadn't diminished with his kiss. He hadn't felt such a pull toward a woman since he was a youth. Here was a unique opportunity to exercise his control. As much as he may wish to steal a few kisses, he didn't trust her, and he would wager she was the thief he was trying to catch. The thefts hadn't started until after she had arrived in Middle Hutton and ingratiated herself into the squire's household.

As he walked past the vicarage, Mrs. Ulster leaned out of her doorway. "Yoo-hoo, Mr. Savernake."

Colin looked up at the woman. She had a bright grin on her face and was smashing a bonnet on her head as she rushed to the gate to greet him.

"What a wonderful surprise to see you."

He had the distinct impression that she had stood by her door until some unwitting wanderer passed her door.

"We had such a delightful evening last night."

"As did I, Mrs. Ulster."

"Although I must say the missing wine caused me such a fright. I wasn't sure I would sleep last night." The excited gleam in her eyes belied her words.

"I do hope you didn't distress yourself too much." He wasn't worried.

"A woman of my sensibilities must be careful, but I daresay I shall get over it. Where are you headed?"

"I'm just on a stroll to acquaint myself with your charming village."

"Then I shall join you and point out the sights." Mrs. Ulster unlatched the gate, stepped into the lane, and latched on to his arm. "Mother Ulster is sleeping, so I have some time. Although I mustn't be away too long."

"I promise I shan't keep you." He wasn't thrilled about his walking companion, but he could think of no way to extricate himself from her company.

As they made their way through the streets of the village, Mrs. Ulster told him stories about the occupants of every building they passed. He wasn't sure he could bear the chattering for much longer. His control had been tested enough with his visit to Lady Anthea. In the next moment, a flash of inspiration struck him.

He turned to his companion with a charming smile. "Mrs. Ulster, as the wife of the reverend you must know everyone in Middle Hutton?"

She batted her eyelids in an attempt to be coy. "I pride myself on my ability to relate to people."

"And I'm sure the villagers in Middle Hutton are grateful for your efforts. You must provide a great deal of comfort to them if needed."

"Indeed I do. So few people realize the burden of a vicar's wife." She let out a great theatrical sigh.

"I imagine you were a great solace to the dowager countess when she arrived."

"The poor dear. To lose her husband and then her home in such a short time. And to have five unmarried daughters." Mrs. Ulster clicked her tongue. "The late earl left them with nothing, you know. They live at Skettle Cottage by the largesse of the present Earl of Fortesque. He gave them a home. Such generosity."

Colin didn't know if he would call sending six women to live in a dilapidated cottage in a remote corner of England generous, but he kept his opinion to himself. "They seem to be a loving family."

"Yes. It's such a shame they were left penniless." Mrs. Ulster lowered her voice. "I heard the late earl squandered his money on women and horses until he had nothing left to give his family. And then he died."

"How inconsiderate."

"Indeed. Poor Anthea was getting ready for her

second season when her father took ill. Then the mourning period followed, and she never had another. None of the girls will. Of course, Anthea will marry well. The squire has enough money for the entire family. But the others—" Mrs. Ulster shook her head.

"What of the others?"

"That Violet is too brash, and Iris is, how shall I put it? Ill? No, that would be unkind, but accurate. Fragile. Yes, that's the word. But she's young yet. She might grow stronger. And the twins." Mrs. Ulster clicked her tongue. "Two more wild and precocious children you could never meet. It's hard to believe their father was an earl."

"They can't help the circumstances of their birth."

Mrs. Ulster stared at him. "Pardon me?"

"A weak joke. Forgive me."

"I don't know what the family lives on. They're too proud to take charity, although the village would gladly give them help." Mrs. Ulster patted his arm. "I do hope your questions don't indicate an interest in one of them."

Colin raised his eyebrows. "Why not?"

"You're the first young bachelor to come to Middle Hutton in a while. We have so many lovely ladies who would enjoy meeting you. You must wait for my daughter to return from her visit to my sister. She's such a dear child."

"Your daughter?"

"Yes. My Eugenia."

If Mrs. Ulster's daughter had the same capacity for locution as her mother, he wasn't sure he wanted to meet the girl.

A large wagon stood in front of them on the street. Colin looked up at the driver. "Good day, Joe."

The big man looked down at him and shook his head. "Not Joe. Bob."

Colin examined the fellow. A few more lines creased the corners of his eyes, and his chin was a little sharper, but the man looked enough like his brother that they could be twins. "Forgive me, Bob."

"Don't matter. Folks is always mixing us up."

"Well, good day to you, Bob." Colin eyed the muscled forearm that held the reins. He didn't want to make this man angry any more than his brother. "We haven't met yet. I'm—"

"I know who you be. Joe told me." As if an afterthought, he snatched the cap from his head. "Good afternoon, Mrs. Ulster."

"Good afternoon, Bob. I didn't see you at church on Sunday," said Mrs. Ulster in a scolding tone.

Bob flushed as crimson as a coxcomb. Under the shock of red hair, his bright face looked like a glazed apple. "No, ma'am. There was a cow fixing to calve."

"I expect to see you next Sunday," she said.

"Yes, ma'am. We'll be there." The big man's head bobbed up and down in an effort to assure her of his sincerity.

"What brings you to town today?" Mrs. Ulster asked.

"I made a delivery for young Master Hobblesby. He asked me to bring—"

"I'm sure she's not interested in what you were carrying, Bob." Dougal appeared beside the wagon. "Good day, Mrs. Ulster, Savernake."

Colin glanced down the overgrown lane. He saw no evidence of a house or building from where Dougal might have come.

"But these aren't your father's properties. There's nothing in this direction but that vacant cottage. I've

forgotten its name. I heard it sold recently. You don't
by chance know who bought it?" asked Mrs. Ulster.

"No." Dougal offered nothing further.

"So your father didn't snap it up like the others in
town?"

"No, he still has the empty one in town. He doesn't
need two empty houses." Dougal climbed into the
wagon.

Mrs. Ulster nodded in a display of sympathy. "Poor
Mrs. Parker. She died three months ago. She was so
spry for a woman of eighty-seven, but it was her time,"
she said, tugging on Colin's arm to get his attention.
She turned back to Dougal. "The butcher's son is
newly married. Perhaps they might be interested."

"Thank you. I'll tell Father." Dougal faced the road.
"Let's go, Bob. We have chores at home."

"Yes, Master Hobblesby," said Bob. He picked up
the reins and clicked his tongue. The horses stepped
into motion.

"The squire is such a fortunate man to have a son
he can depend on," said Mrs. Ulster. "I wouldn't mind
if he took an interest in my Eugenia."

"Indeed?"

"Of course, no one will win my Eugenia's heart easily. Her tastes are quite refined." Mrs. Ulster patted his
arm. "But I think you will pass her muster."

He had to escape before the woman had him engaged and married off. If nothing else, the fear of
having Mrs. Ulster as a mother-in-law would make him
keep his distance from her daughter. "May I escort
you back to your house, Mrs. Ulster? I'm afraid I must
return to my duties with the squire."

"That's not necessary. Mrs. Brown lives just there. I
shall visit her." She unhooked her arm from his.

"Good day to you, Mr. Savernake. I look forward to your visit when my Eugenia returns."

"Good-bye, Mrs. Ulster." He gave her a curt bow and hastened from her side.

When he was far enough from her, he slowed his pace. He hadn't learned much in his talk with her, except to reinforce his suspicions about Lady Anthea. The family was in desperate straits. The wedding had been postponed twice, cutting her off from access to the squire's wealth. Could she have taken it upon herself to borrow from her future husband without his knowledge?

The image of her face rose in his mind—her green eyes sparking with intelligence, her cheeks in a soft blush, her lips parted, moist, ready to receive his kiss.

He froze. With a grunt of impatience, he banished those thoughts from his head. She was the most likely thief. He had better remember the reason for his visit to Middle Hutton before he made a fool of himself.

With brisk strides, he set off toward the Grange, pondering the turn of his thoughts. Lady Anthea might be beautiful, but he had no interest in her save whatever role she played in the squire's thefts. Once he left Middle Hutton, he would forget her, dismiss her from his mind as easily as one dismissed a servant. Her aristocratic blood had no hold over him.

Chapter 7

Anthea climbed to the top of the hill. The green fields rolled over the landscape like waves on the ocean. The stone walls meandered over the fields in no set pattern, like whitecaps, giving more life to the illusion of waves. Despite the summer, the early morning air was invigorating. Anthea drew in a deep breath. The view was spectacular. She'd never miss London with views like these to look forward to.

That was a lie.

She did miss London, the parties, the friends, their country home. She missed pretty dresses, the rich food, and all the good books. Soon she would have money enough for those things, but what chance had she as Hobblesby's wife to see London again? The squire had never left Yorkshire and wasn't likely to in the future. She'd never travel to London again, and she didn't have need for the fancy dresses in Middle Hutton. In addition, the squire shouldn't eat rich food any longer, and as his dutiful wife, she would see that it never reached their table. At least she'd be able to afford books.

She sunk to the ground, laced her fingers around her legs, and laid her head on her knees. A few tears trickled out of the corners of her eyes. The squire might be a good man, but she didn't want to marry him.

If she had become a governess, she might have found satisfaction for herself, but her income wouldn't have been much help to her family. The same held true if she had taken a position as a companion. Besides, she had trouble enough holding her tongue now. If her job depended on her demeanor, she would fail. And she didn't have a talent for storytelling like her sister, even if Violet had never finished a book.

Anthea allowed herself a few moments of self-pity, then wiped her eyes. She would make the squire a fine wife, and she would help her family. As mistress of the Grange, she could see her family's cottage received repairs. Instead of embroidering tea towels, which she sold for a mere pittance, her mother could raise the twins to be proper ladies. If Anthea saved enough out of the money the squire gave her, perhaps she could give Violet and Iris a season. Unless Violet actually finished her book, sold it and could pay for her own season, which Anthea didn't think possible anytime soon.

So her only alternative was to marry the squire. She couldn't blame his children for thinking she only wanted his money. It was true, but she swore to herself she would make him a good wife, even if that meant taking the abuse of his offspring. Besides, Hobblesby knew her reasons for wedding him. Although he had never said so, his actions made her believe so. He put her on display to his friends and announced to anyone who would listen that she was the daughter of an earl. A fair exchange, in her opinion. He would help her family, and she would raise his level of importance.

She held back a snort of laughter at that thought.

As if being the daughter of an earl had made a difference in her life. She'd probably eat better if she were the daughter of the butcher.

"Sorry, Papa," she whispered to the air around her. A twinge of guilt hit her. She had loved her father. He had been a kind and gentle man, full of humor and love for his family. It wasn't his fault he had made terrible investments and believed every huckster who had come to their door. Well, not entirely his fault.

Her fingers played with the medallion on her neck. Her father had given it to her when one of his outlandish schemes had actually succeeded. It was nothing more than a Chinese coin, but he had told her it was a good-luck charm. She had been a child at the time, and his story about the coin had fascinated her. No need to wonder where Violet got her gift for stories. Papa had threaded the coin on a ribbon, and she had worn it ever since. When he died, they sold everything to pay his debts, but the medallion had no value, so she had been able to keep it. It was the only gift from her father she had kept.

She no longer believed in luck or childhood fantasies. Romance was not for her. She had willingly sacrificed those dreams for practicality. Hobblesby might not be her ideal, but he would give her children to love and safety for her mother and sisters.

The image of Savernake rose in her mind. For a moment, she let herself think of the handsome man; then she did let out a laugh. Why should she spend her time mooning over a man who had made his aversion to her so plain? In one moment, he watched her with an accusatory glare; in the next, he was kissing her; and in the next, he acted the perfect gentleman. She couldn't understand his actions, nor did she wish to try. To be fair, he had kissed her only once, but she thought about the kiss so often, it seemed like more. Besides, even if they did get caught up in a romance, he wouldn't want to be saddled with the responsibility of an entire family. Not on a secretary's salary.

Money, money, money. If people could hear her thoughts, they'd think she was little better than a mercenary. Maybe she was.

Anthea rose from the ground and took in the view again. With a rueful smile, she had to acknowledge that the stark beauty of York appealed to her. That was some comfort at least.

With a sigh, she started on the way to the Grange. Hobblesby wanted her to learn about sheep, and today her lesson would include shearing the beasties. Wool was ever so much nicer when it came on a bolt and couldn't look her in the eye.

Colin reread the letter in front of him. It confirmed his suspicions about the Fortesque family. The late earl had made too many bad investments and succumbed to too many outlandish schemes. He had fallen ill three years ago, just when Anthea should have been having her second season. She had rejected several offers in her first. Sensible, considering how young she had been, but not practical, given the outcome of their situation. She could have been a countess in her own right by now. For some reason, a sense of uneasiness flitted through him. He didn't like the thought of suitors vying for her attention.

Colin shook his head. Emotion had no place in this investigation. He read on. When the earl died, his creditors descended upon the family. Everything that wasn't entailed had to be sold to pay off enormous debts, leaving his family with nothing. The present earl had allowed the women to live at their former home for a year until he consigned them to Skettle Cottage, a minor holding worth little. At one time the house had been used as a base for hunting, but it hadn't been used in two decades. Colin had seen the cottage in its present condition. Gad, what state had it been in when the women first arrived? He felt a streak of rage at the present earl.

But this information left little doubt in his mind. However noble the cause, he couldn't allow the thefts to continue.

"Mr. Savernake?"

Colin lifted his head from the papers on his desk and looked toward the doorway. His elbow brushed some papers to the floor, and a long-forgotten cup of tea teetered closer to the edge. He pulled the cup away from disaster. "Mrs. Pennyfeather. Do come in."

"I trust you're finding everything you need to make you comfortable," said the housekeeper.

"Yes. I imagine that has a lot to do with you. Lord Stanhope had a treasure in you."

"Thank you, Mr. Savernake." The housekeeper blushed. Her sudden youthful appearance took Colin by surprise. He realized Mrs. Pennyfeather wasn't as old as one imagined a seasoned housekeeper to be, and she was still a handsome woman. "I enjoyed my time with Lord Stanhope."

"I imagine the squire's house is quite a change for you."

"Aye, sir, but as you know, our stay here is temporary. Although I'm trying to instill the quality of Lord Stanhope's house here at the Grange."

"I have to confess to a little trepidation on my part before I arrived, but I've found everything satisfactory. Even the food has been a pleasant surprise."

"Aye. Cook could find work anywhere, but she wants to stay in Middle Hutton."

"I'd be willing to hire her myself."

"Indeed, sir." Mrs. Pennyfeather smiled.

"In any case, I don't expect to enjoy the squire's hospitality for much longer."

The housekeeper widened her eyes. "Have you found the thief already?"

"I believe so. I need some solid evidence, but I believe I shall finish here in a matter of days."

Mrs. Pennyfeather clapped her hands together. "This is good news, Mr. Savernake. I had been dreading telling you about the latest theft, but now I'm sure you'll find the tray soon."

"What?"

"The reason I came to speak with you, Mr. Savernake. There's been another theft."

"When?"

"This morning, near as I can tell. I do know the tray was in its place at breakfast, but when I went to fetch it for lunch service, it had disappeared."

He hadn't considered the thief would strike again so soon. He felt a rush of irritation with himself. "Which tray? Can you describe it?"

"A large silver one. Embossed flowers cover the surface and the handles are vines. I believe it comes from the time of George III."

"Bloody hell."

Mrs. Pennyfeather clicked her tongue.

"Do forgive me, good lady. I forgot myself." He was angry. How could he have allowed himself to get complacent? His job wasn't completed yet. This newest theft only emphasized his arrogance. "Are you sure the tray hasn't been misplaced?"

"Quite sure, sir."

He drew his hands down his face. "Was Lady Anthea here this morning?"

"Yes. She arrived just before breakfast. I believe the squire wanted her to witness the sheep shearing."

While she did some shearing of her own. "Thank you, Mrs. Pennyfeather. I'm sure I shall recover the tray soon. As much as I have enjoyed my stay in Middle Hutton, I am eager to return to my home. I suppose you and Fletcher will leave as well."

"As soon as our work is complete," said the woman. She lifted the cup of cold tea from the desk. "May I bring you a fresh cup?"

"Thank you, no. Has Lady Anthea left yet?"

"No, I don't believe so."

"Good. I need to speak with her."

"Shall I fetch her for you?"

"That won't be necessary." *I'll find her myself.*

Anthea didn't care if she ever saw another sheep again. They were smelly, stupid creatures. One had butted her into the mud. Another had chewed a hole in her skirt. Thank heaven she was wearing her working clothes. Sheep had no place around crinoline. Or was it crinoline had no place around sheep? It didn't matter. She was just glad the morning was over. She didn't think she ever wanted to eat mutton again either.

In the large washing sink, she scrubbed her hands up to her elbows. Her clothes would have to wait until she returned home.

Mrs. Pennyfeather entered the kitchen. "Will you be staying for lunch, Lady Anthea?"

Anthea shook her head. "I don't have anything decent to wear."

"Tosh. The men have all been working outside. Except the squire, of course, although he says his foot is much better today. This isn't a formal lunch. You look fine." Mrs. Pennyfeather reached for a plate. "I'll set another place."

Anthea wasn't fooled. She knew Mrs. Pennyfeather wanted to see her fed. The woman realized how tight the funds ran at the cottage. "Thank you, Mrs. Pennyfeather. I shall be sorry to see you go."

"What makes you think I am leaving anytime soon?" asked the housekeeper.

"You only came to replace old Mrs. Davies when she inherited that money from a cousin. You're too efficient to stay here long. Someone is sure to come along and steal you from us." Anthea dried her hands on a towel. "You only became available to us because your last employer died."

"You mean Lord Stanhope?"

"Yes. I met the man when he was traveling here last winter. He mentioned he knew my father, but I might be mistaken."

"Lord Stanhope was a good man," said Mrs. Pennyfeather with a smile. "He was always planning something."

Anthea paused. "I wonder how the squire met the earl. Lord Stanhope didn't seem to be the type of man the squire usually befriends."

"Why do you say that, my lady?" Mrs. Pennyfeather looked bemused.

Because Lord Stanhope was too refined to travel in the

same circles as the squire, and the squire likes to lord his success over others. He couldn't do that with Lord Stanhope. But she couldn't say that out loud. "The squire never had an earl stay before."

"Lord Stanhope wasn't a man to place much stake in a man's title." Mrs. Pennyfeather gathered up a napkin and silverware.

"Neither was my father. Perhaps they were friends after all." Anthea sighed just as her stomach growled.

"There, you see, my lady. You are hungry. Luncheon won't be a moment." Mrs. Pennyfeather took the place setting and hurried into the dining room with it.

Anthea decided to wait for the meal in the parlor. Only a few books stood on the shelves. Ornate figurines and pieces of porcelain filled the rest of the space. Hobblesby wasted no effort in showing off his refined taste. She examined a statuette of a bull with a girl on its back and wondered if Hobblesby was even familiar with the story of Zeus and Europa.

"There you are, my dear," said Hobblesby from the door.

Anthea turned to him with a smile to hide the guilt of her stray thoughts. "I heard you were feeling better."

"Indeed I am. Look at me. I'm almost walking normal." Hobblesby took a few steps leaning on his cane.

"I'm pleased."

"Perhaps we should move the wedding up after all."

"I would like that." Anthea cast her gaze to the floor.

Hobblesby laughed. "No need to be shy with me, my dear." He limped forward and sat in the armchair. "I received another letter today about Brody."

Anthea hurried to his side. "Is he better?"

"He's coming home. He should arrive in two days." Hobblesby's face took on a serious mien. "He'll need some help. I've asked Savernake to find an aide for him, but I'd feel better if he wasn't always with a stranger."

"He doesn't know me, but I'll be happy to help in any way I can."

"I know, my dear, but you have enough to worry about without taking on another invalid." The squire laughed and touched his bandaged foot with his cane. "We'll worry about it later. Now where is the house-keeper, that Feather woman?"

"Mrs. Pennyfeather?"

"Right. Pennyfeather. What kind of name is that anyway? Bother with her. I'm hungry."

"She was just setting the table. I'm sure we can go in." Anthea helped her betrothed to his feet and let him lean on her as they made their way to the dining room.

Dougal was already seated, and Savernake came in behind them. She didn't look at him as she helped Hobblesby into his chair, then took her own. To her surprise, she felt Savernake's hands on the back of her chair, helping her to the table.

"Thank you," she whispered.

Savernake nodded, then took his own place.

Jane lumbered in a moment later. Savernake jumped to his feet as the woman entered.

Jane gave him a beatific nod of approval. "It's nice to see a gentleman amongst you."

"I don't have to be a gentleman with my own sister," said Dougal. "You can find your own fops."

"She's right, Dougal," said Hobblesby with his usual chuckle. "Forgive me, my dear little Jane. Your father can't get up easily yet."

"Oh, Father, I don't expect it of you." Jane sent

Hobblesby a disarming smile, then turned her gaze to Anthea. "I see you're eating here again. Isn't the food good enough at the cottage?"

"I must admit Cook outdoes anything I or my sisters could possibly concoct." Anthea folded her hands in her lap.

"I suppose we should get used to seeing you at our table. If Father is determined to marry you."

"I am," said Hobblesby. "In fact, I was just thinking that my recovery is getting along so nicely we may have to move the wedding up."

"Please, Father, I'm in no condition to attend a wedding. You must wait until after your grandchild is born," said Jane.

"Very well, but you must remember I'm not getting any younger." Hobblesby let out a blast of laughter.

"Nonsense, Father. You're not at all old," said Jane.

"More's the pity," mumbled Dougal.

Savernake helped the pregnant woman to her seat, then sat again just as Fletcher appeared with the first course.

"Brody will be here in two days," said Hobblesby.

"He's well enough to travel?" asked Dougal.

"That's what the nurse wrote. They're sending him by train. I think I should meet him. Welcome him home, make him comfortable and all that. Savernake, make sure my calendar is clear for Thursday."

"Yes, Squire," said Savernake.

"And tell Mrs. Bird—damn, what is that woman's name?"

"Pennyfeather, sir," answered Savernake.

"Right. Tell her I want the boy's room cleaned and aired. We also need to move some of the things out of there. Give him more space."

"Are you sure you want him here, Father? He might be more comfortable somewhere else," said Jane.

"He's my boy, and this is his home," said Hobblesby in a tone sharper than usual. Then his features softened again. "He'll do fine. I've already asked Savernake to find an aide for him."

The room fell into silence. Fletcher cleared the soup plates, then brought out the roast. A waft of steaming juices floated over the room.

Jane wrinkled her nose. "What is that smell?"

Hobblesby inhaled with a loud intake of air, then grinned. "If I'm not mistaken, that's one of our prize pigs."

"No, not the meat." Jane sniffed again and turned toward Anthea. Her lip curled, and a look of disdain covered her features. "Goodness, Anthea. Didn't you wash before sitting down?"

Heat flooded Anthea's face, but before she could answer, Hobblesby laughed. "That's the smell of country living, girl. Thea's been learning about the farm. Today sheep. Next time, we'll show her the pigs, eh, boy?"

"Aye, the pigs," said Dougal. His smile was filled with wicked anticipation. "Now, there's a smell you never thought to experience, wouldn't you say, Lady Anthea?"

"I can't say that I ever did," said Anthea. She pushed at the meat on her plate, her appetite gone. First sheep, now pigs. She didn't think she wanted to see another animal ever again.

Chapter 8

Anthea started the long walk home from the Grange. Mrs. Pennyfeather had packed a large basket for her to take to her family, and the neck of a bottle of wine stuck out from underneath the linen cloth that covered the food. She was grateful for the food, since she knew her appetite would return with a vengeance. The basket was heavy, but she didn't mind the burden. Her youngest sisters would enjoy the strawberry jam the housekeeper had packed for them.

"Lady Anthea."

She recognized Mr. Savernake's voice at once. She stopped and turned to him.

He sprinted up the drive to catch her. "May I walk with you?"

"I can hardly keep you from walking where you will," she said, then bit the inside of her lip. She had no reason to be rude to the man, even if he did make her uncomfortable.

"No, I don't suppose you can. Nevertheless, I shall ask your permission."

"You may walk with me. I shall be glad of the company." She adjusted the basket on her arm and continued up the drive.

He reached for the basket and unhooked it from

her forearm. "May I? The drive is steep, and I imagine the basket is heavy."

"Thank you, Mr. Savernake."

"It's quite a climb from the Grange."

"One grows accustomed to it quickly. If you stay for much longer, it won't even cause your breath to quicken as much as the sight of a pretty girl." Why had she said that?

As he took the basket from her, he peeked inside. "Food?"

"Yes. My mother and sisters . . ." She felt a twinge of embarrassment that he had discovered her habit of bringing food home.

He seemed disappointed with the contents. "Glad to see it doesn't go to waste."

She breathed a sigh of relief. "The squire doesn't like to eat the same thing in succession. His workers dine well because of it."

"I imagine they do." He paused for a moment, then looked at her. "The squire is generous with his own."

"He is."

"How would he respond to someone who disappointed him?" His gaze never wavered from her.

What an odd question. "I've never seen him angry with anyone, but I know he requires respect. He considers himself the patriarch of his family and the local nobility, and, as such, he is in charge. I imagine he would be unforgiving if someone betrayed him."

"Even a member of the family?"

"Especially a member of the family. He would take great offense if one of his children stood against him."

"What if the person wasn't a member of the family?"

"Then I imagine he would cut them out of his life."

"No matter how close they were?"

Anthea stopped walking. "Do you have a purpose to your questions, Mr. Savernake?"

"I'm afraid I do." Savernake eyed her with a cold gaze. She spotted the same look of disdain on his face as she had seen the first time they met. "Did you have someone else bring the tray out for you?"

She stared at him. "Pardon?"

"The tray. It's not in the basket, although I imagine it's too big to fit in there anyway, and you don't have it tucked under your skirts. They flow too freely for that."

Ire stirred in her. "Have you been watching my skirts?"

"I don't care about your skirts. The tray, Lady Anthea. What did you do with the tray?"

"I haven't the slightest idea what you're talking about."

He snorted in disbelief, then enunciated each word with care, as if speaking to a dim-witted dog. "The tray that went missing this morning. Did you have someone bring it off the property this morning, or have you stashed it somewhere to pick up later?"

"I have done nothing with a tray." She pulled herself upright. "Are you accusing me of stealing some tray?"

His eyes narrowed. "Who else has such easy access to the Grange and the squire's belongings? Who else has such a need for money? We both know the desperate straits your family faces. How easy to help yourself to a few things before the wedding. They'll be yours anyway in a few weeks."

"Oh, my stars! You *are* accusing me of being the thief." For a moment, her surprise was greater than her anger.

"There's no need to deny it. I know all about your father's investments and how you were thrown out of your home. I know you need money."

"Yes, we need money, but why would you think I'd steal it? Especially not from the squire. He's been nothing but kind to us."

"And that's reason enough to marry him?"

"What do you know of my reasons for marriage? He knows I want to help my family, just as I know he thinks I am a good acquisition. In any case, it doesn't concern you." Rage coursed through her.

"No, it doesn't. But the thefts do concern me. You are the most logical choice for the thief."

"And just how did I remove a case of wine from the cellar? No, wait. I carried it, right?"

"You have an accomplice."

"Of course, my sister Violet. She and I together could have carried a case of wine up those stairs and out of the house without tripping on our skirts. Tell me. Were we wearing trousers that day to make our job easier?"

"Your sarcasm doesn't prove your innocence."

He was chiding her? After his accusation, he had the gall to chide her? Anthea placed her fists on her hips. "And just what did I do with my ill-gotten gains?"

He shrugged. "Sold them."

"Right. That's why I have so many nice dresses, and my jewelry box is overflowing."

"I didn't say you spent the money on extravagances. You bought food or medicine for your ailing sister."

"Ailing sister? Which one of my sisters is ailing?"

"Iris."

"Who told you Iris was ill?"

"Mrs. Ulster."

The man's audacity no longer surprised her. "You should know better than to believe anything that old gossip has to say. Iris is as healthy as a fox. She may be pale, but that's because she prefers to read, and she is withdrawn because she is painfully shy. I'll admit she is an unusual girl, but she is not ill. Now, the twins had chicken pox in March, one right after the other, but Mother took care of them, and they didn't need medicine. Not that I should have to explain anything to you."

Savernake furrowed his brow. "So you spent the money on food or repairs to the house."

"Exactly. That's why I spent the other day on the roof moving the tiles so we wouldn't have any leaks. You remember that day, the day you broke our ladder? Oh, yes, I bought new shutters for the windows to keep out the cold drafts, but I hung them as crookedly as possible." The wind whipped her skirts around her legs, making her feel much like an avenging fury. "Perhaps you might want to ask my sisters how much they had to eat all winter. With all the money I brought home, they should be rather fat by now instead of clutching their stomachs when we don't have enough for breakfast."

His lips thinned. "Damn it. I don't know what you did with the money. That isn't my concern."

"Then just what is your concern? Accusing me of stealing?"

"If not you, who?"

The conviction in his voice was weaker now, but Anthea took no joy in that. She gave him a sardonic smile. "Well now, that isn't *my* concern, is it?"

"I may not have concrete proof that you're the thief, but if another item goes missing, I shall tell the squire my suspicions."

"Fine." She snatched the basket from his arm. She faced him and gave him her haughtiest glare. "I've changed my mind about walking with you. In fact, I'd prefer if you never spoke to me again." She stormed off in the direction of the cottage, leaving him standing at the top of the drive to the Grange.

For a few minutes, she didn't allow herself to think. She waved at the villagers she saw, but didn't register whom she waved to. When she passed the last of the gray stone houses that lined the square, she let her fury reign. Of all the nerve. How dared he accuse her of stealing from the squire? Her steps grew faster and more staccato. As if she didn't have a proper upbringing. As if she didn't know right from wrong. As if she hadn't faced enough hardship in the last year. She had never felt this angry in her life.

Or this hurt.

With that thought her shoulders drooped. She shouldn't care what he thought of her. As a betrothed woman, she had no right to want his good opinion, but she did. With a little cry of despair, she acknowledged that the dreams of a love hadn't quite been extinguished by her betrothal to the squire.

Anger returned, blotting out all other emotions. Mr. Savernake could rot. Why should she feel any remorse for a man with such little sense?

With a firm nod of her head, she turned down the lane toward Skettle Cottage and heard the shouts and laughter of her youngest sisters.

Colin sat in the study and looked over his notes. She was the only logical choice. He closed his eyes and let out a hiss of frustration between gritted teeth. What was it about Anthea that made him lose his sensibilities? Since the confrontation with her two days ago, he had struggled to come up with a new answer, but couldn't. Was he just being stubborn? His usual powers of reason seemed to have deserted him, and he couldn't dismiss the image of her in high dudgeon from his mind. Lord, but she was glorious in her fury. He had no proof the thief was she, but he had wanted to give her a chance to deny it.

She had not.

Oh, she had taken offense, and turned his questions into fodder for her sarcasm, but she had never said she wasn't a thief outright. Her protestations sounded sincere, but he had seen actresses move audiences to tears with their performances too many times to believe her. And he had wanted to believe her.

"Savernake, any word yet on that aide for my son?" asked Hobblesby, poking his head into the room.

Colin stacked the papers into a neat pile. "I've narrowed it down to two candidates, Squire. Both have excellent qualifications, and both have served as batsmen in the army. Perhaps you'd like to glance at their résumés and make a decision?"

"We've got time for that later. I'm off to fetch Brody at the moment. Will you join us?"

"I think he might be more comfortable with just the family."

"Good thought. See if his room is ready."

"Yes, Squire." With a wry smile, he acknowledged that the squire had grown comfortable with treating him no different from the other hired staff. Colin wondered if the squire remembered that he was here to help put an end to the thefts and wouldn't stay on as his actual secretary. As soon as he had proof against her—

He didn't want to think about what would happen

then. He could only hope her indignation was justified, but he never had believed in wishful thinking.

Colin left the study and found Fletcher. "The squire wants to know if Brody's room is ready."

"Yes, Mr. Savernake. We have cleared out the rug and extraneous furniture until he grows accustomed to the space."

"Excellent. I hope he finds it comfortable. His aide should arrive soon."

"I'm sure you have done your best, sir." Fletcher nodded with approval. "Mrs. Pennyfeather tells me that you've almost solved the squire's little problem."

He shook his head. "I've had a little setback."

"What a pity. I'm sure you'll sort it out in the end."

"I plan to."

Fletcher smiled. "Ahh, the refreshing arrogance of youth. Although I daresay you've earned the right to boast. Lord Stanhope told me a few things about your exploits."

"He spoke of me?"

"Does that surprise you? You've made quite a name for yourself."

Colin eyed the odd-looking butler for a moment. "Tell me, Fletcher. Why are you here? You speak of Stanhope with fondness. Did he leave you no income?"

"On the contrary. He left me very well provided for. But he had a few projects he wanted to take care of. Unfortunately, he fell ill before he could complete these tasks. I was happy to step in when he asked."

"And when these tasks are done?"

Fletcher gazed off into nothingness and smiled. "I shall retire to a small cottage somewhere and enjoy myself."

For a moment, Colin said nothing. Fletcher seemed

well content with his role and his future. "I believe I envy you, Fletcher."

"Me, sir?"

"I am filled with a restlessness I can't define, and you have your life mapped out and waiting for you."

"Oh, dear, that does sound dull." Fletcher smiled.

"In any case, when I solve the squire's problem, I shall return to London and the mundane crises of the aristocracy, and you will be off to your cottage."

"Not yet. There is one more task," said Fletcher.

Colin looked up at him with interest. "One more?"

"Yes, sir, but it requires none of your skills." Fletcher rose. "If you will excuse me, I must see how the dinner is coming along. The squire wants everything perfect for Master Brody's homecoming."

"Of course." He only hoped that nothing would mar the celebration.

Chapter 9

Violet trudged up yet another hill. How Anthea could enjoy traipsing up and down the countryside she'd never understand. Violet gazed out over the view hoping for inspiration. Nothing. Her book had stalled, her characters weren't speaking to her, and she didn't know what happened next in her story. The walk hadn't helped her any. At least she had found those currant bushes. Since moving to Middle Hutton, all the Fortesques had gotten into the habit of taking a basket with them whenever they went out. Now her basket was full with the bright red berries. She could taste the currant jam her mother would make with them.

Violet turned and let out a yelp. A man, face upturned to the sun, stood near her at the top of the hill. He snapped toward her at her cry. "Who's there?" His clear blue gaze seemed to pierce her.

"Violet Fortesque."

"What are you doing here?"

"Nothing. I'm just out walking."

"Here?"

Violet frowned. "Yes, here. I don't see why it should concern you where I walk."

"Only when you're on my father's land."

She squinted at him. "Who are you?"

He placed his cane in the grass in front of him and stepped forward. His foot hooked a stone that lay in front of him, and he tripped. His hands thrust forward, looking to catch his fall. Instead, the cane struck her basket, sending the contents over the ground before being flung to the side. The man stumbled forward another step, colliding with her and knocking both of them to the ground.

"Get off me, you oaf," said Violet. She pushed him off her legs and scrambled to her feet. She surveyed the scattered fruit and let out a moan.

"Are you hurt?" The man stood on unsteady legs and gazed around him as if lost. He took a step to the side.

"No, not there," yelled Violet. Then she let out another groan as a handful of currants squished under his boot.

"What was that?" he asked, stepping away from the mess. Two more handfuls fell victim to his footwear.

"Stop." Violet grabbed his arm to keep him still, but he jerked it free.

"I don't want your help," he shouted at her.

"I don't want yours either, but you keep stepping on my currants. Can't you see where you're going?"

He faced her with a scowl. "No, I can't."

That's when Violet noticed the lack of focus in the clear blue gaze. She gasped. "You're blind."

"Brilliant, Miss Fortesque." Several more berries became jam prematurely.

"Hell," said Violet, her voice rising. "Now I'll be ridden with guilt for treating you so ill, and it's all your fault."

He stared toward her for a moment, taken aback. Then he laughed. When he caught his breath, he said, "You're angry with me."

"Yes. I hate feeling guilty. I'm not very good at it."
Her voice was more calm now, but she still frowned.

He chuckled. "Neither am I. Tell me, Miss Fortesque,
is it safe for me to sit here, or will any more currants
succumb to my actions?"

Violet glanced at the ground. Red berries, or better
said, the pulpy mass of several berries, littered the
ground around him. "No, not there. Wait." She hurried
forward, picked up a few whole berries and returned
them to her basket. "There. Now if you walk about five
feet straight ahead, there's a clear spot."

"Right." He moved forward with surprising confidence. "Here?"

"Perfect."

He sat on the grass and looked around. "Won't you
join me?"

"No."

"Why?"

"First, I have to collect the rest of the currants."

"And then?"

"And then it isn't proper for me to sit with a man
whose name I don't know." Violet bent to her task.

"Brody." He stretched his legs out in front of him.

She froze. "Brody Hobblesby? The squire's son?"

"I take it you've heard of me."

"Oh, yes. You may have met my sister."

"Your sister?"

"Anthea."

"My father's Anthea?"

"The same."

He said nothing for a moment, then turned his
head in her direction and squinted at her as if trying
to see her. "Forgive me, but how old are you?"

"What an impertinent question."

"I know. Will you answer anyway?"

She paused. "Twenty."

He laughed. "And your sister isn't much older than you."

"She's twenty-two."

"That explains the irritation I hear in Dougal's voice when he speaks to her. I couldn't figure out why Dougal and Jane sounded so annoyed whenever they spoke of her." He laughed. "The old dog."

She glanced at her half-full basket. She'd have to stop at the bush on her way home to fill it again. "What dog?"

"Father." He felt in the grass with his hands. "If you happen across my cane, would you return it to me?"

She scoured the grass for the cane and spotted it lying a few feet down the hill. She retrieved it and brought it to him. "Why the cane? You don't have a limp."

"It helps me find my way when I walk."

"Obviously not very well, as evidenced by the currant jelly that now covers this hill."

He grinned. "You are a heartless wench. Most women would have been simpering over me in my infirmity."

"Most women wouldn't be sporting bruises from your fists, either."

"I did hurt you."

"No, you didn't. I was jesting." She placed the basket well away from him, then joined him on the grass. "If you can't see, how did you get so far from the Grange?"

"You forget I grew up in these hills. I know these hills better than my alphabet. I've certainly known them longer."

"That doesn't explain everything."

A look of admiration covered his features. "Bright

girl. You're right. My blindness is such that I can see shadows and light, but nothing with distinction. Thus, with the help of my cane, I can get about fairly well. As long as stray stones or hapless fruit doesn't jump into my path."

"Will you get any better?"

"Most likely not."

She examined his face. He showed little trace of his father in his visage. Lean lines angled his lightly stubbled jaw, and his nose was more aquiline than bulbous. His hair was longer than fashionable, and lighter stripes streaked the rich brown, giving proof to time spent in the sun. And his beautiful blue eyes shone like the facets of a diamond. With a small sigh, she realized she found him rather attractive. A Hobblesby? Attractive? But she did. She cleared her throat. "You seem resolved to your fate."

"Some days are better than others. I must admit the company of a beautiful young woman brings out the best in me."

"How do you know I'm beautiful?"

"Logic."

"Now this you must explain."

He folded his hands as if ready to give a speech. "My father is engaged to your sister. If she weren't beautiful, he wouldn't be marrying her. If she is beautiful, then as her sister, you must also be beautiful."

She laughed. "I've known too many siblings with whom I could prove just such a supposition false. But you've forgotten one thing. My father was an earl. Your father would marry Anthea just for her lineage."

"Damn, I knew I had forgotten something."

"Your language is atrocious. Especially in front of a beautiful lady," said Violet, her voice in no way scolding.

She was enjoying their easy banter. She had forgotten how pleasant it was to spend time with a handsome young man.

"Forgive me. One forgets after time in the army. Few women, terrible manners."

She laughed. "But you're correct. I am beautiful."

"And clever."

"And clever."

He nodded. "And conceited." His grin took the sting out of his words.

"Why shouldn't I think highly of myself? I am by far the most talented and lovely lady in the county."

"What of your sister?"

"Anthea's too good and dutiful to be as beautiful as I."

"I thought as much. So, you're beautiful, clever, and the daughter of an earl. By rights I should call you Lady Violet, then."

"Yes, you should."

"Or maybe I should just call you 'Auntie.'" He winked at her.

"God forbid." Violet broke down into laughter. "Although when Anthea and your father marry, I shall be your aunt."

"Tell me, Auntie, why is it I never knew of you before?"

"We've been here just over a year. We had to come when Father died." Her voice cracked at the thought of the life she had left behind.

"I'm sorry." He said nothing for a moment. Then he closed his eyes, and his face sought the sun again. "Do you think they've missed me by now?"

"Who?"

"Father and the rest. They were so busy arguing over what to do with me, I doubt they even noticed I left."

Violet shot to her feet. "What a cruel thing to do to your family. Come along, nephew. We're returning to the Grange this minute." She tugged on his arm.

He rose to his feet with reluctance. "Would you have them shut me in my room?"

"Certainly not. But you mustn't worry them. They don't know what you are capable of yet."

"Neither do I. I haven't been blind very long."

"Which is clear from the poor job of shaving you did this morning."

He ran his hand over his chin. "I didn't do this myself."

"Then the person shaving must have been blind as well. Come along, Mr. Hobblesby. We have to get you home before the squire sends out the dogs after you."

Planting his cane in front of him, he turned toward the Grange. "I don't need your help."

"I didn't offer it."

"In that case, you may accompany me." He held out his arm.

She took it. "You are a stubborn man."

"This after only a few minutes friendship. What will you think of me after we are better acquainted?"

"I shall probably find you unbearable." She gave him a wide smile, and then said, "I'm smiling now."

He grinned at her. "I know. It nearly blinded me."

Ten minutes later, they topped the final hill before the house.

"There he is."

Brody sighed as he recognized his brother's voice. The thunder of several footsteps rumbled through the ground to meet him on the side of the hill. He wasn't ready to leave this remarkable girl he'd found. For the first time since his injury, he had found joy and laughter in a day. She hadn't treated him as an invalid, and he hadn't felt like one. He didn't know what had possessed him to leave the Grange, but he was glad he had.

"Brody, boy, where have you been?" asked his father, huffing and puffing after climbing the hill to meet them.

"I was taking a walk," he said.

"You can't do that," said Dougal.

"Of course he can," said Violet. "His legs aren't broken."

"Stay out of this, girl," said Dougal. "You should have known better than to take him out."

"She didn't take me out. I took myself out," said Brody.

"Now, Dougal, we must be thankful to Lady Violet for returning your brother," said Hobblesby.

"I didn't return him. We walked here together." Violet's grip on his forearm tightened. Her nails dug into his skin. He hadn't known her long, but he could recognize her annoyance with his family.

"You expect us to believe you? The man's blind," said Dougal. "Father's been out for hours on his sore leg when he should be resting."

"My foot is better," said the squire.

"I didn't take him on a walk," said Violet. Her voice rose a pitch.

"In point of fact, Doug, I found her and brought her here," said Brody in a calm voice.

"No need to protect her. We all know the girl," said Dougal.

"Perhaps, but you don't know me very well." Brody turned to Violet. "Thank you for the company, Lady

Violet. From the angle of the sun I would guess that dinner is drawing nigh. Won't you join us?"

Violet pulled back on his arm. "I couldn't. Your family doesn't . . . I need to get home. Besides, I look terrible. My dress . . ."

He looked straight at her, wishing he could see more than her shadow. "Trust me. You look beautiful."

"If Brody wishes it, you are more than welcome, Lady Violet. This way he can get to know another member of his new family." Hobblesby took his son's arm. "Step this way, son. Dougal, take his other arm."

Her hand slipped from him, and he found himself missing her warmth. The two men walked with the care given to a newborn. "Lady Violet, are you there?"

"I am." Her voice came from behind him.

"Good. I wouldn't want you to get lost."

Violet: Is any life more of the sun I would I and that
attract is drawing up to Mom, marking or

Rich: I will be back on the arm. I wouldn't. long
much deeper. I need hard lead beaches book
toward a times.

He looked into her, asked into his brown and she saw.

Violet: ...spaces. "Patricia. You look beautiful."

"I shook at best I you, are more than welcome

I... I used I came. He can came it is a mother
outside a darken Patty, I believe a just illusions
now, once the was, son I began into the hard, say.

For was slightest from that, and I realize himself
hand his parents. The people to spoken with the
own guests or many... I saw was that your man.

"...the once, other you behind you.

Rich: "I wouldn't care you..."

Chapter 10

Anthea found it difficult to eat. Savernake sat on her left, so she made conversation with Hubert, Jane's husband, to her right throughout the course of the meal. He in turn could speak of little more than his impending fatherhood and the joys of being Hobblesby's son-in-law. She was ready to scream by the end of the first course.

But even her unpleasant dinner companions couldn't keep Anthea from noticing Brody paid more attention to Violet than his meal. Who would have thought the squire could have such a pleasant son? Brody didn't look or act at all like Dougal. Or Jane for that matter.

"Brody, what do you think of your father, eh, boy?" Hobblesby's voice was a bit muffled from the roll he had just stuffed in his mouth. "What do you think of me marrying again?"

"If it makes you happy, who am I to stand against it?" Brody shrugged his shoulders.

"That's my boy," said Hobblesby.

"That's because he hasn't been here long enough to understand the consequences," muttered Dougal beneath his breath.

The next course came out. Fletcher placed it on the table.

"Do I smell lamb?" asked Brody.

"Indeed you do. Good for you, lad." Hobblesby beamed around the table as if he had recognized brilliance in his child. He slid a thick chop on Brody's plate.

"Let me cut it for you, Brody dear." Jane leaned over and started to carve at the meat. She speared a piece and said, "Open wide."

"Oh, for heavens sake, he can feed himself. He's not helpless," said Violet. "I daresay he can cut his own meat as well."

"What would you know of it? He's blind," said Jane.

"Blind, not stupid," retorted Violet. "He might have some difficulty at first, but you needn't treat him like an infant."

Anthea leaned forward. "Perhaps, Violet, you're being a little harsh."

"Harsh? I wager we could all cut our own meat if we shut our eyes. If he needs help, he'll ask."

The dinner companions fell silent at her outburst. Violet looked from one to the other, then at Brody, and her eyes filled with tears. Anthea wanted to comfort her sister, but she couldn't find the words.

"Does this mean I couldn't convince you to peel my grapes for me either?" said Brody. Mock disappointment dripped from his words.

Hobblesby laughed. A sense of wonder filled Anthea. In the five days since Brody's arrival, the man had shown little sign of humor. Now in one afternoon, he seemed a changed man. She glanced at Violet. Brody's hand slid across the tablecloth until he touched Violet's fingers. He gave them a little squeeze. Violet smiled.

Anthea cocked an eyebrow. *Interesting.*

As the meal finished, Hobblesby stood and lifted his glass. "My family. Since my gout has now gone, and Brody is home with us, I had a smashing idea. I want to move up the date of my wedding. What say you, Anthea, my dear?"

Anthea coughed into her napkin. Panic seized her for a moment. Then she drew a deep breath. "Whatever pleases you, William."

"It pleases me very much," said Hobblesby. "We don't need much time to prepare. Three weeks should do it. A small ceremony, then a small reception, just the county. Was there anyone you wished to invite, my dear?"

"No, no one really. My family of course." She bunched up her napkin and twisted it in her lap.

"None of them will fall sick this time, I expect." Hobblesby laughed. "Lift your glasses. Let's toast to my wedding."

Anthea gripped the stem of her wineglass until she feared it might snap. She sipped the red liquid without tasting a drop. Three weeks. She could do this. But three weeks was such a short time.

She shot a glance at Savernake. He arched one brow high over his eye, then returned his glass to the table without drinking. His actions told her of his lingering doubts about her. She lifted her chin higher.

"Congratulations, Father," said Brody. "And, of course, to you, too, Lady Anthea."

Dougal didn't bother to hide his lack of participation in the toast. Jane sipped, but never smiled. Hubert drank his fill. Anthea had long since learned that Hubert supported the views of whosoever fed him. Tonight it was the squire. Tomorrow, in his own home, he would deride her along with his wife.

Violet shook her head, but drank anyway. Anthea hated the undercurrents she noticed at the table. She was tired of defending herself to the squire's family and her own. And to Savernake.

"Savernake, I'm putting you to work on the wedding. Speak with the reverend and start planning everything. Mrs. Pennysmith will help you with the menus, but I want Anthea to give her approval before anything is set."

"Mrs. *Pennyfeather* and I shall start in the morning, Squire," said Savernake.

"Excellent." The squire turned to the sisters. "I suppose you're eager to give the news to your mother. Will you be wanting the gig, my dears?"

"The gig would be lovely." Anthea rose, and the other gentlemen stood at their places. "I'll just go and collect my things."

"Will you bring your sister the next time you visit?" asked Brody.

Anthea looked at the young man, then at the blush that tinted her sister's cheeks. "I believe I shall."

Jane clicked her tongue. "I suppose we shall have to grow accustomed to having various members of your family underfoot."

Violet gave Jane a most insincere smile. "Yes, but do be careful when the twins come. You just never know what they might be putting under your feet next."

Jane dropped her mouth open, then clapped her jaws shut and threw her shoulders back. "Harrumph."

"Come along, Violet." Anthea pulled her sister from the dining room. A din of hurried speech followed them, as well as a few chuckles from Brody.

* * *

Opening the large trunk that sat at the foot of her bed, Anthea pulled out the dress she intended to wear for the wedding. Her mother had worn it at her wedding. The intricate beadwork speckled the room with glints of light. The dress was entirely old fashioned, but still beautiful. It was also one of the few possessions they hadn't sold to pay off Father's debts. She brushed an imaginary speck of dust from the front, then folded it back into the tissue paper and returned it to the trunk. Somehow the thought of wearing the gown when she married the squire didn't sit well with her. Maybe she would save it for Violet when she got married.

Anthea came down the stairs and heard voices from the parlor. With a grimace she recognized Mrs. Ulster's voice. Who else could know of the impending marriage so quickly?

"You must be so proud. She has caught such a staunch and stable man," said Mrs. Ulster. "And so prosperous, as well."

Anthea stepped into the room.

"There she is. The blushing bride." Mrs. Ulster rose, took Anthea's hands, and pulled her back to the sofa. "Such exciting news. The entire town is abuzz with anticipation."

Lady Fortesque waved her hand toward the other occupant of the room. "Thea, Eugenia's returned from her visit."

Anthea nodded at Mrs. Ulster's daughter. "How nice. How was your visit to your aunt, Eugenia?"

"Uneventful. I missed everything here." Eugenia wasn't much older than Anthea, but she had the pinched look of a girl who had disappointed her parents by not marrying in time.

"Lady Anthea, you must tell Eugenia of the newest bachelor to arrive," said Mrs. Ulster. "Mr. Savernake is quite handsome. Tell her."

"Mo-ther." Eugenia frowned.

"He is quite eligible, and you're not on the shelf yet, my girl. Eugenia Savernake. It has the perfect ring to it." Mrs. Ulster eyes glazed over with her dreams.

"Mr. Savernake is quite the gentleman," said Lady Fortesque. "He came to see us one day and tried to save Thea from falling."

"How heroic," said Mrs. Ulster, sounding as if she were about to swoon.

"Except that I was in no danger of falling, and he broke our ladder," said Anthea. She wasn't about to play up the man's virtues when she believed he had none.

"So tell us, Lady Anthea, what are the plans for the wedding? Will it be a grand affair?" Mrs. Ulster's face had an expression of ecstasy on it.

"I'm leaving the details to the squire. He's asked Mr. Savernake to arrange things."

"Such a capable man," said Mrs. Ulster. "Are you listening, Eugenia?"

"Yes, Mother." Eugenia sighed.

"But surely you must make some decisions for yourself. For example, who will be your attendants?" asked Mrs. Ulster.

The question took her by surprise. She hadn't thought about attendants. She wasn't sure she would need any. "I don't know. The ceremony should be simple. I expect Violet and Iris shall be the bridesmaids."

A look of crushing disappointment washed over

Mrs. Ulster. She sniffed. "Well, if you should need another, you must remember my Eugenia. The twins are far too young to be bridesmaids."

"Indeed I shall, Mrs. Ulster." Bridesmaids? She just wanted to have the ceremony over with.

The reverend's wife brightened suddenly. "I expect the squire shall invite the entire village. Plenty of opportunity for the unmarried girls to mingle with that nice young Mr. Savernake."

"Mother." Eugenia looked uncomfortable.

"And don't forget the squire's two sons," said Anthea, giving in to her wicked streak.

"Good heavens, no. That Dougal is too old and coarse, and Brody . . . Well, he's not whole, is he?" Mrs. Ulster clicked her tongue. "Such a tragedy."

Anthea was only glad Violet wasn't in the room to hear the woman's comments. She glanced at Eugenia. The girl's cheeks were bright red.

Mrs. Ulster stood. "You must let me know if I can do anything to help, although I imagine if the capable Mr. Savernake is in charge, you'll have no problems."

"Thank you, Mrs. Ulster," said Thea. *You can be sure you're the last woman I'll call on for help.* But a boon to the woman wouldn't hurt. "I would be thrilled if you would help me with the wedding favors."

"Oh, I should be honored." Mrs. Ulster's voice rose a pitch. "I know just what to do. Heart-shaped dance cards for the women and tiny baskets of posies for the gentlemen to gift to the ladies. Or perhaps a sword pin for the gentlemen and a lovely fan for the ladies."

"Why don't you jot down your ideas and we can decide later?" said Anthea.

"Yes, that might be the wisest course. I'll make a list of my ideas, and we can discuss them. I just love weddings. Come, Eugenia. We have several more stops to make before we go home."

Lady Fortesque rose. "Let me see you to the door."

"That's very kind of you, Countess." The three left the room.

Anthea flopped back on the sofa. If Mrs. Ulster's visit was any indication of the rigmarole to follow, she had better rest up to gather her strength for the upcoming days.

"Are they gone?" whispered Violet.

"Coward," said Anthea with a smile. "Yes, they're gone."

Violet came in and sat beside her sister. "I don't mind Eugenia. She doesn't say much, but her mother . . ."

"I know."

The sisters looked at each other and laughed.

"Are you really going through with it, then?" asked Violet.

"Yes."

"You can't tell me you want to marry Hobblesby. I won't believe you."

"Violet, look around you. Is this how you want Rose and Daisy to live? What of Iris's dreams? Do you want to see Mother work herself to death?"

Violet cast her gaze to the ground. "No, of course not."

Anthea took her sister's hand. "And you're not close to selling your book. Don't you see? I can help all of you. The squire—"

"Is a good man. I know. You've said it often enough. It just seems there should be a better way." Violet snatched her hand away. "Why did Father have to be so stupid?"

"Violet." Her sister's words shocked her.

"It's true. He was stupid. He was gullible, and trusting, and foolish." Violet's voice hitched. "And I miss him so much."

"Me, too." Anthea hugged her sister.

"He wouldn't have let you marry Hobblesby."

"No, we'd both be in London, batting the young men away with our fans."

"Or sending them on silly errands."

"Or making them buy us flowers."

"Or write us bad poetry." Violet laughed, then sobered. "I didn't mean it when I said Father was stupid."

"I know. He did make mistakes, but he also loved us."

"Yes, but he might have left us a little money."

If only . . . No, she wasn't going to waste her time on wishing for something that couldn't come true. "But he didn't, so we have to make the best of what we do have."

"I couldn't do it, you know," said Violet.

Anthea smiled. "I know."

Chapter 11

Colin scowled and threw down the quill. He didn't want to help plan the wedding. Of all the distasteful tasks the squire might have set him to, this was the worst. He didn't trust her—she was the most likely thief—but he couldn't explain to himself why he hadn't warned the squire about her yet.

Yes, he could.

Colin closed his eyes and rubbed his forehead. If he allowed himself perfect honesty, he knew exactly why. Because he wanted to believe her. He wanted to believe her indignation sincere and not an act. Her refusal to speak with him since that day was real enough.

Furthermore, he had to admit to himself he hated planning the wedding because he hated the thought of a beautiful young woman marrying a man like the squire. And not just any woman. Anthea.

He needed proof. Something irrefutable he could take to the squire. If Anthea was the thief, the squire wouldn't marry her. But if she wasn't . . .

He wouldn't think about that now. Colin grabbed a fresh sheet of paper, dipped the quill into the ink, and thought for a moment. He needed a trap. In his mind, he sorted through the various items around the house that were valuable and easy to take. The idea solidified in his mind. With the help of Pennyfeather and Fletcher, he might be able to place a valuable object in an accessible location and wait for the thief to strike. Definite weaknesses existed in such a scheme, but it was better than waiting around for the whim of the thief.

But what to use as the lure? Jewelry might be the best lure, but why would the squire leave jewelry lying about the house. Perhaps a jeweled figurine, or that Chinese vase—

Jumping from his seat, he rushed into the parlor. There was the ideal item—a gift Brody had sent from India. The small figurine depicted a sari-clad woman holding a large pearl to the sky. He swept the statuette into his palm and strode from the room. The table in the hall would serve as the perfect spot to draw out a thief. As he placed the figurine on the table, the light glistened off the pearl. Perfect.

Returning to the study, Colin grabbed a sheet of paper. He would need to schedule times for the three of them to watch—

"Yoo-hoo, Mr. Savernake." Mrs. Ulster strode into the room, dragging a young woman behind her. "The butler told us you would be here."

Colin suppressed his grimace and stood. "Good day, Mrs. Ulster. How may I help you?"

"I've just been to see Lady Anthea. We've been talking about the wedding." Mrs. Ulster pulled the woman forward. "May I present my daughter, Miss Eugenia Ulster?"

Colin bowed. "Charmed."

"You remember my telling you of Eugenia."

"How could I forget?"

Mrs. Ulster sat in one of the chairs beside the desk. "Do be seated, Mr. Savernake. You, too, Eugenia."

Colin watched the girl look for a seat farther from the desk, but her mother grabbed her arm and pulled her into the chair next to her. He folded his coattails under him as he sat. "You wanted to speak to me about the wedding?"

"Yes. Lady Anthea has asked for our help, and we've come to you. We understand that you're taking care of the details, the invitations and such."

"Yes."

"We shall need a complete list of the guests as soon as possible if we're to make our favors."

"Pardon?"

"The wedding favors. Lady Anthea has put us in charge of the favors for the guests. Hasn't she, Eugenia?"

Eugenia fidgeted in her chair. "Well, I thought she meant you—"

"So you see," said Mrs. Ulster without waiting for her daughter to finish, "we shall need the list just as soon as possible. Eugenia is quite the artist, but she needs time to complete the task."

The younger woman's face took on a pinkish hue. "Mother, I don't think—"

"Dear me, where is my reticule? Don't tell me I've left it in the front hall. Do excuse me while I fetch it. You young people talk. I'm sure you have much in common." Mrs. Ulster jumped up and dashed from the room before Colin could rise.

"She did this on purpose," said Miss Ulster, fighting to keep her expression from showing her embarrassment. She didn't succeed. Miss Ulster's face took on a vivid hue. "Do forgive her. Mother is forever plotting to have me meet men."

"I doubt she has to try very hard," said Colin, trying to ease the young woman's plight.

"You're very kind, but you needn't worry about me." Miss Ulster lifted her gaze to him and shook her head. "I suppose I should be used to it."

Colin searched for something to say. "I'm sure she means well."

"I wish she would stop. I don't need her help."

Colin examined the woman. She wasn't unattractive, but she had a long-suffering look that had nothing to do with the present situation. He'd have that same expression if that Ulster woman were his mother. "Does that mean you have a beau?"

"It means Mother shouldn't worry about me any longer." Eugenia folded her hands in her lap.

He nearly chuckled. His questions had been thoroughly dismissed. "Does that mean you won't be needing the list of wedding guests?"

"No, we do. Lady Anthea did ask for our help. Mother is so pleased."

He did chuckle then. "As soon as I have it, I'll send the guest list to you."

Mrs. Ulster flounced back into the room. Colin stood, but the woman was in the chair before he had completed the movement. "How are you children getting along?"

"Just fine, Mother."

"I heard laughter. You must be enjoying yourselves. Mr. Savernake, you must come to dinner at the vicarage," said Mrs. Ulster. "How about tomorrow? Then you can continue your conversation with Eugenia."

An expression of pain crossed the daughter's face as she closed her eyes. "We were only discussing the guest list, Mother."

"Excellent. We can help you complete it." Mrs. Ulster rose. "Come along, Eugenia. We have much to do."

Colin stood yet again as the ladies collected themselves.

"I expect to see you tomorrow evening, Mr. Savernake." Mrs. Ulster gave him a simpering smile. "I'm sure Eugenia is looking forward to your company."

The girl's face flushed red again.

A surge of pity for the younger woman shot through him. *His* parentage wasn't ideal, but at least he didn't have to deal with a personality like this mother's. "It was a pleasure to meet you, Miss Ulster."

"Likewise, Mr. Savernake."

"So formal," said Mrs. Ulster with a disapproving cluck. "After tomorrow evening, you will be fast friends, I'm sure."

As soon as the two women left the study, Colin let out a sigh and dropped into his chair. He would have to send his regrets, for no power of heaven or earth could bring him to the vicarage for dinner tomorrow evening.

He returned to his list and made a few notes, trying to work out the details of his plan. He didn't succeed. His glimmer of an idea had vanished after the lengthy interruption. Perhaps if he concentrated . . . A few fruitless minutes passed. Just as he laid down his quill in frustration, Mrs. Ulster popped her head back in.

"Do forgive the interruption, Mr. Savernake."

Colin jumped to his feet. "Mrs. Ulster. I thought you had left."

"I stopped to speak with Mrs. Pennyfeather to offer my assistance with the wedding. When I turned around, Eugenia had vanished. I thought perhaps she had returned to speak with you." Hope filled her visage as her gaze covered the room.

"I regret I must disappoint you. She isn't here."

"How odd. I wonder where she went. She probably didn't realize I stopped and is waiting for me outside. Ah, well. If you see her, send her home, will you? Ta-ta." Mrs. Ulster waved and disappeared again.

He had no hope of recapturing his concentration now. He needed some air. Leaving the study, he passed through the house, taking special care to check before he turned a corner, lest he encounter Mrs. Ulster again.

"Who's there?" Brody Hobblesby stood at the end of the hall.

"Savernake, Master Hobblesby."

Brody's face drew into a grimace. "Horrible. Please don't call me that."

Colin smiled. "Then what shall I call you?"

"Damn good question. I wasn't blessed with a tripping last name." Brody walked down the hall with the aid of his cane. "I'm no longer in the army, so Lieutenant is out, and Hobbs would be atrocious. Sounds too much like some long-dead philosopher, and I am alive, thank you very much. How about Brody?"

"I think I can manage to remember that, Brody."

"Were you heading somewhere?" asked Brody.

"Just outside. I felt the need of air."

"Mrs. Ulster cornered you, eh?" Brody grinned.

The man's perception startled him. "How did you know?"

"My hearing's not gone. I hid in my room until I heard her leave. Didn't want to take the chance she might spot me. Hideous woman. She tried foisting her daughter upon me before I entered the army." Brody leaned closer to him. "The girl's not ugly, but can you imagine *that* for a mother-in-law?"

"*She* certainly can."

Brody laughed. "Good God, man. We have to rescue

you. It's too bad Eugenia wasn't married off before you arrived." The blind man started to the door. "May I join you on your walk?"

"By all means."

The two men started up the hill that rose behind the house. Once or twice, Brody stumbled over stones or roots in his path. Colin reached forward to help him, but the man seemed to detect obstacles with his cane.

"You're adept with that cane," said Savernake.

"They taught me in the hospital. I haven't the skill I'd like yet."

"Your father has asked me to hire you an aide."

"That's probably best. I haven't mastered shaving yet, either. Or dressing. I can't tell if I'm wearing purple with orange." A hint of bitterness tinged Brody's voice. He drew his hand along his jaw. "Father helped me this morning, but I would prefer not to trouble him."

"I'm sure he doesn't mind."

Brody walked farther up the hill. "You're my father's secretary?"

"Yes."

"Why does my father need a secretary? What do you do for him?"

Colin hesitated for a moment. "At this moment, I'm making wedding arrangements."

"Ah yes, the wedding. That should keep you busy for the next few weeks. And then what?"

"Pardon me?"

"What shall you do then? We both know my father doesn't need a secretary. I may be blind, but I'm not stupid. Dougal does most of the work at the Grange, and Jane's husband handles most of the mill business.

And now I've returned. I admit I'm not much use yet, but I shall be. My father likes to put on airs, but I won't stand for someone bilking him."

"Someone is bilking your father, but it isn't me."

Brody stopped. "What do you mean?"

"Hasn't your father told you about the thefts?"

"No. Tell me."

"Someone has been stealing from your father, most recently a silver tray."

"I didn't know." Brody paused. "That's why you're here."

The man was sharp. "Why do you say that?"

"Several reasons. First, you don't fit in. From what Dougal tells me, your weeds are too elegant for a mere secretary. Second, your speech is far too refined for Middle Hutton. The last time I heard diction like yours was in the army. Lieutenant Chesterfield was the second son of an earl. He spoke exactly like you."

Colin chuckled. "Anything else?"

"You ask too many questions."

"Forgive me."

"No, no. I mean you are always asking questions. You ask about people and their background, not about your duties."

Brody was too perceptive by far. Colin weighed his next words. "You could explain my questions as natural curiosity."

"Perhaps, but I'm right, aren't I?"

"If I am here to deal with the thefts, how can I tell you without compromising my confidentiality?"

"You needn't worry about me. In fact, I may be able to help. Most people ignore me now. They believe my injury has impaired my mental capacity as well as my sight. I may hear something."

Colin hesitated only for a moment. "Then I suppose I may trust you."

"I knew it."

The note of triumph in Brody's voice made Colin smile. "You were able to discover the truth about me too easily. If I hope to succeed in my endeavor, I shall have to be more careful."

"I doubt anyone else would notice. You forget all I can do is listen.

"Do you suspect anyone?" Brody's voice had an eager tone.

"I do, but I prefer not to say anything until I've found proof."

"But if you tell me, I might help you find the proof."

Colin wouldn't betray Anthea. Not yet. "I cannot. I wouldn't want to influence you unduly."

Brody nodded. "I understand. You're an upright chap, Savernake."

"I try."

From below them, a voice cried up to the men, "Mr. Brody? Mr. Savernake?"

"Here, Joe," called back Brody.

The big man reached them with little effort. His breathing was as easy as if he'd been walking down a lane rather than climbing a hill. "You're needed at the house, Mr. Savernake. Fletcher sent me for you."

"Thank you, Joe." Colin turned to Brody. "Will you be all right?"

"He'll be fine," said Joe. "I'll carry him back to the house."

Brody looked horrified. "You'll do no such thing, Joe. I'm quite capable of walking."

"But, Mr. Brody. You can't see." The big man shook

his head. "You'd best let me take you back afore you get hurt."

Brody clenched his teeth together. "I don't need your help."

"Aye, but you do." Joe bent down and grabbed Brody's arm and leg.

"If you don't release me at once, I shall tell Father to dismiss you."

"Where would I go?" Joe frowned, but released him.

"Joe, what if I promise to take Mr. Brody back to the house with me? After all, I brought him out here," said Colin.

"The master made me promise no harm would come to Mr. Brody," said Joe.

"And I promise none shall. Now, what say you?" asked Colin.

"If Mr. Brody agrees," said Joe.

"I agree, I agree," said Brody.

"I'll be off, then. I want to see to the horses anyway. Good day to you both." Joe lumbered away as if nothing unusual had happened.

"Of all the humiliating experiences," said Brody with a groan. "He would have slung me across his shoulders like a ewe."

"And carried you with as little effort as well." He eyed Brody. "You're not a small man either."

"Joe and Bob grew larger than I think even they know," said Brody with a laugh. "I'd hate to come to blows with those two."

Colin watched the colossus amble toward the stables. He and his brother had strength enough to walk away with a case of wine or an ox. If Anthea somehow convinced them—

"Thank God they are loyal to my father," said Brody. He straightened his jacket and dusted off his trousers. "Shall we get back? They are waiting for you."

"Of course." He shifted his gaze from the retreating figure. "Shall I carry you?"

"You are not amusing," said Brody, and he started down the hill toward the house.

"But I promised to deliver you safely," said Colin, catching up with him in a few steps.

"I'm not sure I want to help you any longer," Brody said with a smile.

"But I have a pact for you. You won't tell my secret, and I won't speak of your humiliation."

"Done." Brody stopped and thrust his hand forward. Colin shook it. "I'm pleased we could reach an understanding."

Fletcher met them at the bottom of the hill. "Mr. Savernake. I'm glad you've returned so quickly."

"What's the matter?"

Fletcher cast a glance at Brody, but Savernake waved his hand. "Go ahead. Brody knows."

"It's Lady Anthea, Mr. Savernake. She's been found stealing from the squire."

Chapter 12

"For the last time, Jane, I did not steal the pearl." Anthea bit back the words she wanted to scream at the woman. She clenched her teeth together, but never averted her gaze. They stood in the parlor glaring at each other. The squire sat in his armchair.

Jane said, "Admit it, Anthea. I caught you. You are the thief. Isn't that so, Father?" Jane's eyes sparkled with a malicious glee.

"Let Thea speak, Jane," said Hobblesby. The squire turned to her. "Tell me, my dear, why did you have the statue in your basket?"

The basket sat on a low table, and the offending figurine stood beside it. It was the figure of a sari-clad woman holding a pearl to the sky. The Pearl Dancer was one of the squire's favorite pieces.

Anthea shook her head. "I don't know how it got in there. I didn't put it there."

"She won't tell the truth, Father. I don't see why you're wasting your time."

Squire Hobblesby let out a loud sigh. "I don't know what to think."

"What's happening here?" Savernake entered the room. Brody followed.

Anthea closed her eyes as she felt frustration swamp

her. Savernake would never believe her innocent. She knew what would follow. Savernake would tell the squire of his suspicions, and then Hobblesby would dismiss her from his house, or worse, summon the constable. Of all the people at the Grange, why did Savernake have to come in now?

"Anthea is a thief," said Jane, her voice dripping with satisfaction. "I caught her."

Savernake's gaze moved to the figurine on the table. "Is this what she tried to steal?"

"Yes. She slipped it into her basket."

"I didn't do it." She knew the denial was in vain, but she couldn't prevent it. Her fingers reached for the medallion at her throat. The round metal brought no comfort this time.

Savernake turned his gaze to her. Anger blazed in his eyes, but something more as well. Disappointment? Betrayal? She couldn't recognize it.

With a grim expression on his face, Savernake faced Hobblesby. "Squire, you know I've been working on the thefts that have been plaguing you."

Hobblesby straightened up. "You can't mean you've solved it."

"Logic led me to one conclusion, but I had no proof. Now we do."

The squire looked at her, then back at Savernake. Her stomach dropped, and a sick feeling filled her. They would accuse her of something she didn't do, and she was powerless to stop them.

The squire drew his brows together. "Thea? I don't believe it."

"Forgive me, Squire, but the facts fit. She has access to your house, and her family needs money. And now she has stolen this." He pointed to the statuette.

Hobblesby inhaled loudly. "I admit you make sense, but I still find it hard to believe. She's the daughter of an earl."

"I have met many earls, Squire. Not all of them are noble outside of their name." Savernake gave her a cold look.

"Father, her pretty face and fine manners have deceived you. She is little more than a common thief," said Jane.

Anthea didn't care what Jane said. The woman's words held little surprise for her. She glanced at the squire. His crestfallen expression made her insides twist with apprehension. He believed them. She could see in his face that he was starting to believe them.

"Have you nothing to say, Thea?" asked Hobblesby. The pleading in his tone angered her.

"What would you have me say? I could plead my innocence until I talked myself hoarse, but I doubt I would convince Jane or Mr. Savernake."

"And me?" Hobblesby held his palms forward in a gesture of resignation.

"I have already claimed my innocence in front of you. Do you need me to do so again?"

Hobblesby said nothing. He dropped his hands into his lap.

Jane smiled. "I'm glad to hear it's settled. I'll just return this to its rightful place." She picked up the Pearl Dancer and started to walk from the room.

Savernake started. "Where are you going?"

"To return the gem to the hall," said Jane.

"That's not where it belongs," said Anthea. "It belongs on the bookshelf in here."

"Nonsense. It was on the table in the hall," said

Jane. Her gaze darted from Anthea to Savernake to her father.

Savernake took the figurine from her. "I moved it to the hall this morning, hoping to lure the thief into taking it."

"And she did," said Jane.

"Except you wouldn't know the statuette had a new home unless you had seen it there." Savernake placed the figurine on the shelf.

"So I saw it in the hall. That doesn't prove anything." Jane's voice held a hint of panic.

"Even Lady Anthea knows the gem belongs in here." Savernake placed the figurine on the shelf. "If she had taken it from the hall, she would have thought the squire or Mrs. Pennyfeather had moved it, and she wouldn't have corrected you. She didn't know the pearl was ever there."

"But I . . ." Jane looked at her father.

"Jane, what have you done?" asked Hobblesby.

"Father . . ." Jane pouted. "I'd never steal from you."

"I never said you stole from your father," said Savernake. "I just wonder how the pearl got into Lady Anthea's basket."

"She stole it." Jane pointed at her. "I saw her slip it into her basket."

"My basket was in the kitchen. I didn't bring it into the house," said Anthea.

"Then I don't know how it got there. I just know I found it there." Jane wrung her hands.

"Your story has changed," said Savernake. "Did you see Lady Anthea steal the figurine or not?"

"I . . . I . . . I don't remember," said Jane with a wail. Like a sudden summer storm, tears fell from her eyes, and she sobbed. "Father, why are you letting them treat me this way? My baby—"

"Your baby will be fine," said Hobblesby. "Jane, did you put the statue in Anthea's basket?"

Jane hiccuped. "Yes."

Hobblesby sighed. "Why?"

"Because I don't want you to marry her," said Jane, riding on the crest of fresh tears. "She's younger than I am, and she's going to take you away from us."

"Jane, Jane, you silly girl." Hobblesby clicked his tongue. "I can't change her age, but I can promise she won't take me from you."

"What of the other things?" asked Savernake.

"I didn't take anything else. Why should I steal from my own father?" Jane's tear storm finished as suddenly as it had started. She placed her fists on her hips.

"Of course you didn't. Savernake, stop this nonsense at once." Hobblesby rapped his cane on the floor to emphasize his words.

Jane shot Savernake a triumphant look.

Hobblesby pointed at Jane with his cane. "Now apologize to Thea."

The triumphant look vanished from her face. "Do I have to?"

"Yes," said Hobblesby.

With a loud sniff, Jane turned to face Anthea. "I apologize for causing you such trouble."

What about the attempt to smear her name? She was sorely tempted to walk out on all of them and flee to the comfort of her family, but it was concern for the comfort of her family that enabled her to swallow her anger and nod. "Very well, Jane. I accept."

"I owe you an apology as well," said Savernake.

"Perhaps next time you'll believe me when I say I

didn't do something," said Anthea. She wouldn't look at him.

"It seems we all must apologize to you, my dear," said Hobblesby. "For a moment I believed what they said, but I should have known you aren't capable of such behavior. But I expect you'll have time enough to scold me after our wedding."

"I apologize as well," said Brody.

She glanced at him in surprise. "Whatever for?"

"Father said we all have to apologize. I'm just being an obedient son." Brody grinned.

Hobblesby laughed. "Brody, boy, it's good to have you home." He faced Jane again. "I trust we shall have no more incidents like this one."

"No, Father," said Jane.

Anthea couldn't help but compare Jane's behavior to the twins'. Jane acted more like a child than the grown woman she was. Anthea didn't believe the sincerity of the woman's apology. She was sure Jane would hate her more after today's events.

"Glad that's settled," said Hobblesby. "No more talk of Anthea being a thief. In fact, I think we should plan something for the two families. Bring them together. A picnic."

Anthea watched Jane's expression change to one of horror. "I can't possibly attend a picnic in my condition."

"Balderdash. You have to eat anyway, Jane."

"Are you sure you want the twins there?" asked Thea.

"Most definitely. Keep you young, children do. Tell Pennypound we're having a picnic tomorrow, will you, Anthea? I leave it in your hands. Oh, and be sure your family knows." Hobblesby crossed to Brody.

"Let's go to my study and share a brandy. I haven't had much of a chance to talk to you yet."

"An excellent idea, Father," said Brody.

Hobblesby took his son's elbow and placed his other arm around his shoulders. "Come along, then. I shall be your guide."

Jane watched the two men disappear. "I need to leave as well. Hubert is expecting me." She walked from the room as fast as her unwieldy gait could carry her.

Anthea sat for the first time since being brought to the room for the accusation. Her legs trembled, and her hands shook. She tried to swallow, but her mouth was too dry. She ran her tongue over her lips, then rubbed them together, but it brought no relief.

"May I get you a drink?" asked Savernake.

"I don't want anything from you," said Anthea.

He had the grace to look chagrinned. "I meant my apology. I misjudged you."

"Again."

"Again," he said, nodding.

"It seems every time we meet, you end up apologizing to me." Anthea straightened in her chair. "Mr. Savernake, I wish you well in your quest to find the thief, but I don't want to see you anymore. Not alone, not in a group."

"That might prove difficult since I work for the squire."

She ignored her pounding heart. "I shall use whatever influence I have to convince the squire to dismiss you."

"No doubt you shall try." He didn't sound nervous.

"Then we understand each other." She stood. "Good day to you, Mr. Savernake. Or better said, good-bye."

"We shall see. But I feel I should point out that I am

not convinced you are innocent, and I shall be watching you despite your wishes."

Anger boiled over. She was tired, shaken from Jane's accusations, and he stood in front of her and had the gall to question her integrity. She snatched up a Meissen figurine. "Then perhaps I shouldn't disappoint you. This would fetch a pretty penny I'm sure."

"What are you doing?"

"Making your job easier." She placed the figurine in her basket.

"Lady Anthea—"

"No, wait." She took it out again and crossed to the shelf. Thumping the statuette on the wood harder than the porcelain warranted, she snatched up a book instead. "This is a rare book. And it's in French. The squire can't read French anyway. He'll never miss it. I could sell this for a goodly amount."

"Anthea—"

"Better yet, I'll take the pearl." She shoved the book onto the shelf, not caring that pages folded between its covers as she did. "No one would accuse me now of taking the Pearl Dancer. I've been proven innocent in advance." She grabbed the figurine.

"Stop it." He crossed to her.

"Stop what? I'm just carrying out my natural behavior. I'm a thief, remember?" She replaced the Pearl Dancer. "No? This Chinese vase is perfect. And China's all the rage now. It will fetch a handsome price."

She reached for the vase, but his hand shot out and grabbed her arm. He spun her around to face him. "I said stop it."

"Why?" Her heart hammered in her chest, but she felt only fury. "Perhaps you don't want to help the squire. If you catch me, there won't be a wedding, and you won't have a job. Hmmm, maybe I should help you reach your goal. If you leave, we'll never have to see each other again."

"You're being ridiculous."

"Accusing me of theft isn't ridiculous, though. You haven't liked me since we met. Perhaps you're frightened of me. Perhaps I remind you of the family you should have had."

He leaned over her. "Don't speak to me of my family."

"Why? Are they ashamed of you? If this is how you behave with them, I can't blame them."

"You know nothing of my family."

"I know they denied you a title. Perhaps that's why you hate me so much."

"Yes. Just look how much your title has bought you. A husband who could be your father, a house that should be torn down, and a family that doesn't have enough to eat. Oh, yes, I should envy you your title." He thrust her from him.

The push wasn't hard, but she stumbled back. Her arms flailed and struck the Pearl Dancer. It wobbled on its small platform, then toppled off the shelf. It landed with a loud ping, then shattered on the floor.

"Oh, no." Anthea covered her mouth with her hands. Her eyes filled with tears. She knelt down and tried to pick up the shards.

Savernake knelt beside her. "Forgive me, I didn't mean to hurt you."

"You didn't hurt me. It was my own clumsiness." Her voice hitched. She picked up the pearl still clutched in the arm of the tiny dancer. The tears spilled over Anthea's lids.

Savernake looked shaken. "You mustn't cry. It was an accident. The squire will understand."

She gathered up the rest of the dancer in her skirt. "I don't have the money to replace it."

"Hobblesby won't expect you to."

"Whether he expects me to or not, I broke it. I wish I were the thief. Then I could steal something to pay for it."

"I'll pay for it."

She stared at him. "But how can you afford—"

"How doesn't concern you."

"I can't let you—"

"You can, and you shall."

She narrowed her gaze. "Why would you help me? You think I'm a thief."

"I never said I wasn't a fool." Savernake pivoted and left the room.

Anthea shook with anger. The arrogance of the man unnerved her. She wanted to scream with frustration. If she were a man, she could call him out for the insult to her name. If she were a man, her threats would be taken seriously. If she were a man . . .

If she were a man, she would be Earl Fortesque, and her family wouldn't need to depend on her marriage to save them.

She sighed and rose from the floor, cradling the broken pieces in her skirt. Wishing for the impossible was as pointless as counting grains of sand. She'd leave the wishing to dreamers like Violet and concentrate on the things she could change, such as making the squire see how unsuitable Mr. Savernake was as a secretary.

But first she had to tell Hobblesby about the Pearl Dancer.

Chapter 13

Anthea grumbled to herself as she came down the stairs of the cottage. "Miserable, arrogant, loathsome—"

"Thea, what *is* the matter?" asked Violet, coming up beside her. "You've been in a foul mood since yesterday."

Thea pursed her lips. "Nothing much. Savernake called me a thief."

Violet's mouth dropped open. "I beg your pardon?"

"Savernake decided to accuse me of stealing from the squire."

"You can't be serious."

"Jane slipped a statuette into my basket, then made a production of discovering my duplicity. Savernake augmented the situation by explaining to the squire that he believed I had been the thief all along."

"The lout." Violet balled her hands into fists. "How dare he? You can't let him get away with such behavior. I'm going to march right over and give him such a tongue-lashing that he blisters."

"There's no need, Violet. I've already spoken to him."

"But he has no right—"

"I've taken care of it, Violet." Anthea smiled despite herself. She loved her sister.

"How did the squire react?"

"He didn't want to believe it at first, but Jane and Savernake convinced him."

"That's one good thing come of this. Now you don't have to marry him."

"The squire believes me now. Jane confessed to the scheme. The constable is not coming after me."

"You still don't have to marry him."

"Violet." A pang of irritation passed through her. "We've discussed this before."

"I know, I know." Violet sighed. "Will you at least let me yell at Jane when I see her?"

"For shame," said Anthea in a mock scolding tone. "Remember her delicate condition."

"Horrors." Violet clasped her hand to her heart with a dramatic flair. "I forgot. She's as delicate as an elephant."

"Who's as delicate as an elephant?" asked Iris as she came up behind them.

"Jane," said Violet.

Iris shuddered. "I don't see how you put up with her, Thea."

"I keep telling her she doesn't have to, but she won't listen." Violet frowned as the three sisters entered the small parlor.

Iris shook her head. "You don't understand, Vi. Thea is so much stronger than the rest of us. I'm sure I couldn't marry the squire, but I'm ever so grateful she is."

"I don't want her to sacrifice herself for me." Violet's voice grew louder.

"She isn't. She's doing it for all of us," said Iris. "I don't think I shall ever be able to repay her, but I don't believe she wants me to."

Anthea looked at her younger sister in surprise. Her insight was remarkable. For a young woman who had little patience for others, Iris had keen perception.

"Thea isn't a martyr. Yes, she's marrying a man much older than herself, with an unpleasant family besides, but she will have a good life." Iris shrugged. "By marrying the squire, she can help us, and I imagine she will enjoy our happiness almost as much as if it were her own. It's like reading a riveting book. You live through the characters. Besides, anything can happen between now and the wedding."

Violet wrinkled her nose. "The wedding is in three weeks. Do you really think some handsome stranger will come and sweep her away? He'd have to be rich, too, for her to consider it."

Iris gave a mysterious smile. "One never knows, does one?"

"You may stop speaking of me as if I weren't here." Anthea shook her head. "I'm not waiting for some man to rescue me from a fate worse than death. Now, you all may get ready for a picnic. The squire has decided that our families need to understand one another better."

"No, thank you, Thea. I found a book in the attic. I want to read it." Iris showed her the tome in her hand.

"Yes, you will, young lady. The picnic is for the whole family."

"Even the twins?" asked Violet.

"Even the twins," said Anthea. "Besides, Mother knows already and approves."

Iris twisted her lips into an expression of disgust. "What a waste of time."

"You may bring your book," she said in a cajoling tone.

"That's something at least." Iris left the room as if she floated on air.

"If she weren't my sister, I might be frightened of her," said Violet. "I'll go, but I'm not happy about it. I was hoping to get some writing done today. Not that that's likely with the twins in the house."

As if to prove her words true, a shout echoed through the hallway, followed by a squeal of laughter. The twins burst through the door and stopped short when they saw their sisters frowning at them. Rose twisted her face into a grimace. "I don't suppose you'll let us climb out through the window."

"Mother wants to teach us how to do our numbers again," said Daisy.

"Absolutely not," said Anthea.

"But, Thea—" they began in chorus.

"Don't expect pity from me. If you had learned it properly the first time, Mother wouldn't have to teach it to you again."

"But if she would only teach us something interesting like pirates, or knights, we'd love to listen," said Rose.

"You should be ashamed of yourselves," said Violet. "Mother has enough work without having to chase you around the house. Have you no consideration for her? She cooks and cleans for you. Do you think she enjoys chasing you as well?"

Daisy hung her head. "I'm sorry."

"We don't mean to make trouble," added Rose.

"Well, you should think about her a little more often instead of just yourselves." Violet frowned at them.

Anthea put her hand on her sister's arm just as her mother came into the room. "There you are, you imps. Come back to your slates at once or no picnic for you."

The twins ran over to their mother and threw their arms around her. "We're sorry. We didn't mean to give you more trouble," said Rose, her voice hitching with unshed tears.

"We'll sit still until we learn the numbers. We promise," said Daisy. She sniffed and wiped her cheeks on her mother's apron.

"What's this?" asked Lady Fortesque in surprise. "There, there, my dears. No need for tears. Perhaps you've been working too hard."

"No, Mother, we want to learn. Really." Rose's eyes glistened with wetness.

"We'll be good." Daisy nodded until her curls bounced like a hundred rubber balls dropped at the same time.

Lady Fortesque looked at Anthea and Violet. Violet had the good sense to turn her gaze. Their mother shrugged. "Very well. I'm happy to see you so excited about your learning."

"Maybe you could tell us one pirate story?" asked Rose.

Their mother laughed. "If you do your numbers well. Come along."

The three left the parlor.

"Did you see how tired Mother looked?" asked Violet.

Anthea nodded. "Now will you stop questioning why I have to marry the squire?"

"Yes." Violet hooked her arm with Anthea's. "But I don't have to like it."

"That's all I ask," said Anthea with a smile.

The brilliance of the day didn't reflect the mood of the picnickers. With a look of utter boredom on her face, Jane sat on one side of the clearing under the shade of a tree. Hubert sat beside her, although he cast the occasional glance of longing at the blanket covered with food in the middle of the field. Dougal lounged under a different tree with a definite scowl on his face. Iris sat under a parasol, her nose in a book, paying no mind to the noise around her. Violet frowned and clenched her fists each time she spotted Jane.

Anthea sighed. The squire's plan to bring the two families together would bear little success on this day. At least her mother seemed to enjoy her conversation with Hobblesby, and Brody didn't appear the least upset with the situation. The twins hadn't settled down enough for Anthea to gauge their moods.

With resignation, she decided to help the squire with his goal. "I think I'll take a plate to Jane," said Anthea.

"Oh, let me, please," said Violet with a glint in her eye.

Anthea eyed her sister. In a low voice, she said, "No, I'd rather have her eat the food than wear it."

Brody chuckled. Anthea shot him a glance. "You weren't supposed to hear that."

"I know." His grin grew broader, but he lowered his voice so his father wouldn't hear him. "Lady Violet, could it be you haven't forgiven my sister yet for her prank?"

"I haven't begun to forgive her. How dare she accuse Thea of theft?" Violet let out a puff of air.

"What of Savernake?" asked Brody. "He accused her as well."

"I am well aware of his actions, I assure you." Violet grabbed a plate and started loading it with food.

"If I've forgotten it, you can, too," said Anthea.

"You haven't forgotten," said Violet. "You just want to keep the peace."

The two sisters filled several plates, then passed them out. Anthea took one to Jane and her husband. Hubert said, "Thank you," which earned him a glare from his wife. Anthea ignored the woman. She only had to tolerate her, not be her friend.

The twins dashed to the blanket when they realized the food was ready. "Ooooh, pheasant," said Daisy.

"And lobster cakes," said Rose, crumbs littering her lips.

"Girls, you will sit and eat like ladies," said their mother. "And don't speak with your mouth full."

Hobblesby laughed. "I had forgotten the exuberance of the young. Tell me, Lady Fortesque, how do you keep up with them?"

"I am sorry to say I often don't," said Lady Fortesque. "I find myself falling into bed at night after chasing these two around all day."

"Send them to the Grange," said Hobblesby. "We'll put them to churning, or better yet to carding, so they'll be too tired to cause any mischief."

"Perhaps I shall," said Lady Fortesque. Anthea heard the lilt in her mother's voice.

"No, Mother," cried Rose.

"We'll be good," said Daisy.

"What a pity. I could have used two workers with a great deal of energy." Hobblesby winked at the girls. Rose and Daisy squealed as they realized they had been teased.

The food was excellent, but as the meal progressed, the separation of the group didn't heal. At least Savernake wasn't with them. Anthea thanked the fates for that simple gift. She looked down the road and groaned. She had spoken too soon. Savernake was walking with Mrs. Ulster, her mother-in-law, and Eugenia.

"Savernake, good to see you," said Hobblesby. He rose from the ground and brushed the crumbs from his lap. "Mrs. Ulster, Mother Ulster, and Miss Ulster. A pleasure. Won't you join us? Have you eaten? We have plenty."

"Thank you, Squire Hobblesby," said Mrs. Ulster, taking a seat on the blanket. "Lady Fortesque. I am ever so happy to see you again."

"Good day, Mrs. Ulster," said Lady Fortesque.

"We are coming along nicely with the wedding favors. Eugenia and I . . ." She gestured toward her daughter, who no longer stood beside her. Mrs. Ulster glanced around and spotted her near Dougal. "Eugenia, come here. Lady Fortesque wishes to speak with us about the wedding."

"Leave the girl alone, Rowena," said Mother Ulster. "She doesn't want to spend time with the old folks."

"Nonsense. She enjoys our company. Not that we're old, eh, Squire?"

"Not I," said Hobblesby.

"Humph," said Mother Ulster.

"Eugenia," Mrs. Ulster called again.

Eugenia shot a glance at Dougal, then returned to the blanket.

"Tell Lady Fortesque about your idea, Eugenia. And don't eat too much. No man wants a fat wife. At least until after you're wedded, and then it's too late." Mrs. Ulster laughed as if she had told a most amusing story.

"Don't know about that," said Mother Ulster. "Eating like a bird hasn't helped her find a husband yet."

"Oh, Mother Ulster, you're so full of humor today." Mrs. Ulster laughed.

Anthea shut her mind away from Mrs. Ulster. The woman would blather for the next hour with very little of import. She watched instead Savernake, who filled a plate and sat beside Brody. She glanced at Violet. Her sister's gaze had narrowed, and she was staring at Savernake.

"Not here, Violet, please," said Anthea.

"I won't do anything." Violet frowned again. "But I can't believe the gall of the man. He's eating as if nothing happened yesterday. If I could just hit him, once . . ."

Anthea giggled. "And then what? I'd have to nurse your knuckles for the next week."

Violet smiled. "You're probably right. And how would I write then?"

The twins jumped up from their spots. "Mother, may we be excused?"

Their mother sighed. "Yes, but don't leave—"

The girls darted off.

"—your plates . . ." Lady Fortesque shook her head.

"Don't worry, Mother. I'll take care of their dishes." Anthea took their empty plates and scraped the remnants into a bush. She returned the dishes to the hamper.

The squire clapped his hands together. "There's enough of us for a game of Pall Mall. Savernake, would you fetch it for us. It's in the back of the wagon."

"No games, Father. I have to get back to the Grange." Dougal stood. "The horses and cows can't wait." Without waiting for his father to answer, Dougal headed down the road.

"And I can't play, Father," said Jane. Anthea wanted to slap the smugness out of her voice, but it just wasn't polite to hit an expectant mother.

"I'm willing to play," said Brody.

They all stared at him.

He shrugged. "A joke."

Violet stifled a giggle.

"Perhaps we should enjoy the sunshine," said Lady Fortesque in a gentle tone.

The twins burst from behind a tree. "Look what we found," shouted Daisy.

Rose thrust out her hand. A small, heart-shaped stone lay in her palm. Anthea smiled at their exuberance. She noticed Savernake and Brody with their heads together.

"It's only a rock," said Iris.

"It is not," said Rose. She thrust out her bottom lip.

"May I see it?" asked Savernake.

Rose handed it to him.

"Hmmm, interesting." Savernake stroked his chin. "What do you think, Brody?"

"But he can't see," said Daisy.

"Daisy," said Mother in a sharp reprimand.

"Not with my eyes," said Brody, as if he hadn't heard Lady Fortesque.

The girls edged closer to him. "Then how?" asked Daisy.

"With my fingers." Brody opened his hand.

Savernake laid the stone in Brody's palm. Brody picked it up and ran his fingers over the edges. "Most definitely, I should say."

"I thought so," said Savernake.

"What did you think?" asked Rose.

"Elves," said Savernake.

Daisy and Rose opened their mouths in wonder.

"They live around here, you know," added Brody.

"They do?" asked Daisy in a whisper.

"Haven't you heard them?" asked Brody. "Their music keeps me up almost every night."

"I haven't heard them," said Rose.

Brody struck his forehead lightly. "I forgot. You see, when you go blind, they say your hearing becomes more acute. Since my eyes don't work, my ears can hear what you can't. I don't suppose the rest of you have heard them either."

"No. It's such a tragedy," said Violet. Her eyes gleamed at joining the game.

"Do you really think elves made this?" breathed Daisy.

"Who else would leave a heart in the woods?" said Savernake.

"Listen. Did you hear that?" asked Brody suddenly.

The girls tilted their heads and strained to hear.

"I'm sure I heard laughter." Brody turned his head to the woods. "There it is again."

"I didn't hear it," said Rose.

"Neither did I," said Daisy.

Savernake shook his head. "I didn't either, but if Brody says they're there, they are."

"Maybe we can catch them," said Brody.

"Oh, yes, please," cried the girls together.

"Mother, may we go on an elf hunt?" asked Daisy.

"Very well, but if you catch one, you may not bring him home," said Lady Fortesque. "I have enough trouble keeping the house clean without someone else living with us."

"We promise," said Rose.

Brody rose. "I suppose I should accompany you. I can hear them better than you. Lady Violet, will you help me?"

Violet took his arm. "I would be honored."

"An elf hunt, eh? I remember those from my youth." Mother Ulster winked at Violet.

"Well, I'm not going," said Jane. "An elf hunt. How ridiculous."

"No one asked you to come, sister," said Brody. He and Violet started for the trees at the edge of the field.

"Hurrah, let's go," shouted Daisy. She shot over the clearing and into the trees. Rose was a mere three steps behind her.

"Not too fast, girls," shouted their mother after them.

"Eugenia, you must go as well," said Mrs. Ulster. "Perhaps Mr. Savernake will accompany you."

Eugenia flushed a bright pink. Her gaze shot down the road toward home. "I don't think—"

"Nonsense. You must go on the elf hunt. You and Mr. Savernake."

Savernake offered his arm to Eugenia. "It would be my pleasure."

"Anthea has to go as well," said Iris.

All gazes switched to the girl whose nose still hadn't come out of her book.

"And why is that?" asked Anthea, crossing her arms in front of her.

"Because someone has to watch the girls, and I'm not going," said Iris.

"She's right, Thea," whispered her mother. "I would feel better if you were there to watch them."

"You could make Iris go," said Anthea with a sinking feeling in her stomach.

"I could, but you know she would resent every minute away from that book. You'll watch the girls instead of moping."

"Go along, Thea," said Hobblesby. "It's far too soon after my gout for me to attempt such a climb."

Anthea plastered a smile on her face and followed Savernake and Eugenia.

Chapter 14

The woods were cool and dark after sitting in the sun. Colin smiled at the woman on his arm. Why he had agreed to accompany her he'd never know. "Are you enjoying yourself?"

Eugenia looked startled at the question. "Are you speaking to me?"

"Whom else would I address?" Strange woman. Shy as a mouse. Not that he could blame her, with a mother like hers.

"You could be speaking to her." Eugenia pointed behind them to Anthea.

"Not likely. If you haven't noticed, the woman barely tolerates me."

Eugenia smiled. "I should think not after you accused her of being a thief."

"You heard?"

"The village is small, and my mother . . ." She shrugged. "There is little that happens in this town my mother doesn't know."

The woods were thicker now. He heard the gurgle of a beck somewhere to his left, but the laughter of the children ahead of him drowned out all other sounds. He envied them their exuberance.

"Slow down, you two," said Anthea. She brushed

past them and hurried forward to the others. "If you fall into the water, I'll make you wear your wet clothes for the rest of the day."

Brody drew to a stop ahead of them. "Shhhh, did you hear that?"

The twins returned to his side without a peep. They listened. Then Daisy frowned. "I didn't hear anything."

"That's because you're so loud," said Rose.

"Am not," said Daisy.

Brody shook his head. "How do you expect to hear the elves if you bicker. They hate loud noises."

The girls fell quiet again.

"If I'm not mistaken, there's a little pool along the river here. If I were an elf, I would make my home there."

The girls scampered toward the water. "We'll find it," said Rose over her shoulder.

"Wonderful," muttered Anthea. She picked up her skirts and followed the girls.

Violet laughed. "You should have seen the look Thea gave you, Brody."

"Not happy with me, is she?" He chuckled.

"We found it," came the cry from between the trees. Colin couldn't be sure which twin shouted, but he knew it wasn't their eldest sister.

"They don't know the meaning of quiet," said Violet with a sigh. "Now you know why I can't write at home."

"Lead me to them," said Brody. "They'll need my help to find the elves."

Colin started forward, but Eugenia lagged behind. "Miss Ulster?"

"Now, really. An elf hunt? I have no desire to hunt for elves. Such silly nonsense." The woman frowned.

So the mouse had fangs. "Do you wish to stay here?
I cannot leave you alone."

"Nonsense. What could possibly happen to me?"

"Your mother wouldn't approve."

Eugenia sighed. "No, I suppose she wouldn't. I'd
better go with you."

Following the sounds of the children, they pushed
through the bushes until they reached the others. A
small, deep pool bowed out from the swiftly running
stream. A little farther downstream, the water cas-
caded over rocks forming a waterfall. The still water
was clear. He could see a trout swimming at the bottom. Stones surrounded the river here. The twins
scampered over them like mountain goats without a
care. They leaped from boulder to boulder, spreading
their arms wide as if in flight. Anthea followed behind
them, albeit at a slower pace. Colin admired her lithe
grace. Her skirts flipped at her calves, but didn't seem
to hamper her movements.

"Have a care," said Anthea. "These stones are wet.
You may slip." She jumped onto a stone where the
twins had stood a moment before. As if her own words
cursed her, the rock bobbled, tipping her to the side.
Her arms flailed in the air.

"Anthea," he shouted. He released his hold on Eugenia and jumped toward her, but he knew he wouldn't
reach her in time.

With a cry, Anthea fell backward into the pool.

"Thea," shouted Violet.

The splash flicked water over him, but he ignored
the cold drops. Anthea came up, sputtering for air,
then went under again. Heedless of his boots, he
stepped into the pool, and reached for her. Her skirt
brushed against his hand. He clasped the material in

his fist and pulled her toward him. Sliding his hand under her head, he lifted her face clear of the water. She coughed.

He pulled her from the water. Her sodden dress must have added five stone to her weight. Little wonder she had difficulty righting herself. As he climbed up the banks of the beck, his leather soles slipped on the rocks, but he found a foothold and hoisted himself the rest of the way out.

"Thea, you've scared away the elves for sure," said Rose with a pout.

"Are you going to make yourself wear your wet clothes for the rest of the day?" asked Daisy.

"Hush," said Violet. She hurried to her sister's side. "Are you hurt, Thea?"

Anthea shook her head and coughed again. Then she drew in a ragged breath. "My foot hurts a little, but I'm fine." She shivered.

Colin peeled off his coat and spread it over her shoulders.

Anthea shook her head and shrugged out of the coat. "No. I've already caused you enough trouble."

"I'm fine." He looked at her. Her shivering was worse, and her lips had taken on a blue tinge. He pulled his coat on her again. "We need a blanket," said Colin.

"N-no. I'm s-sure if I walk, I'll w-warm up." Her teeth chattered. She stood, but buckled as she placed her weight on her left foot. "Ouch."

"You must have twisted it," said Violet.

"Lady Violet, take Brody and the children back to the picnic area. I'll meet you there."

"But we haven't found the elves yet," said Rose.

"The elf hunt is over for the day, poppet," said Colin.

"Oh-h-h." The drawn-out protest from Daisy brought a half smile to his face.

"Don't worry. We'll come back another time and search for them."

"And you'd better not give me any trouble on the way back, or I'll leave you for the Gypsies," said Violet.

"You will not," said Rose.

"And how can you be so sure?" Violet planted her fists on her hips.

"Because that would make Mother sad," Rose said.

"You're too smart for your own good," said Violet. But she smiled and drew them near. "Thea's been hurt, and we have to get help. Promise to be good?"

"Yes, Violet," said Daisy. "We know Thea needs our help."

"I'll be following behind you with Lady Anthea," said Colin.

"Following? How?" asked Anthea. "I can't walk."

"I'll carry you."

"What?" Anthea squeaked.

Violet led Brody from the stream back through the woods. The twins dashed in front of them.

"You c-can't c-carry me," said Anthea. "You'll g-get wet."

"I'm already wet." He knelt beside her to scoop her into his arms, then paused. Her eyes shimmered with tears. "What's wrong?"

"You've ruined your b-boots," she said as the drops spilled over her lids. "And I'm c-cold and my f-foot hurts."

Her lips were bluer now. He took her hand. The bluish tinge extended to her fingernails as well.

"We've got to get these clothes off you."

"I b-beg your p-pardon?"

"Not here." He lifted her from the ground.

"I'll ruin your c-clothes." But even as she protested she wrapped her arms around his neck and snuggled into his chest.

"Clothes can be replaced." He hugged her closer, trying to stop her shivering.

"I c-can't afford to," she said.

"I never asked you to."

"But—"

"Hush." He glanced down at her. Her green eyes glittered brighter than any jewel. A tear slid down her cheek. "Hush," he said gently.

She said nothing for a minute. As they entered the cover of the trees, a large tremor shook her body. He held her even tighter to himself despite the chill entering his own body. He couldn't see the others, but he knew his pace was slow. With the added weight of her wet dress, she weighed more than a comfortable burden.

"Thank you," she whispered.

"For what?"

"For b-being so k-kind, for not ridiculing me."

That surprised him. "Why should I ridicule you?"

"Because I was so clumsy." She hid her face against him. "I am so m-mortified."

He found a fallen log and set her down. Her hair hung in wet strands, clinging to her skin, and her eyes shimmered. He never thought her more beautiful than now. "You have nothing to be embarrassed about."

She hiccuped. "My f-foot . . . I've made s-such a fool of myself."

He sat beside her. Turning her so she faced him, he cupped her cheeks. "We have to get you warm, but first . . ." He drew in a deep breath. "I believe I am the fool here."

"Why?"

"Because I'm going to kiss you."

Colin leaned to her mouth and touched his lips to hers. They were cold, but after a few moments, he lured heat from them. She let out a small sigh, and he took advantage of her parted lips to delve into her mouth with his tongue. She tasted exquisite, like the exotic mixture of rare spices in creating a gourmet dish.

He pulled her closer, as if he was afraid she might disappear. She received him willingly. Her hand splayed across his back, and her bodice pressed against his shirtfront. Her cheeks warmed under his fingers.

In a dim recess of his mind, a warning rang out, but he ignored it. He wanted more of the headiness that engulfed him as their tongues danced and their breaths mingled. She was his for the moment. She fit.

"This way."

Colin pulled back. He had heard a voice.

"They can't be much farther," said Violet.

Colin looked at Anthea. Her lips were no longer blue and pink blossomed in her cheeks. Her eyes glistened. "They're coming for us."

Her mouth formed an "O." She put her hand to her hair, then dropped it. "Do I look . . . I must look terrible."

"You look wonderful." He turned from her and waved his arms. "Here," he called.

Violet appeared first, followed by her mother. The squire came behind them. Lady Fortesque ran to her daughter and draped the blanket she held over Anthea's shoulders. "Are you hurt?"

"My foot."

"She cannot walk," said Colin. A sharp twinge of disappointment stabbed through him. He didn't welcome the intrusion. He quashed that thought. What right had he to keep Anthea to himself?

"I can't carry her," said Hobblesby. "Savernake, would you be so kind as to bring her farther?"

"Without hesitation." He scooped her up again. Only he noticed the deepening of her cheek color. Much to his regret, her unease with him grew the closer they came to the picnic site. She wouldn't meet his gaze, and she answered her mother's and Hobblesby's questions with as few words as possible.

When they reached the clearing, Hobblesby lengthened his stride to walk beside him. "Put her in the wagon."

Colin placed her on the wagon bed.

Anthea pulled the blanket from around her, then drew the coat from her shoulders. "Thank you for your coat. I'm afraid it's ruined."

"It's only water. It will dry. As should the rest of me." He draped the coat over his arm. He didn't want to cover the spot where he could still feel the imprint of her hand on his back.

"The sun should set you right in a moment, my dear," said Hobblesby. "And perhaps a toddy from Mrs. Birdfeather. You'll stay with me until you recover."

Anthea blanched. She shot Colin a glance, but looked back at the squire in the next instant.

Lady Fortesque shook her head. "I can't let her stay at the Grange. What would people say?"

"Nonsense," said Hobblesby. "Bother the villagers. I insist. I have the room, and Mrs. Pennystone can take care of her. Let Lady Violet accompany her if you're so worried."

"Yes, Mother. I'll go, too," said Violet.

"Very well. Thank you, Squire," said Lady Fortesque.

"Father, you can't be serious," said Jane.

"We'll discuss this later," said Hobblesby. "I have to get Anthea home before she falls ill. Climb in, Jane, or you'll have to walk with the rest."

Grumbling, Jane climbed into the seat with Hubert's aid. Hubert was about to climb up as well, when Hobblesby spoke again. "Not you, Hubert. I'll drive the rig home. You walk with the others. Savernake, may I trust you to clear our things?"

"Of course, sir."

"Wait," said Mrs. Ulster. "Where is my daughter?"

"Don't have time to look for her now," said Hobblesby. He clicked his tongue, and the horses started forward.

Colin shivered despite the sun. His shirt was wet from carrying Anthea, and his coat would be of little use to warm him as it was as wet as his shirt. The walk back to the Grange would warm him. Almost as much as Anthea's kiss. He smiled.

"Eugenia!"

Mrs. Ulster's shout blasted through his thoughts. Where was Eugenia? He turned to Brody. "Didn't she return with you?" asked Colin.

"We didn't see her, and we didn't spend time to look. We thought it more important to get help for Anthea," said Violet.

"My darling daughter is lost," said Mrs. Ulster. "Eugenia!"

"Here I am, Mother. No need to shout." Eugenia walked from the woods, unhurried, unperturbed.

"Eugenia, my dear, dear girl. What happened to you?" asked Mrs. Ulster.

"Nothing. I became bored and went for a walk on my own." Eugenia gazed at the departing wagon. "Did I miss anything?"

"Oh, yes," said Daisy. "Anthea slipped and fell in the water."

"I knew there was a reason I didn't want to go to the river," muttered Eugenia. Colin glanced at her. She shrugged as if defying him to say anything.

"Come along, girls. Let's help Mr. Savernake carry all these things to the Grange." Lady Fortesque stacked plates into the hamper, and in the next moments, her daughters worked beside her.

Mrs. Ulster stared at the woman, then with a slight sniff began to help, pulling Eugenia with her.

Within a half hour, the group had returned to the Grange. Mrs. Ulster bade the group good-bye, then hurried home, no doubt eager to tell the tale of Anthea's dunking. Eugenia trailed behind her mother, her steps less enthusiastic. Lady Fortesque went inside to check on Anthea. Violet and Iris waited outside with the twins, while Hubert helped Brody inside.

Colin carried the picnic hamper around the house to the kitchen door, but before he reached the first step, someone tapped him on the shoulder. He turned to see Dougal standing in front of him.

"Did you wish to see me?" asked Colin.

"Yes." Dougal eyed him with a cold gaze.

"Is something amiss?"

"Nay, not yet, but . . ." Dougal scowled. "I don't like you, Savernake."

He waited for the man to continue, but Dougal said nothing else. "I commend your honesty." He tried to walk past the man. The hamper wasn't light, and he had carried it long enough.

Dougal's hand shot out and shoved Colin's shoulder. The blow wasn't enough to hurt him, but it was enough to knock the hamper from his grasp. He closed his eyes as he heard the dishes smash together and break. Brilliant. He restrained the urge to strike back at the man. "Why did you do that?"

"I'm watching you, Savernake."

What was Dougal talking about? A cold shiver skittered down his spine. Had Dougal seen him kiss Anthea? Impossible. And yet . . . "Is that a threat?"

"Nay. Just a warning. Any misstep, and I'll see it. Now clean this up." The large man walked away.

Colin didn't move for a minute. Thoughts and explanations for the man's behavior whirled through his head, but he rejected each in turn. He knelt beside the hamper and opened it to see what damage had been done.

"Mr. Savernake, let me help you," said Mrs. Pennyfeather coming out the door. She gazed at the broken china. "Oh, dear."

"Don't fret about it, Mrs. Pennyfeather. I shall replace it." With all the things broken or ruined these past two days, he wondered if Stanhope's bequest was worth his expense. He glanced at his boots. He had just worn these boots in to their most comfortable. Plunging them in the cold water couldn't have been good for the leather. Still, the cost had been worth the reward.

He smiled at the memory of the kiss.

"Mr. Savernake, are you ill?" asked Mrs. Pennyfeather.

"No, I'm fine." He shook himself. Anthea was dangerous. He mustn't give in to his weakness for the woman. Dougal couldn't have seen them in the woods, but the man had warned him about something. Dougal's words made no sense, but Colin did reach a single conclusion.

He couldn't trust himself with Anthea.

Take A Trip Into A Timeless World of Passion and Adventure with Kensington Choice Historical Romances!
—Absolutely FREE!

Enjoy the passion and adventure of another time with Kensington Choice Historical Romances. They are the finest novels of their kind, written by today's best-selling romance authors. Each Kensington Choice Historical Romance transports you to distant lands in a bygone age. Experience the adventure and share the delight as proud men and spirited women discover the wonder and passion of true love.

Get 4 FREE Books!

We created our convenient Home Subscription Service so you'll be sure to have the hottest new romances delivered each month right to your doorstep—usually before they are available in book stores. Just to show you how convenient the Zebra Home Subscription Service is, we would like to send you 4 FREE Kensington Choice Historical Romances. The books are worth up to $24.96, but you only pay $1.99 for shipping and handling. There's no obligation to buy additional books—ever!

Save Up To 30% With Home Delivery!

Accept your FREE books and each month we'll deliver 4 brand new titles as soon as they are published. They'll be yours to examine FREE for 10 days. Then if you decide to keep the books, you'll pay the preferred subscriber's price (up to 30% off the cover price!), plus shipping and handling. Remember, you are under no obligation to buy any of these books at any time! If you are not delighted with them, simply return them and owe nothing. But if you enjoy Kensington Choice Historical Romances as much as we think you will, pay the special preferred subscriber rate and save over $8.00 off the cover price!

Chapter 15

Anthea sat up in the bed. The down coverlet fell to her waist, but she ignored it. She hadn't felt a chill since she kissed Savernake.

"Cover up. Mother will never forgive me if I let you get sick," said Violet. She tucked the duvet to her sister's chin.

Anthea pushed it down again. "I'm not cold. Not anymore."

"That's good news. But we don't have to leave yet, do we? I would like to enjoy this a while longer." Violet sat back on the bed she was using and tucked her knees under her nightgown. "I haven't had a bed this fine since Daddy was alive."

Sticking her foot out from under the blanket, Anthea regarded it for a moment. "With an ankle this purple, I'm not going anywhere soon." The joint was swollen and advertised its pain with the dark colors that mottled the skin.

"Yeech. That looks terrible." Violet shuddered.

"Hurts, too. I'm just glad I didn't remove my boots right away. I hate to think how big it would be if I had."

The candles gave the bedroom a soft glow. Anthea appreciated the chance to spend such time with her sister. They'd had few opportunities for simple chat since arriving in Middle Hutton. Usually they fell into bed at night, too tired from their daily chores to do anything but sleep.

"Make sure you elevate that thing," said Violet. She stepped over to Anthea's bed and lifted the injured limb onto the stack of pillows that lay under the covers.

"That *thing* is my ankle," said Anthea with a chuckle.

"No, it isn't. It's taken on a life of its own. I think we should give it a name. How about Dougal?"

A laugh burst from her lips. Then she clapped her hand over her mouth. A moment later, she said, "You are wicked."

"Why? It looks like him in a strange sort of way. I should think he'd be honored." Violet grinned.

A soft knock at the door elicited fresh giggles. Anthea covered herself, waited until Violet had donned her wrap, then said, "Come in."

Mrs. Pennyfeather entered carrying a large tray. "I heard you girls and thought you might like some tea and biscuits."

"Oh, yes," said Violet, eyeing the tray eagerly.

"How can you want to eat after the supper you had?" asked Anthea.

"With little difficulty," said Violet. She filched a thin, sugary biscuit from the plate and bit into it. Her eyes closed. "These are fabulous."

Mrs. Pennyfeather looked approving. "You, too, Lady Anthea. You need to regain your strength after your misadventure. This will warm you." The housekeeper poured steaming tea into a delicate cup.

"But I'm not—"

"Drink, or I'll tell the squire you weren't behaving," said Violet.

Anthea glared at her sister in mock annoyance, but

took the cup. She sipped the hot liquid, then looked at Mrs. Pennyfeather. "Is this a new tea? It tastes different."

"I added mint leaves to oolong. When I'm not feeling well, I find it therapeutic."

"I like it." She took another sip. "But you know the squire only drinks Earl Grey."

Mrs. Pennyfeather nodded. "I bought this especially for you. I'll keep it in a tin in the kitchen for you whenever you would like some."

"How kind of you." Anthea swallowed the soothing brew.

"Just leave the tray outside the door when you are finished. I'll pick it up before I go to bed. I hope your recovery is a swift one, Lady Anthea." The housekeeper left the room.

Violet sighed. "Now I know why you're willing to marry the squire. If I could look forward to this kind of treatment, I just might have married him myself." Violet popped another biscuit into her mouth.

Her sister's words were meant to bolster her spirits, but the sudden sinking in her stomach left little doubt to her mood. Savernake's kiss still lingered on her mouth. The warmth she felt had little to do with the tea. Anthea placed the teacup on the tray and turned her back to Violet.

"Thea?"

"I guess I'm more tired than I thought."

Violet jumped to her feet. She blew out the candle nearest her sister. "I should have realized it earlier. Forgive me?"

"Nothing to forgive. Good night, Violet."

"Good night. I'll just put the tray outside."

She heard the soft clatter of the dishes as Violet removed the tray, then the click of the door latch. The rustle of the bedclothes told her that Violet had climbed into bed. Darkness claimed the room as her sister extinguished the last candle. Soon even breathing from the neighboring bed announced that Violet slept.

Anthea rolled onto her back and stared into the darkness. How could she sleep when Savernake plagued her thoughts? He had kissed her again, and she had kissed him back. And enjoyed it.

Time passed, but still sleep eluded her. She found herself resenting her betrothal, regretting her behavior, and reliving the kiss in turn. She could not blame Savernake. Yes, she could. He shouldn't have made such an approach. And in the next moment, she forgave him.

"Augh," she said to the night. Violet stirred in the next bed. Anthea quieted until she heard Violet settle into slumber again.

At some point she must have fallen asleep, because the next time she was conscious of her surroundings, birds sang outside the window, and light poured into the room. She sat up and glanced at Violet. Her sister still slept. Lucky girl.

She eased the covers from her and glanced at her foot. The swelling hadn't diminished, but she put her feet on the ground to test it. Gritting her teeth, she stood and nearly cried out. Her ankle throbbed. Determined to ignore the pain, Anthea hobbled to the mirror that hung over a dresser. She gazed into the glass. A crease down her cheek gave evidence to her sleep, but the dark arcs under her eyes gave evidence to the quality.

"Thea, you shouldn't be out of bed." Violet scrambled from the bed and crossed to her. "Are you in pain? You look terrible."

"Thank you."

"Lean on me. Let's get you back to bed before you fall down." Violet slipped under her arm and circled her waist with her arm. "Be careful. Why would you do such a stupid thing?"

"I wanted to see how I looked."

Violet gave her a look of disbelief. "You've never been vain before."

"It's never too late to start." She definitely wasn't feeling well this morning.

Violet helped her into bed and arranged the pillow for her foot. "I'll see if I can get you some of that tea you liked." She pulled the nightgown from her shoulders and dressed. "I'll be back in a moment."

Anthea dropped her head onto her pillow. She shouldn't have been so flippant with her sister. Violet could take none of the blame for her poor night's sleep. But Anthea wanted to blame someone. She wanted to blame someone for her lack of sleep, for her sore ankle, for sharing a kiss she shouldn't have, for moving to Middle Hutton, for having to marry the squire. Why did she have to be the strong one? Why did she have to make everything right?

Her breath hitched, and she fought the tears that burned in a lump in her throat. She wouldn't feel sorry for herself. Her fatigue made it impossible to think, that's all, and her mind was playing tricks on her, making her second guess herself. Everything would look brighter in the morning. Or later, since it was morning already. Or tomorrow. She sighed. Or after she slept a little more.

* * *

The next morning, Anthea could stand on her foot, albeit not with her full weight. Not that it mattered. She had had enough of the sickroom and Violet's ministrations. She wanted to go home and talk to her mother. Her restless thoughts had not left her, and she was hoping her mother could spare a few moments to listen to her.

Violet wasn't in the room at the moment. She was probably in the kitchen looking for food. The real joy in staying at the Grange was that they could eat without fear of taking more than their share.

Anthea slipped from the bed and shuffled to the dresser. She drew on her clothes and fastened them as best she could without assistance. She slipped her right foot into her shoe, then tried to do the same with the left. The foot was still too tender to bend much, so she left it unshod. If the Fates were at all kind, she wouldn't wear a hole in her stocking.

As she entered the hall, her heart pounded as if she were carrying out some illicit action.

"Thea."

She jumped, startled by her sister's voice. Turning, she faced Violet, feeling guilty indeed.

"Should you be up?"

"I couldn't stay there any longer."

"I have to admit those four walls were beginning to irritate me." Violet hurried to her side. "Come along. Everyone's in the parlor."

"Why?"

"Good heavens, how should I know? They just are. Lean on me." Violet led her toward the parlor.

Brody sat in the armchair. Anthea looked for the squire, but didn't see him. In fact, no one else sat in the parlor. She turned to Violet. "I thought you said everyone was here."

"Father's convinced Jane to stay until she's had the baby, so he went to fetch her, and Dougal told Father he couldn't be bothered to wait for Jane," said Brody. "Should you be up?"

"Most definitely." Anthea took a seat on the settee.

"Have I missed anything? The squire asked me to join him here," said Savernake as he entered the room. He gazed at Anthea. "Should you be up?"

"Yes." She furrowed her brows. She wasn't sure how to react to him.

"Are you in pain?" asked Violet.

"No, I'm just . . . Oh, stop fussing over me." Anthea crossed her arms over her chest.

Savernake grinned at her as if he read her thoughts. She scowled at him.

"I've brought tea. The gentlemen may prefer to have something stronger." Mrs. Pennyfeather entered the room with a large tray. She placed it on the table. She glanced at Anthea. "Should you be up, my lady?"

"I'm feeling much better, thank you." Anthea clenched her teeth to keep from growling at the woman.

"I'll bring you some of your special brew, shall I?" Mrs. Pennyfeather left without waiting for the answer.

"Special brew?" asked Savernake.

"A tea blend Mrs. Pennyfeather prepared just for Thea," said Violet. She sighed. "It must be nice to have someone who sees to your every whim."

"She hardly caters to my every whim." Annoyance stirred within her.

Mrs. Pennyfeather returned a moment later with a

smaller teapot. "The water was still boiling. Didn't take me any time at all."

"Thank you, Mrs. Pennyfeather." Anthea filled her cup. She hoped the tea would have the same soothing effect as yesterday.

"Tea is ready? Splendid?" Hobblesby entered the room. His eyebrows shot high as he spied her. "Thea, should you be up?"

"Yes, I feel much better."

"Excellent news." Hobblesby grabbed a cup from the tray and filled it from the smaller pot. He took a sip and grimaced. "Gad, what is this dreadful stuff?"

"Thea's special brew," answered Brody.

"Stands to reason. It isn't fit for anyone but an invalid." He poured the remaining tea back into the pot.

"I'll remember that the next time you have an attack of gout." Anthea was fast losing any vestige of sympathy for anyone.

Jane entered the room, followed by Hubert. She looked Anthea up and down with a cold gaze. "Oh, you're up."

Savernake leaned over to Anthea. "Don't say it," he said out of the side of his mouth.

"Say what?" she asked through gritted teeth.

Sotto voce, he said, "Whatever is on that wicked tongue of yours. You'll regret it later."

Her face flushed. "How did you know I wanted to say something?"

"I can read you." His voice dropped to a rich whisper that sent a shiver down her spine. "You forget I've had intimate experience with that tongue of yours."

The heat flared in her cheeks.

"Thea, you don't look well," said the squire.

"It's the tea. It has warmed me." She glared at Savernake.

"Glad to see you warmed up again. I was afraid you'd fall ill after your swim in the river." Hobblesby crossed to her and lifted her hand to his lips. "It's good to have all my favorite girls residing under my roof."

"What? Is she staying, too?" asked Jane.

"Only until I recover," said Anthea. "In fact, perhaps it's time to go home."

"Must we?" asked Violet. Her gaze shot to Brody.

"Nonsense. You must stay one more day, so I can watch out for you, my dear," said Hobblesby.

"No, William. It's too much trouble, and—"

"You'll be living here soon enough. Pennyflake might as well get used to it."

"It's Pennyfeather, Father," said Brody.

"What's Pennyfeather done now?" asked Dougal as he sauntered into the room.

"Nothing, boy. Isn't this wonderful? Everyone gathered under my roof where they belong." Hobblesby grinned and spread his arms out wide. "I include you in that, Lady Violet. You will always be welcome in your sister's home."

"Thank you, Squire." Violet glanced at Anthea and stifled a laugh.

"What? Are they all staying?" Dougal's lip curled as he looked at Jane.

"I am. Hubert's not. It's too far for him to oversee the mill if he lives here." Jane gave her brother a superior look.

"But I'll come visit often," said the hapless man.

"Makes me glad I live in one of the cottages." Dougal's gaze fell on Anthea. "Are you up?"

"Apparently," said Anthea.

Dougal sniffed the air. "I smell something. Mint."

"Thea's tea. Ghastly stuff," said Hobblesby. "Penny-feather made her some sort of brew."

They all stared at the squire.

Hobblesby stared back at them in confusion. "Did I get her name wrong?"

Chapter 16

The room cleared out as Hobblesby went to help settle Jane in her new quarters until only Anthea and Violet were left in the parlor. Anthea tried to stand.

"I *know* you aren't supposed to walk around yet," said Violet.

"I need to speak with Mr. Savernake. Will you help me to the study?"

Violet opened her mouth, but Anthea held up a finger. "No questions, Violet. Please?"

Violet nodded. Anthea braced herself against her sister and hobbled to the door of the study. "Why don't you go see what Mrs. Pennyfeather is fixing for supper?" She held up the same finger. "No questions, remember?"

With a shrug, Violet retreated.

Anthea knocked softly.

"Come."

She pushed open the door. "Mr. Savernake, I—"

"You shouldn't walk yet." He dashed to her side and picked her up.

For an instant, she let herself melt against his chest. Then she stiffened. "Put me down at once."

"I'd wager you'd prefer a chair." He placed her on the brocade cushion of the nearest chair.

"We . . . I . . ." She didn't know how to continue.

Anger would suffice. "Your behavior in there was uncalled for."

"Indeed?"

"What happened between us must never happen again." She could feel her face heat up again. "And no one must learn of what happened either."

"I see." In all manner of calm, he crossed to the desk. "What if I were to speak of it?"

She let out a sniff of indignation. "Why I'd . . . I'll deny it, of course."

"Of course. So you'd be a liar as well as a thief." Savernake sat on the corner of his desk.

Her jaw dropped. "I am not a thief."

"So you admit to being a liar."

She narrowed her gaze. "I am not . . ." She stopped, disbelieving what she saw. He was laughing at her. She was fighting for her reputation, and the man found it funny.

"I wouldn't dream of telling a soul about my lapse in judgment."

Reining in her angry retort, she nodded and ignored the twinge of disappointment his words caused. "Then we can forget about the entire incident."

"Like hell I will." Rising from the desk, he placed his hands on the arms of her chair and leaned over her. "I won't speak of it, but I shall never forget it. You can count on that."

She pressed herself against the back of her chair, but couldn't stop the pounding of her heart. She wanted to lift her mouth and kiss him. God help her, she wanted to kiss him again.

With a sudden push, he straightened and gazed at her as if nothing had passed between them. "Now, I'll take you back to your room."

"No, not my room." Her voice was small.

He arched an eyebrow. "The parlor, then?"

She nodded.

He scooped her up and carried her from the room. They didn't speak. As he set her on a chair in the parlor, he gave her a curious look. "What happened to your shoe?"

She curled her stocking-clad toes in a vain effort to hide them. "I couldn't put it on. It hurt too much to bend my foot."

"You shouldn't be up, but I'll let the squire deal with you." Savernake bowed. "Good day to you, Lady Anthea."

Before she could respond, he pivoted and strode from the room.

She sighed, then looked down at her foot. Her toe stuck out from a hole in the stocking. The Fates hadn't been kind after all.

Anthea and Violet went home the following day. The squire provided the curricle for their use, since Anthea couldn't possibly walk that far yet. For the next few days, her mother insisted she rest, but Anthea couldn't watch her sisters work around her. Anthea helped as much as she could, but she still walked with a limp. Her restlessness had grown worse, but she could find no moment to speak with her mother.

A week passed. Mrs. Pennyfeather sent a message from the Grange. The wedding was to take place in two weeks, and she wanted to settle on a menu. Would Anthea come to the Grange?

"Violet, would you like to come with me to the Grange today? You can find a quiet place to write, and

Mrs. Pennyfeather told me she'll have some tasty tidbits for us to try."

"You just want to use me as a crutch," said Violet with a smile.

"Well, you are handy." Anthea laughed.

"Beast." The shouts of the twins echoed through the small house. Violet grimaced. "But your offer is too tempting. Let me fetch my ink and paper, and we'll be off."

When the girls arrived at the Grange, Violet followed Thea to the kitchen. Mrs. Pennyfeather placed a tray of food in front of Thea. "Cook and I have come up with some recipes I hope will please you."

Before she led herself to a quiet corner of the kitchen, Violet snatched a tart from the tray and popped it into her mouth. The rich buttery crust broke into flavor on her tongue, then mixed with the custard and fruit topping. "Mmmm. If you don't make this for the wedding, can you make some for me just for fun?"

Mrs. Pennyfeather beamed. "You are too kind, Lady Violet."

"Kind is not a word often used to describe me. I'm merely telling the truth. These are wonderful." She reached for a second, but Thea slapped her hand.

"Leave one for me, greedy." Thea picked up the tart and bit into it. She closed her eyes as she swallowed. "Violet's right. These are marvelous."

Violet grabbed a cheese straw. "You know, if you feed the guests too well, they may never leave."

"I'll tell Cook you approve, Lady Violet." Mrs. Pennyfeather handed Anthea a sliced strawberry with a piece of candied ginger in it. "Try this, Lady Anthea."

Violet looked at the fruit with longing, then shook her head. She'd get nothing done if she didn't take herself away from these temptations. She gathered her papers, quill, and ink. "I'm going to find another room. If I stay here, I won't do anything but eat."

"I'll find you when it's time to leave," said Thea.

A maid entered the kitchen. "Excuse me, Mrs. Pennyfeather, but the squire is thirsty. He said you have some cold beer in the cellar."

"I don't think so," said Thea. "He's not going to have another attack of gout if I can help it."

The maid looked startled. "Begging your pardon, my lady. I didn't know you were here."

"You have nothing to apologize for." Thea smiled at the maid. "Mrs. Pennyfeather and I are busy. Would you be willing to make the tea for the squire?"

"Of course, my lady."

"And when you take it to him, don't let him bully you into giving him wine."

"No, my lady." The maid bobbed a quick curtsey, then scurried to the pantry to fetch the tea.

"I wonder if she'll ever get used to me. She still jumps whenever I speak to her," said Thea.

"Well, I'm not surprised, what with the way you shout at her." Violet grinned at her sister.

"You'd better find your spot to work before I yell at you," said Thea. "You should have a good hour or two before we have to leave."

"Thanks, Thea." Violet left the kitchen and walked down the hall to an unused sitting room. Taking a place in front of a small table, she set out her paper, dipped the end of her quill in the ink, then proceeded to chew on the end of the feather. The writing would come if she were patient enough. Trouble was, patience wasn't her greatest virtue.

But after a few minutes of frustration, the words

began to flow onto the page. She worked without interruption for some time, losing herself in the pages of her writing and in the pictures in her mind. She breathed the air of her characters and lived their feelings. The real world ceased to exist as the pages came to life.

Crash.

Violet jumped as her pen skittered across the page, leaving a black slash on the white.

Brody Hobblesby clutched a now-empty stand. He stood among the shards of a broken vase. "Damn it." He shoved the stand so that it crashed to the floor with the vase. Hard lines around his mouth played up his scowl. "Damn it all to hell."

"Careful. There's a lady present," she said.

"Who's there?" He spun toward her.

"Violet Fortesque, and would you mind being a little more quiet? I am trying to write."

"Why didn't you speak up when I entered the room?"

"I didn't see you."

"You expect me to believe that?" He narrowed his eyelids. "Or are you mocking me?"

"As if I had nothing better to do than mock you." She let out a soft grunt of impatience. "I was working, and you've interrupted me."

His blank gaze tried to seek her out. "This is my house."

"Of course. But Thea had to speak with Mrs. Pennyfeather about the wedding, and she invited me to come along. Your house is more quiet than ours. Most of the time. Now if you don't mind . . . " She turned back to her pages.

Brody took a step toward her, but stopped short as the porcelain crunched under his foot. He clenched his fists. "Lady Violet, it seems I need your help."

She looked up. His expression was dark. "What is it now?"

"I cannot walk without stepping on something."

She looked at the floor. With a sigh of exasperation, she crossed to him. Stepping over the shards, she took his arm. "Here. Step a foot to the right, now forward. Wait. There's a large piece right in front of you." She released his arm and bent to retrieve the piece. She tossed it toward the others. It landed with a loud ping.

"Did you throw it?" Astonishment colored his voice.

"Yes. I'm not paid to pick up here." She took his arm again. "Where do you want to go?"

"Does this room still have a settee?"

"Yes." She led him to the small sofa.

Brody sat on the horsehair cushion. "Someone has changed this room around since I was last in it."

"When was that?"

"About five years ago."

"Then it shouldn't surprise you that it's changed." She crossed back to her table and picked up the quill again.

"What are you doing?"

"Writing." She dipped the pen in the ink and scribbled another word on the sheet.

"Ahh, that explains the scratching sound." He stretched his legs out in front of him. "Don't let me keep you from your pages."

The movement distracted her. She lifted her head. For the briefest second, she allowed herself to admire his handsome face. Then she said, "I can't write if you chatter."

For a minute or two, she worked in silence.

"What are you writing?"

She paused in mid-sentence as impatience roiled

within her. "Nothing at the moment. Apparently I'm having a conversation."

He chuckled. "You must be one of those temperamental artists."

"I wasn't the one who walked into the room cursing." She finished writing the sentence in front of her.

"Forgive me."

She set the quill aside. "I suppose I must if I am to have any peace. Why were you so angry?"

He hesitated. "There are times I rail against my fate and my blindness."

"I imagine you would. I often rail against mine."

"What do you have to rail against?"

"Fate and the lack of money."

"I see." He leaned forward as if trying to catch a glimpse of the pages. "So what are you writing?"

"A novel."

"Ahh, I have read one of those once."

"Have you indeed?" A smile tugged at the corner of her lips.

"What is this one about?"

"A man and a woman who overcome great obstacles to find happiness."

Brody nodded. "I believe that's the one I've read."

She couldn't keep the laugh from her voice. "You're incorrigible."

"Alas, 'tis true." He clutched his hand to his chest. "My poor old nurse told me it would bring my downfall."

"And did it?"

"Not in the least. In truth, I never even had a nurse." He grinned at her, stealing her breath with his charm. "May I hear some of your novel?"

She eyed him, wondering if she could trust him with her words. "Only if you promise not to ridicule it."

"But what if it needs ridicule?"

"I've changed my mind. I shan't read it." She gathered the sheaf of papers and held them to her.

He held out his hand toward her. "No, please. I was making a jest. I truly would like to hear it."

For a moment, she didn't move. "Very well."

Violet sat beside him. Turning to the first page, she started reading. At first her voice was soft and filled with uncertainty, but as she flipped through the pages, her tone grew stronger, and her characters' speeches gained life. He listened with a tangible intensity, serious, yet not so grim that he didn't smile at the humor. When she reached the end of the third chapter, she stopped.

"Please continue," he said.

"I cannot. There's no more. Well, a little, but not enough to continue."

"You are a cruel woman. How can you leave me wondering what happens next?" He reached toward her and brushed her arm. Following the curve of her elbow to her wrist, he grasped her hand and lifted it to his lips. "You have a gift, Lady Violet."

"Did you really like it?"

"I wouldn't tell you so if I didn't. What does your family think of it?"

"They haven't read it."

"Then I *am* honored. I would only change the part where the hero kisses the heroine for the first time."

"Pardon? I thought you liked the story."

"I do, but the kiss seemed forced."

For the next few minutes, they argued back and forth about her work. Violet found herself enjoying the exchange of ideas and had to admit Brody was right more often than he was wrong. In fact, he was right every time. Drat him. But her book would be stronger for his help.

"May I read you the next chapter when I've finished it? As loath as I am to admit it, your insight has helped me." Her tone lilted as she spoke.

"You're not offended by my blunt talk?"

"Not in the least."

"Then I shall expect you when you've finished the next chapter. What shall you do with it when it's finished?"

"Sell it and help my family. I don't want to have to marry like Anthea." In the next instant she clapped her hand over her mouth and groaned. "I shouldn't have said that," she uttered between her fingers.

"Probably not." He patted her hand. "But it isn't as if I haven't figured out why Lady Anthea is marrying my father."

A cry from another part of the house interrupted them. Brody leaped to his feet and started toward the door, but banged his shin on the low table. "Curse my blindness."

"This way." Violet grabbed his arm and led him as fast as she could to the door. The commotion seemed to be coming from the kitchen.

"What is going on here?" asked Brody from the doorway.

A maid was sobbing into her kerchief. "It's the master. I went in to take his cup away, and he was lying there on the floor."

"Where's Anthea?" asked Violet.

"The young miss is in with the squire right now. Mrs. Pennyfeather went to fetch Mr. Savernake and Mr. Fletcher."

Brody turned to Violet. "Take me there."

Chapter 17

Colin dashed into the parlor well ahead of Fletcher and Mrs. Pennyfeather. Hobblesby lay sprawled on the floor, his back in a rigid arch, his arms and legs twitching and flailing. His eyes, wider than Colin had ever seen them, stared at nothing. Dougal cradled his father in his arms, flinching whenever his father's arms struck him. Anthea knelt beside them. An overturned cup of tea sat on the table, marking the wood with a large stain. A few last drops remained on the saucer. Colin hurried to the cup. "Has anyone touched this?"

"Why are you worried about the cup, fool?" asked Dougal. His face was pale, and panic rode in his mien. "Your first concern should be my father."

"No one has touched anything," said Anthea. Her face was as white as paper, and she didn't blink.

Mrs. Pennyfeather entered the room. "Dear heaven."

Fletcher followed behind her and hurried forward to the suffering figure.

"Help me get him to bed," said Dougal. He hooked his arms under his father's shoulders. Fletcher grabbed the squire's legs. They lifted him from the floor, trying to subdue his thrashing as they carried him.

"I'll see that his bed is ready." Mrs. Pennyfeather

darted in front of the two men and rushed down the hallway.

Fletcher and Dougal carried the squire from the room.

"What happened?" asked Colin.

Anthea rose to her feet and swayed a little as she stood. "I don't know. Mrs. Pennyfeather and I were in the kitchen when the maid burst in screaming that the squire was dying. I ran here to find Dougal cradling his father. You came in soon after."

"What's wrong with my father?" asked Brody from the door. He was leaning on Violet's arm.

Anthea crossed to him and laid her hand on his forearm. "Your father has fallen ill. He's been taken to his bed. We don't know what's wrong yet."

"Have you sent for a doctor?" asked Brody.

"I'll go," said Violet. She released Brody's arm and ran from the house.

"He's in his bed?" asked Brody.

"Your brother took him to his room. Can I take you there?" asked Colin.

"No, I can find my way." Brody disappeared from the doorway.

"Perhaps I should join them." Anthea stared after Brody, but didn't move.

"I think you should sit." Colin led her to the settee and with a gentle push seated her. He eyed the overturned cup on the table.

"He looked as if he were in great pain," said Anthea in a whisper.

"Try not to think about it. The doctor will be here soon."

She popped back to her feet. "No, I should go help." Her face was whiter than before.

"You'll faint before you get there. I'll fetch you a cup of tea."

"I don't want tea." Her eyes filled with tears. "Goodness, I feel so helpless. Do you have a kerchief?"

Colin stared at her. "Pardon?"

"I thought I'd start to clean this mess up." She knelt beside the table and reached for the cup.

"Don't touch it!" He leaned over the cup. No visible signs of any foreign substance remained in the spilled liquid or the porcelain. He dipped his finger into a droplet and touched it to the tip of his tongue. He winced. Too much sugar. "I thought the squire didn't like the mint tea."

Anthea blinked. "He doesn't. He only drinks Earl Grey."

"Well, someone doesn't know that. This tea has mint in it."

"Then he wouldn't have had any."

"That may have saved his life." Colin wasn't sure, but he would wager the tea was poisoned with strychnine. The copious amount of sugar would mask the bitter taste.

"So you think he'll live?"

He glanced at Anthea. "I think it would take more than a mouthful of diluted strychnine to kill him."

Anthea gasped. "Strychnine?" The blood drained from her face. She pitched forward.

Colin caught her before she hit the table. Her breathing was even, but she felt cold to his touch. He laid her on the settee and pulled his kerchief from his coat pocket. A vase of flowers stood in the corner. He pulled the flowers from the water and dipped his kerchief into the mouth of the vase. Letting the flowers fall to the floor, he hurried back to her side and mopped her face with the cool cloth.

His fingers slid over her smooth skin, and the tiny pulse point at the base of her throat drew his attention. He drew in a deep breath. Now wasn't the time to think of her as anything more than someone who needed help. A strand of hair brushed the back of his hand as he swiped his kerchief across her forehead again. It was as soft as he had expected. He gritted his teeth. She needed to awaken soon, before he allowed his imagination free rein. Why didn't she carry smelling salts like other women?

A moment later—or was it an eternity—her eyes fluttered open.

"Shhh." He put his hand on her shoulder to keep her from sitting up.

"What happened?"

"You fainted."

"I never faint."

"You did today."

Anthea gasped. "William. How is he?"

"I don't know. I was taking care of you."

She pushed his hand away and sat up. "I should go see him."

"What can you do that the others can't?"

"I am to be his wife."

"But you aren't his wife yet." Colin handed her the kerchief. "Press this against your head. You still look pale."

The doctor arrived a moment later, and a few minutes after that, Dougal and Brody returned to the parlor.

"I don't like that man." Dougal paced the room. "I don't see why we couldn't stay."

"Fletcher was helping him, and we were in his way." Brody slid his feet forward until they tapped a chair. "He'll be out as soon as he knows anything."

"I don't trust him," said Dougal.

"We've known Dr. Rosenthal since we were children."

"Doesn't matter." Dougal stopped in the middle of his stride and scowled at Anthea. "I didn't see you inquiring after Father."

"Anthea fainted," said Colin.

"How do you feel now, Lady Anthea?" asked Brody.

"What does it matter how she feels? Father should be our only concern." Dougal leaned over her. "So much for your pretense of loving Father."

"Leave her alone, Dougal," said Colin.

"Are you threatening me?" asked the larger man.

Colin didn't flinch. "Only if you persist in hounding her."

"I'll take care of you, just as soon as I know Father is fine."

"You may try."

"Please," said Brody. "We've had enough unpleasantness today. Let's just wait to see what the doctor says."

Colin glanced at Anthea. Her face had a little more color, but she didn't look well. She had twisted his kerchief into a thick knotted jumble. He returned his gaze to the two men. "What do you gentlemen know about poison?"

"What?" Dougal whirled to face him. Bright red spots mottled his cheeks.

"What are you saying?" asked Brody.

"There's a good chance your father may have been poisoned. This tea—"

"What do you know about such things?" asked Dougal.

"Enough to know your father's illness wasn't natural." Colin pointed to the cup. "It's minty."

"That doesn't prove anything," said Dougal with a growl.

"Perhaps not, but his symptoms do." Colin checked Anthea's expression for another sign of swooning. She was still pale, but she listened calmly.

The doctor entered the room. Dougal ran to him. "Well?"

"He's resting now. We gave him an emetic to empty his stomach." The doctor rubbed his forehead. "Have you been having rodent trouble lately?"

"I don't want to talk about farming now, Dr. Rosenthal." Dougal glared at the man.

"Neither did I. Have you bought any strychnine to poison the vermin?"

"Is that what it was? Strychnine?" asked Brody.

The doctor nodded, then remembered to whom he spoke. "Yes."

Dougal shook his head. "It doesn't make sense. Who would want to harm Father?" He froze, then faced Anthea. "We never had any trouble until you arrived. First the thefts, now this."

Colin took two steps toward the man. Even Brody shot to his feet, but Colin stopped himself when he heard Anthea speak.

"I understand your shock, Dougal, but I didn't poison your father." Anthea drew in a deep breath. "Doctor, what does the squire need?"

"Rest. Let him sleep. When he wakes, don't let him get too active. Strychnine is hard on the body. I've left further instructions with the butler." The doctor crossed to her. "I know you had planned to wed soon, but perhaps you should delay—"

"I have already considered it," said Anthea. "Thank you."

"No need to see me out." The doctor left the room.

For a moment, no one spoke. Then Dougal said, "He can't keep me from seeing my father." Dougal strode from the room, his every step clomping with urgency.

"He didn't mean what he said, Lady Anthea," said Brody.

Anthea smiled with resignation. "Yes he did. But it doesn't matter. The only thing I care about now is the squire's health."

Colin examined her expression. She looked relieved at the squire's prognosis. No hint of fear crossed her face. For an insane moment, Colin felt a rush of relief at that.

Violet flew into the room. She searched for her sister, then rushed to her side. "I came back as fast as I could. I told Hubert in town. Jane was asleep in her room. Is there any news?"

"Father will be fine," said Brody.

"Thank heaven," said Violet. "What happened?"

"Poison," said Anthea. "The doctor thinks it was strychnine."

Violet gasped. "He must be mistaken."

Colin shook his head. "I'm afraid not."

Violet looked at her sister. "You don't look well, Thea."

"She fainted," said Colin.

Anthea scowled at him.

"Thea has never fainted." Violet put her hands on her sister's cheeks. "You poor dear. I think you should come home with me."

"I can't right now, Violet. I need to stay until the squire is awake." Anthea removed Violet's hands from her face, but held them in her own. "Tell Mother what happened. And that the wedding will be delayed."

"Again?"

"Yes." Anthea sighed. "It was good of you to fetch Jane."

Violet shrugged. "I didn't do anything."

Brody stood from his chair. "I'll help you gather your pages, then see you out."

Violet smiled. "I'd like that." She took his arm, and the pair left the room.

"How are you feeling?" asked Colin. "Your sister is right. You needn't stay if you're ill. There are plenty of people to watch the squire."

"No, I'm fine. My place is here." Anthea gazed up at him. For a moment, he thought she would say something to him, but she looked away.

"Shall I leave you? After our last meeting, you may not want my company."

"No, please stay. I don't want to be alone."

He nodded. An awkward silence descended over them. He knew she was thinking about their argument as much as he. Turning to the table, he poured the remaining tea from the saucer into the cup. Where might he have the contents tested? Perhaps the doctor would know—

Jane burst into the room. For a woman in the advanced stages of pregnancy, she moved with surprising agility when she wanted. "Where's my father?"

"In his room," said Anthea. "He's resting now."

"I'll see for myself." Jane started for the door.

"The doctor said not to disturb him. Dougal and Fletcher are there."

Jane stopped and whirled around. Her gaze narrowed. "You can't keep me from my father."

"I don't intend to, but the doctor said he'll be fine. You shouldn't worry."

"Shouldn't worry?" Jane let out a harsh laugh. "Does Dr. Rosenthal know what happened? How can we be sure he won't have a relapse?"

"He said it's poison. Strychnine."

Jane blanched.

Anthea rose from the settee and crossed to her. "Oh, Jane, I'm so sorry—"

The woman twisted out of reach. "You should be. I have no doubt you did this to him."

Chapter 18

Anthea sent her gaze skyward. Jane's father lay ill in his room, yet the woman still had time to give voice to her aversion of Anthea. "I didn't poison him, Jane."

"Why should I believe you? This could be one more trick to keep him in your power." Jane crossed her arms on top of her stomach.

"My power?"

"Don't act as if you don't understand me. You can't fool me. You've had him in your power since you arrived. Why else would he want to marry you? Why else would he stop listening to his children?"

Anthea shot a glance at Savernake. He looked thunderstruck. About how she felt. She said, "If you think anyone could sway your father from his chosen course, you don't know him very well."

"Don't speak to me of my father. I've known him better and longer than you."

Hubert entered the room. "Don't upset yourself, Jane. I could hear your shouting in the hall. You must think of the child."

Jane flung herself into her husband's arms. "Do you see how horrid she is? She's ruining our lives and killing Father."

Savernake threw his arms in the air. "This is ludicrous."

Jane whirled on him. "You believed her a thief, and now you believe her innocent? She's a witch, I'm telling you. She has you all under a spell." Jane burst into tears and buried her face against her husband's chest.

"There, there, now," said Hubert.

Anthea opened her mouth to say something, but she didn't know what, so she closed it again. This entire situation was beyond belief. It was beyond *dis*belief. She didn't have the words to describe it. How Jane must hate her to believe such terrible things. Her legs grew wobbly again. She dropped onto the settee.

"Mrs. Fanning, perhaps you'd better leave this room and find someplace you can calm yourself," said Savernake. A muscle twitched in his cheek as if he were clenching his teeth. "You won't do yourself or your father any good in this state."

"You're just a servant," Jane shouted. "You can't tell me to go."

"Then we shall go." Savernake crossed to Anthea and grabbed her hand. "Fanning, take care of your wife."

Anthea let Savernake pull her from the room. She wanted to protest, but leaving was the sensible thing to do. He led her to the study and closed the door behind them before he released her hand. He studied her, but said nothing.

"I don't know whether to thank you or yell at you," she said finally.

"I think we've heard enough yelling for today."

"You may be right." She folded her hands in front of her. "Thank you for defending me."

He shook his head. "I should have done a better job, but I simply couldn't believe her accusations."

"What makes you so sure I'm not a murderess?"

"Logic."

"Do explain."

"If you kill the squire before the wedding, you can't marry him, and if you don't marry him, you can't help your family."

"True. It doesn't paint a good picture of me, though." She sought a chair. Her legs were still weak, and the encounter with Jane hadn't helped her regain her equilibrium. She sank into the chair. "It seems we are at a truce again."

"Maybe not after I say what I must." His expression filled with chagrin, he crossed to her. "I want your help."

"Pardon?" she squeaked when she could speak again.

"It's presumptuous of me to ask, but I need your help."

"With what?"

"We need to discover who tried to murder the squire."

Anthea gave him a strange look. "Shouldn't we leave that to the constable?"

"The same one who's trying to solve the thefts? I should think you wouldn't have confidence in his abilities."

"You're right. He's not very clever. But what can we do? I'm only Hobblesby's betrothed, and you're just his secretary."

Colin paused. He wasn't ready to tell her the real reason for his presence in Middle Hutton. "We may find something to help him."

Anthea furrowed her brows, but nodded. She reached for the medallion at her neck. "But what can I do?"

"You know everyone, yet can still view people with an outsider's eye. They trust you—"

"Jane does not—"

He held up his hand. "If not trust necessarily, they must tolerate you. You are privy to conversations I cannot hear because of my position. And I am convinced you possess a keen intelligence."

"Thank you for that, I think," she muttered under her breath.

"Will you help?" His gaze latched on to hers. The dark, stormy depths didn't look so unfriendly to her now. Instead they offered a strong haven from the horrors of the day. She *would* rather be active in the search for the squire's enemy.

She let out a long breath. "Very well. I shall help you."

"Excellent. For now I'd like to concentrate on the poisoning, but if another thing goes missing—"

"I know. You're still determined to prove I'm the thief." She paused. "I suppose it wouldn't help to tell you I'm not the thief."

An unreadable expression crossed his features, and then he laughed. "No. I don't believe you can change my mind on that issue."

"I didn't think so. You are a stubborn man."

A knock at the door interrupted her thoughts. Mrs. Ulster strode into the room without waiting for an invitation. Behind her, a reluctant Eugenia entered, her gaze darting back to the door every few seconds.

"Oh, my dear. You poor, poor thing." Mrs. Ulster enfolded Anthea into an embrace, and she found herself suffocating in the woman's bosom.

"Good day, Mrs. Ulster." Savernake stepped forward. "Miss Ulster."

Startled, Mrs. Ulster straightened. "Mr. Savernake. I didn't notice you in my distress."

Anthea drew in a deep breath. She would have to remember to thank him later.

Mrs. Ulster drew a handkerchief from her reticule and dabbed her eyes. "I came as soon as I heard, didn't I, Eugenia?"

"Yes, Mother."

I imagine you did, thought Anthea.

"I saw dear Lady Violet running through the village. I knew there must be trouble, so I followed. She's much faster than I. By the time I reached the village square, the doctor had already mounted his horse and was riding in this direction. And when I saw Violet run to the Fannings' house, I just knew there was a crisis at the Grange, so I came to offer my comfort."

"That's kind of you, Mrs. Ulster," said Anthea.

"They told me at the door the squire fell ill. How is he?"

"He'll survive," said Savernake.

"What happened?"

"He fell ill." Anthea gave the answer in a rush. The last thing she wanted was for Mrs. Ulster to know the squire had been poisoned.

"Yes, dear, I know. They told me at the door." Mrs. Ulster patted her arm. "You must be distraught."

"Indeed I am." Anthea hoped the woman wouldn't ask about the cause of Hobblesby's illness again. The gossip would learn about it eventually, but Anthea had no desire to talk about it now.

"Was it apoplexy? His heart?" Mrs. Ulster leaned forward to catch her words.

Savernake stepped forward. "Will you forgive us,

Mrs. Ulster? I hesitate to mention it in front of Lady Anthea. I don't wish to cause her further grief."

Mrs. Ulster clasped her hands to her breast. "Of course. You are such a caring, sensitive man. Isn't he, Eugenia?"

"Yes, Mother." The girl glanced at the door, refusing to look at Savernake.

Anthea dropped her gaze, afraid Mrs. Ulster might see the relief in her eyes. "You are too understanding."

In the next instant, the woman gasped. "What of the wedding?"

"I've decided to postpone it until we know how the squire is recovering." She didn't have to hide her emotions at that statement. Another delay meant a longer struggle for her family.

"Surely not. You've worked so hard on the arrangements. Eugenia and I were coming along nicely with the favors as well." Disappointment stretched her vowels out to whines.

"I think it for the best. I wouldn't want to tax the squire's strength."

"Naturally," said Mrs. Ulster. She clicked her tongue. "This day has brought a double tragedy, then."

"May I still depend on you for your help with the wedding?"

The woman raised her handkerchief to her eyes again and wiped delicately. "Anything you need, dear Lady Anthea. My wish is but to serve. We're happy to help in any way. Isn't that so, Eugenia?"

"Yes, Mother." The girl's gaze shot to the door again. She must want to escape.

"Eugenia, could I trouble you to look for Mrs. Pennyfeather for me?"

"Yes," said the girl, and she darted from the room.

Anthea bit back a smile.

"What a good child I've been blessed with. Isn't she a joy, Mr. Savernake?" asked Mrs. Ulster.

The predatory gleam in the woman's eyes startled her. Mrs. Ulster was staring at Savernake with a hunger that was frightening. Anthea wrinkled her brow. The woman couldn't be in love with the man. She was twice his age—well, not twice, but she could be his mother. That was it. She didn't want him for herself; she wanted him for her daughter. A sense of relief filled her for a moment, which turned to aggravation as well. Eugenia was no match for a man of Savernake's strength.

Anthea chided herself. What did it matter whom the man married? He was no concern of hers.

But she watched him speak to Mrs. Ulster with a guarded jealousy despite her resolve.

"I'm sure she's a treasure, Mrs. Ulster," said Savernake.

"Such a pity our dinner didn't work out. We'll have you over soon, though. After the squire has recovered a bit and things are settled."

Mrs. Pennyfeather knocked on the open door and entered the room. "Did you need something, Lady Anthea?"

"Yes." Anthea searched her brain for an idea. She had sent Eugenia on her errand without thinking about the consequences. "I was wondering if we had some broth for the squire when he woke."

"I've already taken care of it, my lady."

"Has Jane been to see her father yet?"

"She's with him now," said the housekeeper.

"Would you let me know when she's left? I would like to visit him when there isn't a throng beside his bed."

"Certainly, Lady Anthea. May I bring you some of your tea or a little something to fortify yourself?"

"No tea. Bring brandy instead. I'm not sure Lady Anthea has recovered from her swoon," said Savernake. He turned to Mrs. Ulster. "Dear lady, forgive us, but perhaps you should come back when the squire is ready for visitors. We'll be sure to tell him of your visit."

"Say no more, I am on my way." The woman gazed into the hallway and frowned. "Have you seen my daughter?"

"She left the house a few minutes ago, ma'am," said Mrs. Pennyfeather.

"I don't know what's gotten into that girl lately. Every time I turn around she's disappeared." A second later Mrs. Ulster's cheeks blossomed crimson as she gazed at Savernake in horror. "I don't mean she's flighty. She's a very conscientious girl."

"I'm sure she is," said Savernake with a small bow.

Mrs. Ulster gathered her gloves and reticule. "If you see her, send her home."

"We shall. Thank you for coming, Mrs. Ulster," said Anthea.

"If you need me for anything, you must fetch me." Mrs. Ulster clicked her tongue. "Oh, you poor, poor dear." She lifted her handkerchief to her eyes again and fled the room, a single sob echoing as a reminder of her presence.

"I shall bring you a tray," said Mrs. Pennyfeather.

"Wait," said Savernake. "Set aside the canister you kept the tea in, but be careful not to touch it or spill it. Make sure no one can touch it."

"As you wish, sir." Mrs. Pennyfeather left the room. As soon as both women were beyond hearing range,

Anthea said, "Thank you for not mentioning why Hobblesby fell ill. Mrs. Ulster means well, but . . ."

"The village would have known everything by this evening." He smiled. "I quite understand."

Anthea slumped in her chair. "I'm glad you do. This day has held too much for me to make sense of it. Who do you think poisoned the squire?"

"I don't know. Tell me everything that led up to when we discovered him."

"Violet and I came to the Grange to work on the wedding plans with Mrs. Pennyfeather. Violet went off to write, while Mrs. Pennyfeather and I stayed in the kitchen. The squire asked for ale . . ." She stopped. The blood drained from her face, leaving her skin cold. "Dear heaven. The tea. Do you think the poison was in the tea? I asked the maid to make sure he didn't lace it with rum."

"The maid brought Hobblesby the tea?"

"Yes. Mrs. Pennyfeather and I were busy, so she brewed it. She must have used the wrong canister."

"Who knows the mint tea is yours?"

"I thought everyone knew. Dougal accused me of snobbery, said their tea wasn't good enough for me. Jane wrinkled her nose whenever she smelled it. Perhaps the maid didn't. She always acts frightened of me."

"Frightened? Why?"

"Because I'm the daughter of an earl, I think."

"Do you think they would hate you enough to make it look like you poisoned the squire?"

"They?"

"Dougal or Jane."

She couldn't prevent the tears from welling up in her eyes. "Perhaps, but I can't believe they would poison their own father to hurt me."

"Neither do I." He stared at her. "No one else drank the tea?"

"Mrs. Pennyfeather on occasion."

"And the squire?"

"He hated it. I already told you that. He drank ale whenever I wasn't here and only drank Earl Grey to appease me."

Savernake froze. "Then we may have another possibility."

"What possibility?"

"The squire was poisoned by accident. Someone may have wanted to kill you."

Chapter 19

As Brody stood against the doorjamb, Dougal shoved past him. Brody rubbed his shoulder, but didn't say anything. He knew his brother was upset. Brody tried to peer into the room, but the shadows were too great for him to discern where the bed might be. Not that it would matter. He couldn't see his father even if he stood beside him.

Jane was in there now, sobbing and clinging to their father's hand. His father let out a soft moan.

"For God's sake, leave the man alone. He needs to rest," said Brody.

"Don't be so heartless," said Jane with a growl. "I don't want him to die."

"He isn't about to die. The doctor said he would be fine. In a few days. If. He. Had. Quiet."

"You don't care," said Jane on a new wail. "You don't care if he dies."

With a groan of disgust, Brody abandoned his brief vigil in the doorway and escaped Jane's theatrics. He loved his father, but he also believed the doctor.

He counted the steps until he reached the end of the hall. Right turn, ten more steps. Reaching forward, he touched the door and found the latch. Fresh air had a way of clearing one's thoughts, even if those thoughts were of an annoying little sister.

He stepped outside. Blast. Another of England's famous gray days. Sun made navigation easier. Squaring his shoulders, he followed the sound of the stone path until he reached the garden. He had run these paths playing Blind Man's Bluff. Little had he known how useful those games would be to him now.

The crunch of the gravel and the smell of the roses told him the way. A low shrub brushed against his trousers, and he corrected his position. Just about here should be a stone bench.

Ouch.

His shin found it. He patted the seat to make sure it was dry, then sat. The air was cool. The heat of the sun couldn't penetrate the thick clouds. If he tried, he could remember how the colors of the flowers muted on such days. Their fragrance was as vivid as ever.

"It was horrible."

He cocked his head at the voice. Dougal? In the garden? Dougal had always hated the garden. He thought it a waste of the land.

"He almost died," said Dougal.

"But he didn't."

To whom was he talking? Brody knew it was a woman, but who?

"If you had seen his eyes, his pain—"

"Shhhh, it's over now," said the woman.

The footsteps crunched closer, then stopped. Brody knew they had spotted him.

"What are you doing here, Brody? Is Father worse?" Anxiety gave Dougal's voice a higher pitch than normal.

"No, Father is fine. I'm not sure about Jane, though. She's almost hysterical."

"Doesn't surprise me. She can be a stupid cow at times."

Brody paused. "Who's with you?"

"No one."

Surprised, Brody blinked in a vain effort to clear his vision—an old habit he couldn't seem to rid himself of. But Dougal's words stunned him. His brother didn't lie. He could be mean, stubborn, and a bully, but he didn't lie. At least, he never had before. Brody frowned.

"Will you be all right out here by yourself?" asked Dougal.

"Yes."

"Then I'm going to check on Father."

Brody heard the footsteps retreat. Most definitely more than one set. Why was Dougal lying? It made no sense.

No use worrying about it now. He could smell the rain in the sky. As he drew in a deep breath, the first drop hit his face. He stood, pictured the path in his mind, and headed for the house. The rain started in earnest. By the time he wound his way out of the garden, his coat stuck to him, and rivulets ran down his collar.

"Mr. Brody."

He turned toward the voice.

"It's Fletcher, sir. I have an umbrella. May I help you to the house?"

As loath as he was to accept aid, he was no fool. "Thank you, Fletcher. However, I'm afraid I'm already soaked."

"No matter, Mrs. Pennyfeather is laying out fresh clothes for you. You wouldn't want to catch a chill." Fletcher caught his elbow and led him down the path to the house.

When they stepped inside, drops splashed to the floor from his sleeves and trousers and ran down the backs of his hands, tickling him. "I'm afraid I'm creating more work for the staff."

"Don't think of it, sir. It's only water. When someone comes in from the byre, the mess is far worse."

Brody laughed. "I suppose it is."

Footsteps announced the arrival of someone else. "I've brought a towel, sir," said Mrs. Pennyfeather. She pressed the thick cloth into his hands.

"Thank you." Brody wiped his face and ran the towel through his hair. "How's my father?"

"Resting, sir. I shall return to him presently," said the woman. "Dry clothes are laid out in your room."

"Thank you."

"Do you need assistance, sir?" asked Fletcher.

"No, thank you. I can handle it from here." Brody turned in the direction of his room and counted off the steps.

In a few minutes, he was dry and warm again. Grabbing his cane, he made his way to his father's room. "Is anyone here?"

"I am," said Mrs. Pennyfeather.

"I'd like to sit with my father."

"Of course, sir. There's a chair on the right side of his bed. Would you like me to leave?"

"If you wouldn't mind."

"Not in the least."

He heard the scrape of the chair on the floor and the rustle of the woman's skirts as she passed him. He stepped into the room and with his cane felt his way to the bed. A moment later found him seated by his father's side. Reaching his hand forward, he touched his father's arm, then trailed down to his hand. His father's hand was large and warm, the palm callused from years of work at the Grange. Brody smiled. He remembered how his father would take him around the farm when he was but a boy. Hand in hand they'd walk from barn to byre, checking on the animals. His heart was never in farming, but Brody remembered the pride with which his father bought him his commission. How the squire had boasted about his brave son.

Brody sighed. Last year in Burma he had saved his idiot captain, but lost his eyesight in the process. After selling his commission, he invested the money in the markets and had a small income, but he didn't know where to go. With some reluctance, he had come home to depend on his father again as he had as a boy. That fact alone ate at him. How could his father be proud of his blind son now?

An image took shape in his mind. With a wry smile, he corrected himself. It wasn't an image exactly. He had never seen her, but he recognized Lady Violet's spirit. He had only just met her, but he felt more comfort in her presence than anyone's since his injury. She didn't trip over herself to help him or mince her words with him. Hell, she had yelled at him several times. Even his father babied him again. She treated him as a man.

He wished she were here.

With a sharp snort of disgust, he dashed that thought from his mind. What would she want with a blind man? What would any woman want with him?

His father stirred on the bed.

"Father?" Brody lifted his father's hand and clasped it between his own.

"Brody?" Hobblesby whispered. His voice was raw and gravelly.

"I'm here. Do you need anything?"

"No." His father squeezed his hand. "Good to have you home."

Tears stung at Brody's eyes. "I missed you, too, Father."

"Is Anthea—" Hobblesby broke off to clear his throat.

"She's still here. Shall I fetch her for you?"

"No. Don't want her seeing me like this."

His father pulled his hand free. Then Brody heard movement from the bed. He frowned. "The doctor told us you should rest."

"Bother the doctor." A moment later he heard his father panting. "Perhaps I do need help."

"What can I do?" He stared at the bed, willing his sight to return, but his father remained in shadows.

"Savernake."

"I'll get him at once." Brody stood and made his way to the parlor. He heard Jane and Dougal speaking in hushed whispers.

"Brody," said Hubert. "Let me help you." The man grabbed his arm.

He pulled free. "I don't need help, Hubert."

"Really, Brody, you don't have to be so cross. Hubert was just being kind." Jane pouted. He could hear it in her voice.

"Have you seen Savernake?"

"He's with *her* in the study," said Jane. The acid in her tone told him volumes.

"Let me take you," said Hubert, latching on to his arm again.

"Go comfort your wife instead." Brody pivoted and escaped to the hall.

When he reached the door to the study, it was open. He heard Savernake and Lady Anthea speaking.

"Then we may have another possibility." Savernake sounded shaken.

"What possibility?" said Lady Anthea.

"The squire was poisoned by accident. Someone may have wanted to kill you."

Brody's sharp intake of breath whistled. The two occupants of the room fell silent, until Savernake spoke. "You heard?"

He nodded. "I'm blind. The hearing becomes more acute, they say."

"I'm glad it was you at the door," said Savernake.

"As opposed to . . . ?"

"The one who did this. You don't think the strychnine got into the tea by accident?"

Brody sighed. "No."

"There is a seat beside me if you wish," said Lady Anthea. Her soft voice was a marked contrast to the sharp intensity of Savernake's.

"Thank you, Lady Anthea. My father would like to see—"

He heard the rustle of her skirts. "Is he awake? I must go to him."

"Please sit, Lady Anthea. He wants to see Savernake."

"Me?" Savernake sounded surprised. "I'm on my way. Will you sit with Lady Anthea? I fear she hasn't recovered yet." His retreating footsteps told Brody the man hadn't waited for a response.

Brody turned to her. "Recovered? You didn't have the poison?"

"No. I'm ashamed to admit I fainted." Chagrin colored her voice. "I've never fainted in my life."

"Ahh, but you've never faced poison before, have you?"

"No." She let out a sad laugh. "Why doesn't the squire want to see me? Does he think I did this?"

"Perish the thought. He told me he doesn't want you to see him in his state of weakness." He crossed to the settee and sat beside her. "Why would you think he'd accuse you?"

"Jane did."

"For all her years, Jane is a spoiled child. I wouldn't listen to a word she says."

She paused. "You know Savernake thinks I'm the thief."

"But a thief does not a poisoner make." He chuckled, then sobered. He gripped his cane. "I heard your voice when it first happened. Your shock was real."

"They say poison is a woman's weapon."

"Are you trying to convince me that you did poison my father?" He smiled at her.

"No." At last he heard laughter in her voice. "I just needed to know what you thought."

"I don't think you'd hurt my father. I'm reserving judgment on the matter of the thief." He winked.

The swish of more skirts announced the arrival of another woman. "Mr. Brody, I've brought a tray for Lady Anthea, but I can bring more if you're hungry."

"No need," said Anthea. "There's plenty here for both of us."

"Perhaps just a bit more bread, then," said Mrs. Pennyfeather. She left before he could protest.

"I'm really not hungry," said Anthea with a sigh, "but Mr. Savernake thinks I should eat."

"He's right." Brody hesitated for a moment. "Do you trust Mrs. Pennyfeather?"

"Yes. Why do you ask?"

"We don't know who tried to poison my father." He paused again. "Or perhaps you."

A piece of silverware clattered on the table.

"Forgive me. I didn't wish to startle you."

"Too late." The dishes clinked together on the tray. Then she said, "Blast. I can't not eat for fear everything is poisoned. Besides, if someone wanted to kill me, they wouldn't put poison in everything."

"You're right, of course. But Savernake's words warrant attention. You must be careful, Lady Anthea. I would hate to see anything happen to you."

"Thank you." She popped a bite into her mouth. "There, I'm still alive."

He grinned. "I believe you are recovering. You've found your sense of humor. Tell me. Does Lady Violet possess one as well?"

"If you count sarcasm as humor," she said.

"I feared as much. May I ask you an impertinent question? You are to be my mother, after all."

She chuckled. "Yes, and what a wonder of science I am. Younger than my own son."

"Why are you living in Skettle Cottage? It was derelict when I was a boy."

"We have nowhere else to go."

"Is that why you're marrying my father?"

She fell silent.

"I didn't mean to insult you," he said in a rush. "You can't be marrying him because you love him, and although he is fond of you, I don't believe he loves you either. He has wealth, but not the wealth of the *ton*. You're the daughter of an earl. Why aren't you and your sisters in London, having your seasons, finding rich husbands?"

"You *did* mean impertinent, didn't you?" she said,

but he could hear no umbrage in her tone. "We couldn't afford a season even if we wanted one. Our needs have changed in this last year. I hope only to help my sisters find a good life, and ease the burdens of my mother."

"Much as I thought."

"Do you despise me now?"

"Not at all. I understand family. I know my father will enjoy parading his new wife around. You are the daughter of an earl."

"That was in another lifetime."

The sadness in her voice pained him. He wondered if Lady Violet was as determined as her sister. If her book could sell . . .

He smiled. "Lady Anthea, I think I shall be proud to have you as my mother."

Chapter 20

"We've been over it a hundred times," said Anthea. She fell into a chair and closed her eyes. "I'm tired, and I'm hungry, and I can't think anymore."

"Just one more time, to see if we missed anything." Colin poised his quill above the paper.

"Nothing. I can't tell you anything new. I've been over it too many times."

He laid the pen to the side. "Perhaps we should take a break." He glanced at the list of names. It was probably a futile exercise. The tea could have been poisoned at anytime, but at least he felt as if he was doing something.

He crossed to her. "How are you feeling?"

"I told you. I'm tired and I'm hungry."

"No, I meant are you frightened. This can't be easy for you."

She sighed. "No, but I find it hard to believe someone wants to kill me."

He didn't want to argue with her. She was tense enough. "The squire is recovering well."

"Yes, but he still doesn't want me to see him. He doesn't want me to think him weak."

"So much for the vows."

"What do you mean?"

"In sickness or in health . . ."

"I intend to keep my vows."

"Not you, he."

"Are you saying I can't trust him?"

"Not in the least. I'm just saying it's odd he doesn't trust you."

"He trusts me." She paused. "Unlike you."

"I have to admit that so far you've proven me wrong."

A knock at the door put a stop to their strange conversation. "Come in," said Savernake.

The maid entered, wringing her hands. Her face was pale, and her eyes red-rimmed as if she'd been crying for hours. "My lady . . ."

Anthea shot upright. "Is the squire—"

"No, my lady, the squire is fine." The maid drew in a ragged breath, then flung herself on her knees in front of Anthea. "Oh, please don't let them take me to jail, my lady. I didn't mean to kill the squire. The squire's been nothing but good to me and my family."

Anthea blinked. "I don't understand . . ."

"I killed him. I gave him the tea." The woman broke out in fresh sobs.

Her eyebrows arched high, Anthea gazed at Colin. "Do you have a handkerchief?" she mouthed.

He reached in his pocket and pulled out a linen square. He handed it to her.

She opened it with a flick of her wrist. "Here you go. Don't cry." She handed the handkerchief to the wailing maid.

"Th-thank you, m-my lady. You're t-too k-kind." The woman blew her nose with a loud honk.

He'd have to get a fresh one from his room. This handkerchief he'd let the woman keep.

"Now, calm yourself, and tell me what the trouble is," said Anthea in a voice she might use with a child.

"I made the tea, the tea that killed him. I swear I didn't know there was poison in it." The maid's voice held a tremor.

Her words piqued Colin's interest.

"Of course you couldn't know," said Anthea in a soothing tone. "You must remember the squire didn't die. No one killed him, and no one thinks you would harm the squire."

"So you won't be sending for the constable?" said the maid with a sniff.

"No. You must not be frightened any longer," said Anthea.

"But you might be of help to us," said Colin.

"H-help?" The woman turned her wide-eyed gaze on him.

"Yes. We need your help." Colin pulled up a chair to the woman. "Won't you sit?"

"No, I couldn't," said the maid. "It wouldn't be right. Not in front of my lady."

"It's quite all right. Do sit," said Anthea. She gave him a quizzical look.

"If you say so." The woman rose from the floor and perched on the edge of the chair as if afraid to soil the cushion.

"Tell me, uh, why is it that I've never learned your name?" asked Colin.

"It's Lydia, sir. Mrs. Pennyfeather gives me my orders, sir. There's no need for the gentlemen of the house to bother with my name."

"Right. Tell me, Lydia, how long have you worked for the squire?" Colin paced in front of her.

"Just these last two months, sir. My mother thought

I was too young before." Lydia's head swiveled as she followed his movements.

"The day of the squire's poisoning. What happened?" Colin clasped his hands behind his back.

"I was cleaning the parlor, sir."

Colin made another pass.

"Do stop pacing. You're making the poor girl nervous," said Anthea.

Colin glanced at her and then at the maid. "Right. Sorry. Do go on."

"The squire came in and saw me and asked me to fetch him some ale. So I went to the kitchen. My lady told me to make the squire tea, and not to let him drink any spirits."

"Very sound," said Colin.

The maid gave him a timid smile. "The tea canister was out on the sideboard. I measured out the tea and poured water over it."

"The tea canister was out?" asked Anthea.

"Yes. I thought it strange since it was smaller than the usual one, but I figured Mrs. Pennyfeather changed the container."

Colin exchanged a glance with Anthea. Her tea was kept in the smaller canister and placed in a different spot, so that no one would confuse it for the squire's tea.

"I filled a cup with the tea and brought it to the squire." Lydia paused. "I didn't know it had poison. Honest."

"I believe you," said Anthea. She patted the woman's hand.

"Did you add sugar?" asked Colin.

"No, sir. The squire hates sugar in his tea," said Lydia, shaking her head for emphasis.

Yet the tea was sweet. He had tasted it. The sugar must have been added to the tea itself to mask the strychnine. "Was there anything else?"

"No, sir. Then the squire got sick and . . . and . . ." Lydia looked at Anthea and burst into tears again.

"There, there, Lydia. It wasn't your fault. Someone used you for their wickedness, but no one can blame you." Anthea put her arm around the maid's shoulder.

"Thank you, milady. You're too kind."

"Why don't you take the rest of the day off and try to put it from your mind? I'll tell Mrs. Pennyfeather." Anthea smiled at the woman.

"You won't let me go, then?"

"A fine servant like you? I wouldn't dream of it. Go on, now." Anthea rose.

Lydia jumped to her feet. "May I stay at the Grange, my lady? Joe and I are sort of sweet on each other . . ."

"Go find your young man." Anthea acted with all the grace of the lady of the manor.

"Thank you for your help," said Colin. "If you think of anything else, let us know."

"I will, sir." Lydia scurried from the room.

"That didn't help us much," said Anthea.

"No, but it does tell me that you have to be careful."

"You really think someone wanted to kill me?"

"It does seem more likely. It was your tea that was tampered with."

"I just don't want to believe it." Anthea sunk into her chair.

"Who would hate you that much?"

"The only ones I can think of are Jane and Dougal. They don't want me to marry the squire. But to kill me?"

"Greed is one of the reasons people kill." Colin

fastened his gaze on hers. "You must swear to me you won't go out alone or eat anything that others haven't."

"But—"

"Swear." Colin grabbed her shoulders. Her green eyes stared into his, and he knew he was lost. He might have believed her a thief, but he no longer cared if she was. "I don't want to see you die. I can't let you die."

In the next moment, he pulled her to him. He kissed her as if he were trying to solder her to him. Her heat burned his lips, tantalized him, left him aching for more. She trembled in his arms, giving rise to every protective emotion in his breast. He would save her . . . No, she would save him.

She pulled free. "We mustn't."

The ragged desire in her voice fanned his desire into a raging conflagration. "Yes, I must."

He stepped forward so that his legs entwined with hers. The contact jolted through him, leaving him hard. Threading his fingers through her hair, he kissed her again, letting her heat sear through him.

He brought his hand forward to the buttons at her throat. Anthea pulled away slightly, but he didn't let her escape. Her protest died in his mouth.

Her corset pressed up the fullness of her breasts, offering them to him. He traced his fingers over the soft mounds.

She sucked in her breath. "You can't—"

His chuckle rumbled deep in his chest. "Do you know how tempting you are?" He lowered his mouth to trace the line of her jaw with soft kisses. His lips slipped under her jawline and continued down her neck.

"Mr. Sav—" Her breath hitched. "Colin, please."

"As you wish."

"No, I didn't mean—" A low gasp escaped her as he tasted the soft flesh at the top of her breast.

"You are mine. You may not know it yet, but you are mine." He sucked on a spot just above the small ruffle of her corset.

Her head dropped back, and she let out a low moan of pleasure.

When he broke off the contact, a small round mark remained on her creamy skin. He looked at it with a sense of propriety. "You're mine. You can't dispute it any longer."

"I belong to no man." Her voice, tinged with sadness, was quiet. She turned her gaze to his. Passion still glowed in her eyes.

"I want you, and you want me."

"That may well be, but I can't give in to my wants. My wants aren't important." Her fingers trembled as she buttoned the high collar of her dress.

"Your wants are the only concerns that should matter."

She let out a sad laugh. "What of the needs of my family?"

"What of your needs?"

"Food, clothes, shelter, and an occasional book." She pulled the pins from her hair and combed her fingers through the blond lengths. With deft motions, she plaited the tresses and returned the pins to anchor the braid to her head. "The squire will provide me with those."

"You don't love the man."

"Love is an extravagance I cannot afford. I am far past wanting any more luxury than a full stomach."

"You still mean to marry the squire?" His gaze narrowed.

"Yes."

"What if I tell him?"

"Tell him what?" Her voice was stronger now. "That we shared a kiss?"

"He will lose faith in you."

"If he believes you." She faced him. "Tell me something, Mr. Savernake."

"You called me Colin earlier."

Her cheeks took on a pink hue, but she steeled her expression. "Tell me, Mr. Savernake. You spoke of love a moment ago. Can you offer me love?"

He stared at her. The moment passed, then another.

"I thought not." She crossed to the door, then turned back to him. "I thank you for your concern, but you needn't worry about me."

He watched her leave the room, not moving until the wood of the door met the jamb. Then his stomach dropped, and he fell back into the chair behind him. Why had he let her leave? She was in danger, and if she wasn't with him, he couldn't protect her.

Jumping from the chair, he dashed to the door, then stopped. He had no right to protect her. The pain of that thought stole his breath. He wanted to claim her, he wanted to keep her by his side, to love her.

Love?

He cared for her. Despite his best intentions, he found himself thinking of her at all times. She stirred his desires like no woman before. But she was more than an object of his lust. Honorable, graceful, devoted to her family, she embodied her strong values. She didn't fear hard work, faced her future with dignity, and radiated with the gentle power all great women had.

Idiot.

He loved her. The slightly sick feeling in his gut told him the truth of his thoughts. He had no right to her, but he loved her anyway. After all his protestations against the aristocracy, he had fallen in love with the daughter of an earl. The irony brought a cynical laugh to his lips.

Crossing to the sideboard, he poured himself a generous brandy. Clutching the glass in his fist, he sat in the armchair. He needed to think, but first he needed to drink. Too many thoughts whirled in his head—the thefts, the threat to her, the wedding, the squire, damn the man.

He tossed back the amber liquid, savoring the burn at the back of his throat. He didn't know how, but he would claim her. Somehow he would declare his love for her.

But first he had to keep her alive.

Chapter 21

Anthea stared at herself in the mirror. The bright morning sun did little to improve her mood. She buttoned her blouse, but paused as she caught sight of the mark at the top of the swell of her breast. She ran her fingers over the purplish circle. Colin's lips had touched her here. A shiver of delight skittered down her spine.

She closed her eyes as shame washed over her. She had no right to marvel at Colin's touch when she was to marry the squire.

"Thea?"

Violet's voice broke through her contemplation. With a gasp, Anthea clutched the neck of her blouse together.

Violet giggled. "Did I startle you?" She unlaced her nightgown, let it drop to the floor. She grabbed her garments.

Anthea fastened the rest of the buttons in a rush. "You're cheerful today." Anthea snatched up her hairbrush and attacked her tresses with long, vigorous strokes.

Violet slipped into her clothes. Fastening the ties and buttons, she dressed, then folded the discarded nightgown. "I wrote a chapter yesterday, and my characters are speaking to me again."

She eyed her sister. "Are you sure it has nothing to do with seeing Brody today?"

A becoming shade of pink bloomed on her sister's cheeks. "He's helping me with my book, that's all." Violet paused. "You don't think Brody was adopted, do you?"

"Why would you ask that?"

"He's just so different from the other Hobblesbys."

Anthea sent a scolding look toward her sister. "You're terrible."

"I know, but you love me anyway." Violet kissed Thea's cheek. "I'm off. I'm not waiting for you to get ready."

"Say hello to Brody for me." Her sing-song tone brought fresh color to her sister's face.

"Stop, Thea." But Violet grinned at her sister. With a wave, Violet disappeared.

Anthea finished dressing with slow deliberation. She wasn't in a hurry to go to the Grange. How could she face Savernake? Or the squire?

She dallied as long as she could until she knew she had to leave. If she waited any longer, the twins would have to share their lunch with her. With a sigh, she tied her bonnet under her chin and walked the narrow road that led from Skettle Cottage.

She swung her basket in a slow arc, her pace unhurried. Her thoughts, however, jumbled together in a mad rush of guilt. Part of her wanted to savor the memory of Savernake's touch—a secret treasure she could pull out when she needed her spirits bolstered—but part of her berated herself for her enjoyment. Her duplicity ate at her. How could she wed one man when she dreamed of another?

The dull thud of horses' hooves interrupted her

reverie. She looked up at the approaching wagon. Joe and Bob sat on the seat. A large white tarp covered their load. "Good day, boys. Are you off on an errand?"

The two large men looked down at her from the seat. Joe's eyes widened as if in horror, and two red splotches appeared on Bob's face.

Joe cleared his throat. "Miss Anthea. Uh . . . morning to you." As if remembering his manners, he snatched his cap from his head. Bright red hair stood up from the sudden action. He elbowed Bob and pointed to his brother's head.

Bob grabbed his cap and flattened it against his chest. "Miss Anthea. What are you doing here?" He shot a glance at their load.

"I'm on my way to the Grange." She frowned in bemusement. The brothers were a bit slow, but they had never acted so strangely with her.

"Of course you are," said Bob. His face flushed even redder. "We're . . . ah . . . we're—"

Joe nodded with great energy. "On an errand. Yeah, on an errand. Isn't that right, Bob?"

"An errand. That's right." Bob scratched his head. "Important errand."

"She don't need to know, Bob."

"Right." He clamped his mouth shut.

Their behavior perplexed her. She shrugged. "I won't keep you, then."

"Good." Joe smashed his cap onto his head, then pulled it off again. "Begging your pardon, Miss Anthea. I meant to say 'good day.'"

"Yes, good day, Miss Anthea." Bob nodded and returned his cap to cover the thatch of red hair.

Joe clicked his tongue, and the horses pulled forward. The wagon rocked. The tarp opened to a slit, but Anthea saw nothing more than a corner of something.

"Good-bye, boys." She waved to them, but neither noticed her action. Or if they did, they didn't return her gesture.

With a laugh, she dismissed their behavior. The boys were always a little strange, but harmless. They loved the squire and the Grange. She wondered if they'd still call her Miss Anthea after she wed the squire. Knowing the boys, it might take a while for them to grow accustomed to her new name.

She reached the Grange in short time. As she approached the door, Savernake met her at the steps. "What were you thinking?"

"Pardon?"

"Did you forget everything we talked about yesterday?"

Heat flew into her cheeks. "We . . . I cannot think about yesterday."

"Little idiot," he muttered under his breath. She glanced at him in surprise. He grabbed her arm. "Why are you walking alone? Where is your sister?"

"She's already here." She tugged her arm, but he didn't release her.

"Have you forgotten someone wants to harm you? You promised you would take precautions—"

"What could happen to me on the walk from Skettle Cottage?" With a quick wrench, she pulled herself free, but not without some pain. She rubbed her upper arm.

"Anything. Someone could have shot at you, or run you over with a carriage, or—"

She laughed then. "I did see the boys, but they were driving entirely too slow to hurt me."

"The boys?"

"Joe and Bob."

"You aren't taking this seriously." He scowled at her.

"Yes, I am, but I find myself in greater danger from you than from anyone else." She met his gaze and didn't bother to hide the longing she knew shone in her eyes.

"Anthea." His voice softened. He lifted his hand to stroke her cheek.

"Anthea, my dear, I've recovered." The squire's voice boomed through the hall.

She stepped back as Savernake's hand dropped to his side. She turned to her betrothed. "William, you're up. And you've color in your cheeks."

"Yes, my dear. I was well recovered yesterday, but Jane insisted I stay in bed. I hope you've forgiven me for not letting you see me in my sorry state." Hobblesby stepped up to her and kissed her on the cheek.

The brush of his lips left her cold. She smiled at the squire. "I'm not sure I've forgiven you, but I understand."

"Not forgiven, eh?" Hobblesby winked at Savernake. "Hear that, Savernake? She's a spirited one, my Anthea."

"Yes, Squire," said Colin with a subdued nod. "I would speak with you about your accident."

"Not now. We must celebrate my health." Hobblesby took Anthea's arm and led her toward the parlor. The top of his head reached level with her nose. Why had she never noticed how short he was?

"What's this I hear about you postponing our wedding?" Hobblesby asked. He brought her to the settee, seated her, and pulled up a chair for himself.

"I wasn't sure how soon you'd recover. The doctor said you needed rest and quiet, so I thought it better to arrange the wedding for a later date."

"Well, unarrange it. I feel fine. No reason to postpone this thing any longer. I'm not getting younger, you know." The squire guffawed.

Anthea sighed. How many times had she heard this particular jest of his?

Hobblesby turned to his secretary. "How are things at your end? Can we still be married in two weeks time?"

"I'm sure the reverend will be willing to perform the ceremony as originally scheduled. The guests shouldn't be difficult to contact."

"Excellent." Hobblesby leaned forward and grasped her hands. "We don't have to wait much longer."

She forced herself to smile. "That would be lovely."

Hobblesby lifted one hand and kissed the back of it. "I fear if we delayed it one more time, people would start to believe we shall never marry."

Savernake turned his back to them.

Hobblesby stood. "Now, if you will excuse me, my dear, I need to see to my farm. I've been unable to tend to anything these past few days." He chuckled. "We'll see how Dougal did without me."

Hobblesby left the room. Anthea rubbed her forehead. How could she go through with the wedding? How could she not? Her family needed her help. She had had no qualms before . . . before Savernake came. She glanced at him. His gaze was cold.

"You're looking for sympathy in the wrong person." His voice sent an uncomfortable chill down her spine.

She lifted her chin. "I wasn't looking for sympathy."

His laugh held no mirth. "You've learned the lessons of the *ton* well."

"I don't know what you mean."

"Selling yourself to the highest bidder, but not above finding your amusement on the side."

The blood drained from her face. She closed her eyes. She couldn't deny his hateful words, but they hurt nevertheless. A moment later, she steeled herself against his disdain and looked at him. "If my company troubles you so, why don't you leave Middle Hutton?"

"I haven't finished my task here. I gave my word to help. The minute I have, nothing shall keep me here."

"Then you're as much a slave to duty as I." Her voice grew softer with every word.

"The difference being I won't ruin my life when I've fulfilled my obligation." He pivoted and strode to the door, but before he could leave, Fletcher entered the room.

"Mr. Savernake, I'm glad to have found you. There's been another theft," said Fletcher.

Savernake glanced at her, then back at the butler. "What was taken this time?"

"A chest of linens. The squire had ordered them for his nuptials. Mrs. Pennyfeather was changing the bedclothes when she noticed the chest was missing."

Savernake ran his hand through his hair. "How large was the chest?"

"The size of a trunk, sir. One man couldn't lift it by himself, at least not when it was full."

"Which it was."

"Yes, sir. With tablecloths, bedding, Belgian laces. The squire meant it for his bride." Fletcher shook his head. "I'm sorry we didn't see anything, sir."

Savernake shook his head. "You couldn't have expected it. When did you last see the chest?"

Anthea stirred on the couch. "I saw it today."

Savernake turned to her. "How could you have? You arrived and came directly to this room."

"I know, but I saw it in the back of a wagon as I walked here."

"What?" He crossed to her. "You saw the thief?"

She shook her head. "No, I saw the boys. Joe and Bob."

"You're not making sense."

She drew in a deep breath. "As I was walking here, I saw Joe and Bob driving the wagon somewhere. They acted strange when they saw me. A white tarp covered something in the back of the wagon. As they drove away, I caught a glimpse of the corner of something." She paused. "The load was the size of a chest."

Savernake turned to Fletcher. "Where are they now?"

"I don't know, Mr. Savernake."

Savernake frowned. "I'll need to speak to them when they return from their outing."

She shook her head. "No."

He narrowed his gaze. "Don't you want to help your *betrothed?* Or don't you care who steals from him?"

"Don't be an idiot. Of course I want to help William." She fought to regain her calm. "I meant, I don't think *you* should talk to them. You should let me."

"Why?"

"You're an outsider. I'm to be their mistress. You might frighten them. No, you *will* frighten them."

He frowned at her words. She smiled at him.

"What if they try to harm you?" he said.

"If they try to harm *you*, they'll succeed. They're bigger than you. Besides, they won't hurt me."

"How can you be sure, Lady Anthea?" asked Fletcher.

"Because I'll be with her," said Savernake.

"They won't speak if you're there," said Anthea, full of confidence. "No, they won't harm me because they love the squire, and the squire loves me."

Fletcher cocked his head, making the hump on his back look larger. "She makes sense, Mr. Savernake."

"I want to hear what they say." Savernake started to pace. "I'll hide if necessary, but I want to be there."

She nodded. "I think we can do that."

"I'll let you know when the boys return," said Fletcher. The butler left the room.

She looked at Savernake. "Does this mean you no longer believe I am the thief?"

He stopped. Without balking, he gazed into her eyes. "I haven't believed you the thief since I kissed you in the woods."

Chapter 22

Violet laid down the quill. Stretching her arms above her shoulders, she rolled her head from side to side. "Ouch."

"What did you do?" asked Brody.

"I'm stiff." Violet pushed away from the table and walked a few steps.

"You've been working hard, but that last chapter was the best."

She smiled. "It was good, wasn't it? Your ideas were wonderful."

"I didn't do much. Only a suggestion here and there." He faced the direction of her voice.

"You did much more than that." She paused. "In fact, I was hoping you'd agree to help me write this book."

His eyebrows arched. "I? I'm not a writer."

"You are. You see the story so clearly."

"But I see little else." Brody smiled at her.

She placed her fists on her hips. "If this is another lapse into self-pity, I won't stand for it. I can out-pity you. If you knew how my mother—"

With a laugh, he held up his hand. "No, no. I wasn't bemoaning my fate . . . Well, maybe a little." He rose from his seat and started toward her with a careful step. "I was merely thinking that had I my vision as I did before, I would know what you look like."

"Why should you want to see what I look like?" she said in a quiet tone.

"I would like to know if you are as beautiful as you say . . ."

Violet drew in a sharp breath in mock outrage.

". . . or as you sound." Grinning, he took another step toward her. "It's good that you're standing by the window. I can see your shadow. May I look at your face?"

"How?" Her voice was no more than a whisper.

"With my fingers." He reached her. He lifted both hands to her face.

She stood as still as a rabbit when it first hears a sound, ready to take flight, but not ready to move yet. His fingers brushed her cheeks. She closed her eyelids. With a feather-light touch, he moved over her features, gently tapping her nose and forehead, slipping over her eyes, smoothing her eyebrows. When he reached her lips, he used just one finger to trace the curve of her mouth.

He leaned forward and replaced his finger with his lips. His kiss was soft, undemanding, yet Violet sensed he was holding himself back.

He pulled back a mere inch.

"I've never been kissed before," said Violet on a whisper.

"Forgive me. I shouldn't have done it. But I . . ." He shook his head. "If I were a seeing man, I would have stolen a kiss long ago. Perhaps that first day on the hillside."

"Why didn't you?"

"I'm a blind man. What could I possibly offer the daughter of an earl?"

She let out a small cry. "You can be such a stupid man."

She placed her hands on his cheeks and pulled him to her. She kissed him with all the fervor and anticipation she had kept in check since the day she met him. His mouth opened over hers, spreading her lips apart and sliding his tongue over her teeth. Her eyes shot open in surprise, but she welcomed the intimacy. Her heart raced, and she almost forgot to breathe. For an instant, she thought she should remember the giddiness that accompanied his kiss for use in her writing, but in the next instant she could think of nothing but him and the sensation spinning through her.

A long moment later, he pulled back. His expression reminded her of a cat who got into the cream. His grin mirrored the one she knew was on her face.

"Does this mean you'll help me write the book?" she asked in a breathy voice.

Brody laughed. "If you promise such payment in return for my work."

"My word, you are wicked. Just the type of man I need to add life to my story." She tucked her hand in his.

"I do think I'm falling in love with you, Violet," said Brody.

She paused. "Just falling? I suppose I shall have to work harder, then." Her heart hammered in her throat, and she wanted to cry with joy.

He clasped her wrist and lowered her hand. His expression grew serious. "No, Violet. You cannot mean what you are saying. I am blind."

She let out a gasp of mock outrage. "Good heavens. How long have you been keeping this secret?"

He frowned. "Don't jest. I have little money of my

own, and I depend on my father for a home. What future can we have? I have nothing to offer you."

"You're wrong. You have everything to offer me. Your heart, your mind, and your soul." Violet gazed up at the beautiful man and cupped his face in her hands. "Who would have believed I'd ever say such things to a Hobblesby?"

Brody gave her a crooked grin. "Watch your mouth. You're speaking of my family."

"I know, and I can't believe what I'm saying." She lifted his hand and placed it on her lips, so he could feel her smile. "I knew I loved you from the moment you didn't cringe at my displays of temper."

He brushed a kiss on her forehead, then stepped back. "I won't offer for you until I can find some way to support you."

"I already have work for you. This book. With your help, I can finish this book in little time and then send it off to a publisher."

"They might not buy it."

"Then they'll buy the next. You have a real gift for words, Brody."

"But—"

"If you're looking for excuses, you'll always find them."

He shook his head. "I'm realistic, whereas you are a confirmed dreamer."

"Perhaps. But dreams have come true, and I will make mine happen." She kissed his hand. "Now let's get to work. I want to sell this thing before I'm an old maid."

"Very well, but I don't want to see our kiss appear in the pages of that book."

"But it would make such a wonderful moment."

"Violet—"

"I was jesting. I doubt I could find the words to describe what I felt. Perhaps if we tried again . . . " She tiptoed and placed her hand on his chest, touching his lips with hers.

He held her away from him. "You are incorrigible." But he kissed her again. How could he have been so lucky to find a woman like her? It would be years before he could provide for her, but maybe the writing was indeed the means to supporting a wife. Until then, he had to control his desire to be selfish and enjoy what she offered him. He broke off the contact. "We have a book to write. You came here to work, not play."

"You are a brutal taskmaster." Her smile lit up her voice. She left his side, and a moment later he heard her scratching on the paper. Turning toward the brightness of the day, he glanced out the window and wished he could see the grounds instead of just remembering them. A fresh breeze carried the scent of the garden through the opening. Violet didn't understand how difficult it would be to have a blind husband. Perhaps that was better. When a real suitor came for her, she could just remember him with fondness. Whereas he wouldn't forget her.

He stilled. Someone was having a conversation outside. Better said, someone was yelling outside the window.

"Damn it."

Brody recognized the voice of his brother. Dougal sounded angry.

"How were we to know she would walk by just then?" asked a second voice.

Brody thought he recognized it, but he couldn't be sure through the window.

"I told you not to let anyone see you," said Dougal.

What was Dougal talking about?

"She didn't see nothing. We had it covered up."

A different voice, but similar to the other.

"What did you say to her?"

"Nothing, Mr. Dougal. We exchanged greetings, that's all."

"That's saying something. I told you not to talk to anyone either."

"We couldn't let her pass without saying good day. That wouldn't have been right."

"Never mind. I'll take care of her. Any other problems?"

Brody didn't like the tone of his brother's voice. "Violet, come here," he whispered.

"I'm in the middle of a sentence," she said.

"Come here anyway. I need your help."

She sighed, but he heard her footsteps. "Yes?"

"Look out the window, but don't let them see you. Make sure we're both behind the drapes. And keep your voice low."

"We're hidden. What is this about?"

He shook his head. "Not now. Whom do you see with Dougal?"

"I don't know their names. Those two men who work here. Large, with red hair."

Now the voices made sense. He nodded. "Joe and Bob. They're *both* outside?"

"Yes. Why can't I let them see me?"

"Dougal's angry about something. It doesn't make much sense, but it doesn't sound right." He held up his finger to his mouth as the voices came through the glass again.

"She wants to talk to us," said one of the boys.

"You can't. I don't care what excuse you give, but don't talk to her."

"But we—"

"No. Here, take this, and go into the village and buy yourselves a pint or two. Don't come back until morning."

Brody turned to Violet. "What did Dougal give them?"

"A handful of money," she whispered back.

"But my girl, Lydia, is here," said one of the boys.

"She'll live without you one night. She'll probably be glad for the rest."

One of the brothers guffawed.

"Nay, my Lydia's a good girl."

"If all goes well, you'll be able to marry the girl soon for all I care," said Dougal. "Get going, both of you. I don't want to see you until tomorrow."

"Right, Mr. Dougal," said one brother.

"Lydia will be happy to hear that, sir," said the other.

"Go!" shouted Dougal.

Violet touched his arm. "They're leaving now with Dougal glowering at them as they walk away."

Brody pulled back from the window. "Odd."

"Now can you tell me what this is about?"

"I don't know." He drew his brows together. "Who do you suppose the 'she' was whom they spoke about?"

"There are only a few women in your house. Jane, Mrs. Pennyfeather, and I suppose you could count Thea, too."

"Jane wouldn't want to speak to Joe and Bob. She tries to avoid them whenever possible." He paused. Loyalty toward his family warred with the need to share his thoughts. "Dougal's been acting strange for a while now."

"I always thought he was strange," muttered Violet.

He let out a short chuckle. "He's still my brother."

She sighed. "I know. I feel the same when people speak of Iris. How has he been strange?"

"After Father was poisoned, I was in the garden. Dougal was walking with a woman, but when they saw me, they fell quiet. Dougal denied anyone was with him."

"Wait," said Violet. "A woman is coming toward Dougal now. I think she was hiding behind the trees."

"Who is it?"

"Gad, it's Eugenia Ulster. But I don't see her mother anywhere."

"What is she doing here?" None of this made sense.

Violet grabbed his arm and pulled him toward her. "Stay down. She just glanced at the window."

"Did she see me?"

"I don't think so. She's staring down the road after Joe and Bob."

Eugenia's voice was more difficult to hear. Brody was tempted to open the window wider, but knew it would draw attention to them. He leaned forward to catch her words.

"What did they say?" asked Eugenia.

"She saw them and wants to talk to them," said Dougal. "Don't worry, I sent them away for the day. She can't stay here forever."

"Not yet at any rate," said Eugenia. "But if the marriage takes place—"

"It won't." Dougal's answer sounded like a shot.

"She" was Anthea, Brody knew now. Violet's hand tightened on his arm. He knew she realized they were speaking of her sister as well. He laid a hand on her shoulder to comfort her.

"Didn't I tell you she would be a problem?" said Eugenia.

"Aye." Dougal fell quiet.

"You know what we have to do."

"Aye, but I don't like it."

"Neither do I," said Eugenia.

A moment later, Violet gasped.

He bent to her ear. "What happened?"

"Eugenia walked into Dougal's arms. They're embracing. No, wait. Dear heaven, they're kissing." Violet's voice squeaked in shock.

"You must be mistaken," said Brody.

"I know what kissing is even if I haven't had much practice at it."

"It's not that I doubt your word, but it's too fantastic to believe. Dougal and Eugenia? Father has never liked the girl, and Dougal has never spoken of her."

"I'm just telling you what I saw."

"What are they doing now?"

"Please. I have no desire to watch."

"Violet."

"Oh, very well." She moved away from him for a moment, but never released his arm. "They're walking toward one of the other buildings."

"Is it one of the barns?"

"No, it looks like a cottage."

"Dougal lives in one of the outbuildings." Brody pulled away from her.

"What do you think they want from Thea?" asked Violet.

"I don't know. I must think a moment." He reached a chair and sat.

A knock sounded at the door. "Pardon me, Lady Violet, Mr. Brody," said Fletcher. "I've been requested to fetch you both. The family is gathered in the parlor awaiting the arrival of the midwife."

Brody jumped from his chair. "Jane. Is she well?"

"From what I've been told, Mrs. Fanning is at the early stages yet, but she is fine. Your father has asked you all be present."

"I shouldn't stay," said Violet. "I'm not family, really."

"Squire Hobblesby said you were welcome," said the butler.

"He's just being polite. No, I'll go home." She shuffled her papers and tapped them into place. "I had a lovely day, Mr. Hobblesby. I look forward to another."

The promise in her voice made him smile. "I'll let you know what I discover about that other matter," said Brody. As she breezed by him, he could smell the scent of jasmine in her hair. He longed to reach out and touch her again, but knew he couldn't in front of Fletcher. "Good day to you, Lady Violet."

Her footsteps clicked against the wood in the hall. Brody turned to Fletcher. "Lead me to my family. Looks like I'll be an uncle soon."

Chapter 23

Colin observed the occupants of the room. The squire eyed the brandy that stood on a salver as if he wanted to celebrate the birth of his first grandchild before the child was actually born. Brody sat in his chair listening with humor to the sounds and conversations around him. Hubert paced the room, stopping at the door and glancing toward Jane's room with each pass. She had banished him from her presence an hour ago. Anthea was with Jane. Colin wondered how she fared with the squire's daughter. Better than the woman's husband, since Anthea hadn't reappeared.

"Where's Dougal?" asked the squire.

"Fletcher's looking for him," said Colin. "Would you like me to go as well?"

"No. No need for you both to wander about. He'll be here soon enough, I suppose." Hobblesby beamed at the small group. "Exciting, isn't it?"

Hubert paused long enough in his pacing to glare at him.

"We should wait for Jane's opinion on that, Father," said Brody.

Hobblesby snickered. He eyed the brandy again. "You chaps won't tell Anthea if I indulge just a little.

Join me, Fanning. You look as if you need a drop or two."

Hobblesby crossed to the sideboard and poured out two generous portions. "Anyone else?"

"Not for me. It's too early yet," said Brody.

"It's late somewhere," said the squire. "Savernake?"

"No, thank you, sir."

The squire handed a snifter to Hubert, then lifted his own to his lips. When he removed it, Colin saw the level in the glass had dropped to nearly half. No wonder the man had trouble with gout. Hubert stared at his glass for a moment and paced again, clutching the snifter in his hand, but not drinking.

Brody turned his head toward the door, and a moment later, Dougal entered the parlor. He glanced at everyone and scowled. "I don't have time for this."

"Nonsense, boy. Your sister is about to whelp. You can take a little time from the animals." Hobblesby patted his son on the arm. "You'll understand better when you have a wife of your own."

"Where were you, Doug?" asked Brody.

"Out," came the terse answer.

"Alone?" asked Brody.

"Who would I be with?" Dougal's answer sounded more like a growl.

"I don't know. Maybe you had an assignation."

Dougal screwed up his face. "What the hell are you talking about?"

"Don't know. Just seems like you're alone a lot." Brody tapped his chin as if in deep contemplation. "Some feminine companionship might cure you of your sour disposition."

Colin scrutinized Brody. The banter didn't have

Brody's usual lightness. His grin held uneasiness, not mirth.

"What would you know of feminine companionship, 'cept for those who take pity on you?" Dougal glared at his brother.

"Boys, that's enough." Hobblesby downed the rest of his brandy.

"Don't worry, Father. I know better than to take Dougal's words seriously." Brody smiled at his father. "I believe I will take that brandy after all."

Hobblesby scurried to the salver and filled another snifter. Then he refilled his own. He brought the brandy to Brody. "Let's drink to your sister."

Brody lifted the glass to his lips and swallowed. The squire again drained half of his.

Fletcher entered the room. "The midwife, sir."

A plump woman entered the room. Her hair, more gray than brown, smiled at each man. "Good day, good day. A fine day to be born."

"Where have you been?" Hobblesby crossed to her, ignoring the brandy that sloshed over the edge of the glass. "We sent for you hours ago."

His agitation didn't disturb the woman in the least. If anything her smile grew even broader. "There now, Squire. These firstborns like to take their time. There's no hurry even now. I've only come this soon out of consideration of you. Is that brandy? I wouldn't say no to a drop."

Hobblesby stared at the woman for several seconds, then returned to the salver. He spilled a little of the amber liquid into the glass.

The midwife giggled. "It'll take more than that to wet my lips."

"I don't want to blur your faculties," said the squire.

The woman laughed. "It'll take a lot more than that to get me drunk. This is no'but something to splash on the back of my throat. No worries, Squire. I'm the best there is, and your daughter's a fine woman. Broad hips. I'll have little else to do than catch the baby as he comes out."

The squire poured a little more, but not more than a finger's width. He handed it to the woman.

She lifted the glass. "To the health of the child." Tipping her head back, she tossed the contents of the whole glass into her mouth. Closing her eyes, she winced, then swallowed. "Ahh. Perfect. Now, where is your daughter?"

Before the squire could answer, a voice rang in the hall. "Nonsense. I'm sure I'll be welcome. Where are they?" A moment later, Mrs. Ulster blew into the parlor rather like a whirlwind. "Here you are. I saw the midwife leaving town headed this way, and I knew I had to come offer my help. How is Jane?"

On the edge of her skirts, Fletcher followed her in, nearly prancing to keep up with her. "Forgive me, sir. I couldn't stop her."

The squire threw up his hands. "No harm done. Show the midwife to Jane's room, Fletcher." He took back the glass from the midwife.

With a curt bow, Fletcher escorted the woman from the room.

Mrs. Ulster beamed at the assemblage and clapped her hands together. "How are you holding out? First births can be tricky. Have you given the father plenty of spirits to calm him?"

"I don't want to be calm," said Hubert. He still clutched the untouched brandy.

Mrs. Ulster crossed to him and patted his arm. Hubert snatched it out of her reach. "I am needed here, I see," she said.

"Where is your lovely daughter this afternoon, Mrs. Ulster?" asked Brody.

The question surprised Colin. He knew Brody's feelings toward the family.

"She's at home. That is, I left before she returned from her charitable rounds." Mrs. Ulster's voice was twice as loud as it should have been.

"Such a pity we can't enjoy her company," said Brody. "I find Miss Ulster such an interesting woman."

Colin wondered why Brody persisted in the topic. He moved closer to the man.

"I'll be sure to tell her you asked after her," Mrs. Ulster shouted.

"Gad, woman. Brody's blind, not deaf," said Dougal with a grimace.

"Yes, of course." Red flooded the woman's cheeks, and she blinked rapidly. "I forgot."

Dougal shook his head and muttered something under his breath that Colin couldn't hear. Dougal crossed to the door. "I'll be back."

Hobblesby darted after Dougal. "I want you to stay . . ." The squire's voice trailed off as Dougal left the room without looking back.

Colin took advantage of the distraction and leaned over to Brody. "What are you doing?" he whispered.

"I have to speak with you. Later. Alone." Brody leaned back as if he had said nothing.

Mrs. Ulster clicked her tongue. "Youth can be so headstrong. I'm sure your son meant no disrespect."

Hobblesby opened his mouth to respond, but Mrs. Ulster continued. "Where is Lady Anthea? I would have thought she'd be here."

"She is," said Hobblesby. "She's in with Jane."

"Oh, dear, that will never do. She shouldn't witness a birth. She's unmarried." Mrs. Ulster shook her head.

"We'll be married in two weeks," said Hobblesby. "She's as good as wed."

Mrs. Ulster waggled her finger in the air. "'As good as' is still unmarried. I'm glad I came. I'll relieve her." Mrs. Ulster rushed from the room.

The squire fell into a chair. "I will never understand the rules of women. Perhaps another brandy . . ."

Hubert handed the squire his untouched drink on his next pass through the room. For several minutes, no one spoke. The only sounds were the footsteps of Hubert as he trod back and forth in the room.

Colin's thoughts returned to Brody's strange behavior—the goading of his brother and his interest in Eugenia Ulster. Had the man learned something about them? He was tempted to take Brody from the room now and ask, but given the squire's reaction to Dougal's departure, he didn't think it wise.

Brody cocked his head toward the door. Colin looked up to see Anthea enter the room. Just seeing her was enough to send his blood racing. He suppressed the smile he wanted to give her.

Hobblesby jumped to his feet. "How's Jane?"

"As far as I can tell, she's fine." Anthea started toward the squire, but stopped when she saw the two empty glasses in the squire's hands. "I hope those aren't yours."

Hobblesby's face changed into a mask of contrition. "Just a little to soothe our nerves."

"Then I'll have Mrs. Pennyfeather brew some tea."

"No tea," said Hobblesby. "I'm off tea for a while."

"Can't say that I blame you," said Brody.

"Very well, but no more brandy."

The squire crossed to her. "Tell me again how Jane is."

Anthea patted his arm. "She's a strong woman, and she's holding out fine."

"How much longer . . . ?" asked Hubert.

She shook her head. "I don't know. The midwife had only started examining her before Mrs. Ulster threw me out."

"That woman is a menace," said Hobblesby. "She and her daughter both."

"She means well," said Anthea.

"I don't care. I like her husband well enough. Can't imagine how he tolerates her." Hobblesby stretched his arms overhead. "If only we had other proper folk in this town."

Colin stared at the squire. He had heard such words come from his stepmother's mouth. He hadn't expected to hear it in Middle Hutton.

"It's too bad the earl never comes to check his holdings. I could invite him to dinner." Hobblesby tapped his chest. "Imagine me entertaining the earl. Of course, now it's quite possible, once we wed. You are, after all, the daughter of an earl." He lifted Anthea's hand to his lips.

Colin turned away. He couldn't stomach the squire's bluster.

"I doubt he'll want to meet me," said Anthea. "I'm a commoner as much as you."

"Nonsense. We must make the contacts. Think of our children. They'll do better with connections in the *ton*."

The next few hours passed with excruciating slowness. Mrs. Pennyfeather brought a tray of food to the parlor at suppertime. Hubert didn't eat, but the others

248 *Gabriella Anderson*

were grateful for the distraction. Being summer, the sun set late in the evening, but Fletcher lit candles and sconces as darkness fell, and set a fire in the grate.

At last, Mrs. Ulster reappeared. Her hair had straggled from the confines of the chignon, and she looked tired. She fell into a chair. "A boy. Mrs. Fanning and the baby are doing just fine."

Hobblesby whooped and jumped to his feet. "Thank you."

Mrs. Ulster giggled. "Oh, Squire."

Hubert crossed to her and grabbed her arm. "May I go see her?"

"Yes. I think the midwife is finished cleaning her. But don't be too long. Your wife needs her rest now."

"A son." Hubert looked off toward the ceiling. Then he left the room.

"I want to see her as well." The squire started for the door.

"No, wait, William. Let Hubert see her alone first," said Anthea.

The squire stopped. His shoulders drooped a little, but he nodded. "You're right."

Mrs. Ulster fanned herself with her hand. "I'm exhausted."

"Savernake, see that Mrs. Pennyfeather packs some food for Mrs. Ulster and see her home," said Hobblesby.

"Yes, sir." Savernake crossed to Mrs. Ulster and offered her his arm. "May I take you home, Mrs. Ulster?"

"Thank you, Mr. Savernake. I'm sure Eugenia will be happy to see what a gentleman you are."

His smile stiffened. "I'm only doing what any man would do."

"You mustn't belittle yourself, Mr. Savernake." Mrs. Ulster took his arm. "Good night, everyone."

As they left the room, Savernake sent them a pleading glance.

"Hah," said Hobblesby. "Savernake knows that
woman has plans for him. If he's not careful, she'll
snare him for that girl of hers. Now, where's Dougal.
He needs to be told."

The squire rang the bellpull. Fletcher appeared in
a moment. "Sir?"

"Have you seen my son?"

"Mr. Dougal? No, sir, shall I fetch him?"

"Yes, and send Mrs. Pennyfeather in with some
champagne. We need to celebrate."

Soon champagne stood on the table in front of
them. Although Dougal wasn't present yet, Hobblesby
handed Brody a glass, then gave one to Anthea. He
lifted his own. "To my grandson."

Anthea nodded and sipped from the bubbly wine.
The slightly sweet taste reminded her of her father
and the many times he had lifted a glass to celebrate
the launch of a new scheme. They all eventually
failed, but her father had celebrated nevertheless.

When her glass was empty, Anthea glanced out the
window. The last vestiges of daylight had disappeared
from the sky. She placed the flute onto the table. "I'd
better get home. I'll tell Mother the news and be back
early tomorrow. In any case, I doubt Jane needs any
more visitors tonight."

Hobblesby nodded. "That would probably be best.
Thank you for understanding, my dear."

She crossed to her betrothed and kissed him on the
cheek. "Congratulations on your grandson."

"You are a comfort, my girl. We'll see you on the
morrow."

"Good night, Lady Anthea," said Brody.

"Good night."

Anthea made her way to the front door. Fletcher held the door open for her. "Won't you stay, Lady Anthea? It's rather late. Mrs. Pennyfeather can make up a bed."

"No, I'd better go home. They'll want to hear the news."

"As you wish, my lady."

"Good night, Fletcher."

The sky was dark, but the moon gave enough light to see the way. Anthea walked slowly, enjoying the cool of the night. She felt worn, as if she had done more than sit in the parlor all evening. As the lights of the Grange vanished behind her, a shiver snaked down her spine. After the day of waiting, she had forgotten about the possible threat to herself. She shouldn't be out here alone.

Rustling in the bushes startled her. She gasped. Casting a glance over her shoulder, she laughed at herself. Nothing was out here, but in any case she would be careful. She wasn't stupid.

Turning, she started back toward the Grange. She would wait for an escort, or spend the night there. Whichever she decided, she would be more comfortable among people. The darkness seemed to magnify the danger, imaginary or not.

Anthea froze. The moon cast its light on a figure in black just down the road from her.

"Who's there?" she cried.

The figure didn't answer, but started to run toward her.

Anthea didn't ask again. She lifted her skirts and ran.

Chapter 24

Colin congratulated himself on extricating himself from Mrs. Ulster's lair with such ease. As he returned to the Grange, he noticed most of the lights doused in the house. Fletcher met him at the door.

"End of a long day, eh, Fletcher?"

"Yes, sir." Fletcher closed the door behind him.

"Is everyone in bed?"

"Almost, sir. Although I'm sure Lady Anthea hasn't arrived home yet."

"Home? She isn't spending the night?"

"No, sir. I offered her a bed, but she wished to go home."

His unease grew. "Who went with her?"

"No one, sir."

All vestiges of his high spirits fled. "Bloody hell." He pivoted and ran out the door.

The moon provided enough light to see the road, but he hated to think of her alone in the dark. Dammit, she knew better than to walk alone.

He ran, scouring the road for any glimpse of her. Why hadn't she listened to him? The farther he ran, the more his disquiet grew. He tried to reason with himself—she was safe, no one would try to harm her tonight, she was already at home—but he couldn't shake his belief that something was wrong.

A scream tore through the dark.

Anthea.

He plunged through the bushes toward his left. *Scream again. Let me hear you.*

He listened for movement—breaking twigs, leaves crunching, anything. He froze, straining to hear something.

"No!"

There.

He dashed through the thick bracken. Anthea lay on the ground. A figure clad in black loomed over her. She fought against him, striking out with her fists and kicking. Her skirts hampered her ability to defend herself.

Colin leaped forward. He pulled the man away from her, spun him around, and punched the assailant on the jaw. The man reeled back. Colin noticed he wore a mask. He braced himself for another attack, but the man stopped short, whirled on his heel, and fled through the bushes.

Colin rushed to Anthea's side. "Are you hurt?"

The tracks of her tears shimmered in the moonlight. "I'm more frightened than anything else."

He took her in his arms and hugged her to him. Then he held her away from him. "What were you thinking? I told you never to go anywhere alone."

She sniffed. "I know. I was coming back to the Grange when I saw him."

He wiped away her tears. "I didn't mean to yell. He didn't hurt you?"

She shook her head.

He cupped her face in his hands. "Are you sure?"

"Yes," she whispered. "I don't think he meant to . . . you know. He tried to get his hands around my throat."

A wave of anger washed over him. He wished he could throttle the man. "I told you not to go out alone."

Fresh tears coursed down her cheeks as she nodded. "I remembered too late. I tried to come back to you."

He drew her to him. "God forgive me, I don't know what I'd do if something happened to you."

He kissed her then with all the strength his fear gave him and all the sense of protection he had no right to feel. He tasted the salt of her tears on her lips.

Her lips opened under his, and she burrowed into his chest. "Don't let me go," she said.

"I won't."

She trembled in his arms, and he tightened his hold on her. He wanted to banish the memory of the assailant, banish her demons, banish her fear.

"Let's get you home." He helped her to her feet and led her back to the road. With his arm around her, he started walking toward the Grange.

"This isn't the way," she said.

"The Grange is closer, and I think I need to get you warmed up as fast as I can. You haven't stopped shivering since I arrived. The squire won't mind."

She didn't protest again, just snuggled closer to his side. "I don't know why, but I am cold."

"It's the shock. You'll be fine once we get you some tea and a blanket."

Fewer lights glowed now than earlier. Colin reached the door and opened it. Fletcher hurried to them and took in her disheveled appearance with a concerned frown. "Lady Anthea, are you hurt?"

"N-not really." A large tremor shook her.

"We need some tea, and a blanket. Can Mrs. Pennyfeather make up a room?"

"At once, Mr. Savernake. Should I wake the squire?"

"No. She's safe now. He can be informed in the morning."

Fletcher hurried off, and Colin led her to the parlor. He seated her on the settee and lit a single candle.

A minute later, Fletcher reappeared with a blanket. "The tea is coming."

"Thank you, Fletcher." He took the blanket from the butler and wrapped it around Anthea's shoulders. She looked utterly lost. He sat beside her and rubbed her hands. They were cold. "Just a few more minutes, and we'll have you warmed up."

Mrs. Pennyfeather arrived with the tray. She clucked when she saw Anthea and poured a cup of the steaming liquid. Colin took it from her.

"Perhaps a drop of brandy to calm her?" suggested Mrs. Pennyfeather.

"Yes," he said, ignoring Anthea's look of dissent. He held out the cup as Mrs. Pennyfeather poured in a splash of the spirit. He handed Anthea the tea. "Drink it."

She nodded and wrapped her fingers around the bowl of the cup. She took a long draught.

"Better?" he asked.

She nodded.

Mrs. Pennyfeather said, "I have a nightgown laid out for her, and I'll place a warm brick in her bed. Bring her there when she's drunk all the tea." She bustled from the room.

He smiled at the housekeeper's tone. She sounded more like a nursemaid than a servant. "You heard the woman. Drink up."

Anthea wrinkled her nose at him, but took another swallow. It was a good sign. Her spirits were rising.

"Do you need anything else, Mr. Savernake?" asked Fletcher.

"No. Go to bed. I'll see she gets to her room."

"Very good, sir." Fletcher left the room.

The single candle didn't give off much light, but he didn't want to rouse the household. The glow was enough to see her shivering had stopped. She placed the cup on the table. It was empty.

"Good. Now to bed."

"I don't know if I'll be able to sleep."

"The tea and brandy should help. You need to rest and try to forget about what happened."

She nodded. He retrieved the candle and returned to her. Without removing the blanket, he helped her rise, then led her to her room.

He stopped at the door. "Do you need help? I'll fetch Mrs. Pennyfeather."

"No, I'll be fine." She paused. "Thank you. For coming after me."

He didn't answer. Her face was tilted toward him, and in the candlelight her lips glistened, beckoning him toward them. He steeled himself. Not here. Not in the squire's house. Stepping back, he thrust the candle at her. The flame flickered at the sudden movement.

"Good night. You're safe now."

She scrutinized his eyes, then nodded as if she understood his every thought. "Good night, Colin." She stepped into the room and closed the door behind her.

He let out a breath he hadn't been aware he was holding. He didn't know how much longer he could keep himself from her. Turning on his heel, he made his way down the dark hall to his room.

* * *

Anthea's eyes opened with a start. She had been dreaming of walking down the dark road and seeing the menacing figure standing in the moonlight. Her heart raced, and her breath rushed out of her. She gasped after air, panting, until she slowed her breathing to try to calm herself. The events of her dream slowly diminished in intensity, replaced instead by the memory of the actual incident.

Alarm stirred in her as she relived the reality of the attack. She hadn't quite believed Savernake when he told her that her life was in danger. She did now.

A moment later anger swamped her. How dared someone harm her? What reason could they have? She had done nothing to hurt anyone, yet someone wanted to kill her. Throwing back the covers, she paced the floor in fury. Sleep would be impossible now.

Her emotions roiled within her like a storm. This would never do. She forced herself to sit on the bed. Dropping her head into her hands, she tried to sort out her feelings.

It wasn't fair. She had always done everything according to the rules of society. She'd had a single season, but never really enjoyed the frivolity of the *ton*, never received poetry from smitten young men. Rows of new, unused dresses had hung in her armoire at Mansfield, all sold to pay for her father's debts. When her family moved to Middle Hutton, she worked beside her mother to provide for her sisters, and when the opportunity presented itself, she betrothed herself to a man old enough to be her father—a good man, to be sure, but old. He didn't write her poetry or dance with her. Like a dutiful child, she accepted him for what he could provide for her family.

The fear was gone, replaced by righteous indignation. Not tonight. Tonight she would embrace the exuberance of being alive. Tonight she would be selfish and act on her emotions. Tonight she would live for herself and no one else.

She marched from the bedroom before she could talk herself out of her actions.

Making her way down the dark hall, she was careful to walk with a silent tread. It wouldn't do to have someone discover her. In front of the door she wanted, she paused. She fingered the medallion at her neck.

No. Don't stop. Don't think. Feel.

She drew a deep breath, then pushed the door open.

"Who's there?" Colin sat up in the bed. The sheet fell to his waist, exposing the bare skin of his chest.

"Shhh." She shut the door behind her and faced him. She took in the sight of him. "You're a light sleeper."

"Anthea?"

Crossing to the bed, she sat on the edge. "I asked you not to let me go earlier. You said you wouldn't."

He stared at her. "Did you have a nightmare?"

"Yes, but I'm not frightened any longer." She placed her hand on his chest. The warmth of his skin sent a flash of longing through her. His heart thudded under her palm.

He grabbed her hand by the wrist, but didn't lift it from him. "What are you doing?"

"Being selfish. Thinking of myself just this once." She leaned forward and kissed him.

His mouth melted under hers, welcoming her to him. She reveled in his response. With a boldness she didn't know she possessed, she slipped her tongue into his mouth. This was what a kiss should taste like—hot, moist, and exhilarating. She lifted her free hand to rake through his hair. A sound of enjoyment rose from deep in his chest.

To her joy, he wasn't willing to play a passive role in her act. His hand burrowed deep into the tresses at her neck, anchoring her to him. He released her wrist and brought his hand forward. Through the thin material of the nightgown, he cupped her breast. Her breath stopped at the jolt of awareness that rocked through her.

Then he stopped. Pushing her from him, he stared at her. "Why are you doing this?"

"Does it matter?"

"It shouldn't. I should just let myself enjoy this, but I can't. Why are you doing this?"

She traced a circle on his cheek. "I've always done what's expected of me. Just once I need to do something that I want."

"And you want me?"

"Yes. You make me feel things I've never felt before, left me with yearnings that I don't even understand. I want to understand them."

"But the squire—"

"Not tonight. Tonight the squire doesn't exist. Only I do. And you." She leaned forward to kiss him again.

He held her back. "You don't know what you're asking."

"Then show me. Teach me what I don't know. I've come to care for you. I . . ." She paused. She nearly said she loved him. With a shock, she realized it was true. Tears filled her eyes. "Please. Let me have this night."

With a groan of defeat, he pulled her to him. He kissed her, his lips staking a claim to her as words never could. His hands loosened the ties at her neck and

slipped the nightgown over her shoulders. He pushed
the material from her, then leaned back to look at her.
"Beautiful." His whisper was breathy and ragged. In the
next moment, he lowered his lips to her nipple and
took it in his mouth.

She sucked in her breath. She never imagined such
sensations existed. Heat pooled between her legs, ignit-
ing regions with an exquisite fire. One hand stole around
his neck, pulling him closer to her. The other circled to
his back, kneading the strength she found there.

With a swift tug, he divested her of the nightgown.
She felt no shame in her nudity, but a blush warmed
her skin nonetheless. He threw back the sheet that
covered him.

"You sleep without clothes," she whispered. Her gaze
traveled over him. His desire grew more evident at her
perusal.

He chuckled, a sound that rumbled with warmth
through his chest. "Lie down." He pulled her next to
him, then rolled on top of her. Bracing himself on his
elbows, he held himself above her, but lowered his
mouth over hers.

The light hairs on his chest brushed against her nip-
ples. The aureoles puckered, thrusting the sensitive
peaks against his skin. He swayed above her, rubbing
skin to skin, heightening her sensitivity.

He shifted his weight to one arm. With his free hand,
he traced a trail down her shoulder, along her arm, to
her waist. He laid his palm flat against her belly. She
sucked in her stomach. His hand slid lower, until it
rested on the curls between her legs. She thought she
would explode from the heat of his hand, but in the
next moment his fingers parted the curls and delved
into her intimate folds. Her head dropped back, and

she let out a ragged breath. If this was wrong, why did it feel so good?

Colin slipped a finger into her, eased it out, then slid it back in. She gasped and bucked under the attention.

"Shhh." He kissed the corner of her mouth. "Tell me now if you wish to stop. I don't know how I'll manage, but I will."

"No, please. I need . . ." She didn't know what word she searched for. "I want to know you."

His erection rubbed against her thigh. She arched against him and heard him draw in his breath. He hesitated for a moment, then slipped two fingers into her.

"You're almost ready."

Any longer, and she'd be more than ready. A quivering began deep in her belly. He seemed to sense it, because he withdrew his fingers to play with the bud at the apex of her legs. As he rubbed with his thumb, he slid his finger back into her. She did explode then, sending sparks shooting into every corner of her being. She cried out, but he caught the sound with his mouth as he kissed her again.

Before she recovered, he lifted his hips and placed his manhood at the entrance to her core. He lingered there, moving back and forth in inches, until she wasn't sure where she left off and he began. He pressed forward, sliding in on her own wetness, stretching her, filling her.

He paused. "I'm sorry." He thrust forward.

She didn't understand his words, but the next moment a sharp pain ripped through her. She cried out, but even as she did, the pain diminished. He stared at her with concern in his eyes. Reaching up with her hand, she stroked his cheek. Relief filled his expression. He pushed forward until he was sheathed inside her. The wonder of their union brought tears to her eyes.

He withdrew, then pressed forward again. She braced herself for a similar pain, but none came. As his rhythm increased its tempo, she relaxed, until a new tension gripped her—a tension filled with anticipation.

She closed her eyes and held her breath. His movements grew more urgent. With every thrust, her awakening grew, but it wasn't enough. She let out the air in her lungs and lifted her hips to meet his and matched his rhythm.

Each push drove her closer to an elusive point. She took in a new breath and held it. There. She was there. A shower of stars burst behind her eyelids. Her release came with a blaze of joy. Her every nerve tingled as if sparks danced within her.

Above her she felt Colin pull out and twist to the side. He shuddered, then collapsed onto the sheet. His arm curled around her as he turned back to her.

"Is it always like this?" asked Anthea.

With a laugh, he said, "Never. At least not in my experience."

"Then it was special."

He kissed her forehead. "You have no idea how very much."

"I'm glad." She snuggled against him. For a moment, she reveled in the afterglow of their coupling. She brushed a strand of hair from his forehead. "Were you always a light sleeper?"

"Yes." He drew in a deep breath. "I had to be. I never knew when one of my half brothers would try to ambush me in the night. I learned fast not to sleep."

Her heart broke for the child he was. "I'm sorry."

"Don't be." He grinned. "I've never been as grateful for it as this night."

She smiled, but a minute later, she sighed. "I have to go."

"I know." Colin leaned up on his elbow, trapping her with his arm. "I can't let you marry the squire. Marry me, instead."

Tears filled her eyes. "How? How can I ignore my family and their needs. How can I break it off with the squire and not cause a scandal?"

"We'll find a way."

"You don't understand. My marriage gives my sisters a chance to escape my life. If there's a scandal attached to my name, who will accept them?"

He lifted her hand and kissed the back of it. "I can provide for them."

"On a secretary's salary? Have you forgotten I have four sisters?"

"No, you don't understand—"

"No, *you* don't. I can't marry you. Tonight is all I have for me. Tomorrow I belong to my duty again." She grabbed her nightgown and shoved her head and arms through the holes. "I will never forget this night."

"Anthea, wait. I have—"

"No." Dashing from the bed, she ran to the door. She stopped and faced him. "I will always love you." She fled the room.

Colin stared after her. She loved him. Part of him rejoiced in her words, but a part of him raged. She thought him not good enough. The ache of the years with his father flooded through him. He thought he had shut them away forever.

He stopped. Anthea didn't think that way. He knew that in his soul.

Just as he knew he would never her let her marry the squire.

Chapter 25

"There's our hero," said Hobblesby in a booming voice. "Had a bit of a lie-in after the excitement last night, eh? Can't say that I blame you. Anthea and Fletcher told us what happened."

"They did?" Colin glanced at Anthea. To his gratification delightful pink blossomed in her cheeks, but she averted her gaze.

"Can't thank you enough, Savernake," said Hobblesby, his mouth filled with toast and eggs. He reached across the table, still clutching his fork, and patted Anthea's hand. "Saved my girl here."

"I'm just happy I could help." Colin looked around the dining room. He knew he was late to breakfast, and most of the family was already gathered. Hobblesby ate with relish, but he noticed Brody merely pushed the food around on his plate with his fork.

"Where's Dougal this morning?" asked Brody.

"By God, where is that boy?" boomed Hobblesby. "He never did return to see his sister's boy. Fletcher, send for Dougal at once. Tell him if he doesn't come, I'll cut him out of the will. That'll get him moving." Hobblesby gave the table a wink.

"Very good, sir." Fletcher disappeared.

Crossing to the sideboard, Colin filled a plate with

eggs, ham, and bread. He took his customary seat at the table beside Brody.

"You haven't seen my grandchild either, Savernake. A fine boy. Big. Strapping. Lungs of a Hobblesby." The squire let out a hearty laugh.

"Perhaps later."

"You're right, of course. We must give Jane a chance to recover. Hubert's in there now with her. Had Pennystone bring them a tray. A mother has to keep her strength up, you know."

Colin nodded at Hobblesby, but bit into an egg to prevent the need for a response.

"Now tell me about this business last night," said Hobblesby. "What made you follow Anthea?"

Colin swallowed before he spoke. "It goes back to your poisoning."

"Don't remind me. I still can't drink tea. Just the thought of it turns my stomach."

"It occurred to me that if you weren't the target, then Lady Anthea must be. It was her tea that the culprit tampered with."

Hobblesby grew still. His mien lost all signs of joviality. Then he shook his head. "Balderdash. Who would want to harm Anthea?"

"That's precisely what Lady Anthea said. And last night she was attacked."

Brody stopped his pretense of eating. His face was pale.

"Brody, are you ill?" asked Colin.

"No, just angry. I'll wait for you in the study, Savernake." Brody pushed himself back from the table and left the room.

Hobblesby frowned. "Don't know what's gotten into my sons these days."

Dougal entered the room. His jaw sported a large red spot. "I've already eaten, Father. What do you want?"

"What happened to your face, boy?" asked Hobblesby.

"Got kicked by a cow. It grazed me."

"That hasn't happened in years."

"I wasn't careful." Dougal shrugged.

"Have you asked after your sister?"

"She had a boy. I saw him." Dougal scowled, then winced. He lifted one hand to the sore spot on his jaw. His gaze fell on Colin, and he dropped his hand.

"I'm glad to see you care." Hobblesby nodded, pleased with the man's response. "Did you hear about the attack on Anthea last night?"

"No." Dougal looked at Anthea. "She doesn't look too bad."

"Savernake saved her before the fiend could harm her." Hobblesby patted her hand again. "I want you to put out a warning to all the hands to keep an eye out for their women."

"I will." Dougal fidgeted. "Anything else."

"No. Get back to your farm." Hobblesby gave his son an indulgent grin. "You always did love the Grange more than any of my other children."

Dougal hurried from the room.

"I think I should get home," said Anthea. "Mother will be worried about me."

"I'll take her," said Savernake.

Hobblesby focused his gaze on him.

"She shouldn't be out alone, if someone is trying to harm her."

"I'm not completely convinced this wasn't the work of some madman, but you're right. She shouldn't go alone."

"I'll get the gig." Savernake rose from the table.

"No. I will. Have Fletcher get the gig ready. I'll see Anthea home," said Hobblesby. "Besides, Brody is waiting to speak to you."

He had forgotten. He flashed his gaze at her, but she didn't meet it. A jolt of irritation struck him. Was her plan to ignore him? For now, he'd let her play her game, but not for long. They had much to discuss. "I'll tell Fletcher."

Colin left the room. After speaking with Fletcher, he entered the study. Brody stood by the window. He faced outside. Colin wondered what Brody was thinking. Before he could speak, Brody turned to him.

"Savernake? Is that you?"

"Yes. What's wrong?"

Brody moved to a chair. He turned toward him and looked at him with his unfocused gaze. "I know who attacked Lady Anthea."

"What? How?"

"Violet and I overheard Dougal yesterday. He was talking to Joe and Bob. He gave them money and told them to stay away for a day. Apparently Anthea had seen them carrying something . . ."

"Yes. We wanted to talk to them. Dougal paid them to stay away?"

"He was rather angry as well. They said she saw something."

"She did." Dougal knew about the missing chest of linens, this much was clear. "What does this have to do with the attack on Anthea? You think Bob and Joe—"

"I wish. Unfortunately, I think Dougal attacked Anthea." Brody's shoulders drooped, and pain filled his expression.

Colin recognized the conflict within Brody. He

watched the war between the man's reluctance to betray his brother and the desire to retain his honor, but Colin couldn't help the flux of anger spreading through him. "Now I understand your behavior yesterday. You already suspected him. But you didn't say anything. Anthea might have been killed."

"Don't you think I know that? Don't you think I've been hating myself all morning? I was a hero in Burma, lost my eyesight to save a stranger, but I did nothing yesterday. Damn it, Dougal is my brother. I didn't want to believe him capable of such things."

Colin drew in a deep breath. "I apologize. I shouldn't blame you."

Brody nodded. "No apology necessary. You said nothing I haven't already said to myself. I wasn't sure. And I certainly didn't think he would attack Anthea last night. Jane was having her baby. He should have been here with us. If I had . . ." A shudder shook him. "I just didn't think he'd do anything last night. Thank God you went after her."

"Why do you think Dougal attacked her?"

"Because of what happened next." Brody stood, then sat again. "I hate not being able to pace." His frustration gave a growl to his voice.

"Tell me."

"Eugenia Ulster joined Dougal after the boys left. They talked about Anthea." Brody paused. "Dougal's determined that the marriage won't take place."

Colin fell silent. He remembered the bruise on Dougal's face. The man had claimed a cow kicked him, but the mark could have come from a fist. His fist. He crossed to a chair and pulled it up to Brody. "Tell me everything."

Brody related the conversations he had overheard.

The man's fists clenched and unclenched as Colin asked question after question. A half an hour later, Brody could tell him little else. Except . . .

"I don't understand Eugenia Ulster's role in this," said Colin.

Brody drew his hands down his face. "That's the oddest bit of all. Dougal's never mentioned Eugenia. I know she's been an object of pity because of her mother, but . . . Violet saw them embrace and kiss."

"Pardon?"

"That was my reaction. But Violet swears that's what she saw."

Dougal and Eugenia? He didn't know what to make of this information.

Brody continued. "The day my father was poisoned, I went out to the garden. Dougal was there with some woman. He denied anyone was with him, but I heard a woman's voice and two sets of footsteps. I realize now it must have been Eugenia."

Colin thought for a minute. If Dougal knew Joe and Bob had taken the chest, the thefts must be connected to Dougal. But why would Dougal need to steal from his own father? After all Brody had said, he agreed Dougal had something to do with the attacks. He didn't know yet what role Eugenia played in everything, but he would find out.

"Savernake?"

"I'm here. You've given me a lot to think about."

"I imagine I have." Brody shook his head. "What do you think I should do?"

"What do you mean?"

"How can I tell Father?" Brody hadn't looked this despondent since his arrival in Middle Hutton.

"Don't tell him anything yet. We need to get proof."

"What are we going to do?"

"The first thing I need to do is tell Lady Anthea." Colin placed his hand on Brody's shoulder. "Don't say anything to Dougal. I know it's asking much—"

"No. I understand. It's keeping it from Father that will be difficult."

"If you hear anything else . . ."

"I'll let you know." Brody stood and navigated his way from the room.

Dougal. Colin shook his head in annoyance. He should have known. Jane was openly hostile to Anthea, but he couldn't picture a heavily pregnant woman carrying out such a scheme. Even if poison was a woman's tool.

A woman. Could Eugenia have anything to do with the attacks on Anthea? Obviously she played some role, but which? The squire had mentioned more than once that he didn't think the Ulsters his equals. Could Dougal have fallen in love with Eugenia knowing his father would never approve? But then killing the father would make more sense.

As the questions multiplied in his mind, he rubbed his forehead. He couldn't spend more time speculating on the reasons behind Dougal's actions. He had to warn Anthea. Drawing on his coat, he stepped into the hall.

"There you are, sir." Fletcher stopped by the door. He cleared his throat. "Mrs. Pennyfeather found this in your room." Fletcher handed him a thin ribbon with a small medallion on it.

Anthea's.

Colin examined Fletcher's expression.

"I thought perhaps you should return it to the

lady." Fletcher's face revealed nothing. The butler turned before Colin could say a word.

"Damn it." Fletcher knew. Colin looked at the medallion in his hand. He was determined to prevent her marrying the squire, but not by dragging her name into scandal. He could only hope the butler was as discreet as he appeared. Certainly the man hadn't appeared shocked, but then a good butler wouldn't.

He couldn't worry about this now. He had to get to Anthea and warn her about Dougal. If he took the gig, he'd get to Skettle Cottage—

Hell. Hobblesby had taken the gig, and he was sure Dougal wouldn't let him borrow a horse.

He started up the road at a brisk walk. She wouldn't be in danger in these few minutes.

Would she?

Chapter 26

Anthea's mother made a fuss over her when she arrived home, and an even bigger fuss when she heard the story of the attack. The squire left after telling her family about his grandson. Her mother bustled her off into the parlor. "You look tired."

Anthea grimaced. "Well, I didn't get much sleep last night."

"I imagine not. Lie down. I'll bring you a coverlet." Lady Fortesque gave her a gentle push onto the worn cushions.

The legs wobbled as she settled onto the furniture. "I'll be fine, Mother."

"Nonsense. You stay there. I'll be sure to keep the twins away from you." Her mother scurried from the room.

Violet slipped into the parlor. "Is it true? Someone attacked you last night?"

She nodded. Her fingers reached for the medallion at her throat, but found nothing but skin. Where was her choker? Had she lost it in the attack?

"Did you see who it was?"

"No. He wore a mask. Please, Violet, I don't want to think about it."

For a moment, Violet looked as if she would accommodate her wishes. Then she spoke again. "Thea, I have to tell you something about—"

"Not now, Violet," said Lady Fortesque, entering the room, a coverlet draped over her arm. "Thea needs to rest. Go make her a cup of tea."

Violet frowned. "Mother, I—"

"Don't argue, Violet. Make enough for us all." Her mother tucked the blanket around Anthea.

Violet stomped from the room.

"Your sister could use a lesson or two in patience," said Lady Fortesque. She kissed her daughter's forehead. "You don't look like yourself, Thea."

Anthea didn't know how to answer. She wasn't herself, but less from the attack than . . . Oh, God. "Mother, did you love Father?"

Her mother's eyebrows arched. "Why would you ask that now?"

"I suppose because my wed . . . " Her voice cracked. "Because my wedding is so soon."

Lady Fortesque nudged her over and sat beside her. She took her daughter's hand. "I hardly knew your father when we married, but I came to love him very much. That doesn't mean I was blind to his faults, but I did love him. And he gave me such wonderful daughters."

Maybe she would come to love the squire. Her eyes filled with tears. No, she would never love the squire any more than with the fondness of a relative.

"Thea?" Her mother stroked her cheek.

"It's nothing, Mother. I'm tired."

Violet came back without the tea. "We have a visitor."

Eugenia Ulster entered the room. Pulling the blanket off herself, Anthea sat up and wiped her cheeks with the back of her hand. "Good morning, Eugenia."

Eugenia crossed to her and sat beside her. "I came

as soon as I heard. You must have been so frightened, Thea."

"You know already?" asked Anthea.

"News of this sort travels fast in the village." Eugenia cluckled. "Besides, Mother was at the Grange this morning, and I accompanied her. I felt it my duty to come see you, but I would have come anyway. You're one of my dearest friends here in Middle Hutton."

Anthea met Violet's gaze over the girl's shoulder. Violet shook her head. Her sister was right. Eugenia's words made little sense. Eugenia had never made any overtures of friendship with either of them, and she hadn't been at the Grange this morning. Unless Eugenia had arrived after the squire brought her home.

"Come, Violet, let's see how the tea is doing." Lady Fortesque stood and took Violet's hand.

"I think I should stay with Thea," said Violet.

"Nonsense. She has a guest." Lady Fortesque frowned at her younger daughter.

"No, Mother. I—"

"Violet Nightingale Fortesque, you come with me this moment." Mother grabbed Violet's hand and pulled her from the room.

Anthea watched her sister mouth something to her, but she couldn't understand. She turned to her guest. "Thank you for coming, Eugenia, but as you can see, I'm fine."

"Did you see who it was?"

"No. It was too dark, and the fellow wore a mask. He was big, though, but I can't say much else." She reached up to her throat again, but halted the gesture midway. The necklace was gone.

"I don't know how I would have survived such a

thing. My heart would have stopped beating. You are so brave."

"Not in the least. I was terrified."

"It makes me so angry to think someone would try to chase us off our own roads. Mother didn't want me to come here alone. As if I would allow some man to keep me from my friends." Eugenia pursed her lips.

"It makes sense to keep safe," said Anthea. Eugenia had never said so many words in her presence before. This wasn't the usually shy creature who visited with her mother.

"And to mar such a happy day. How dare the fiend bring such gloom to the arrival of the squire's grandson?" Eugenia was looking more and more like her mother. "I know. Let's prove to the beast that he didn't scare you."

"But he did."

"No, I mean let's show him. Come with me. The squire asked me to pick up something from the station for him. He's having some sort of gift for Jane sent by the morning train. Come with me."

"I'm rather tired, Eugenia."

"No, you must. You must prove to the fiend and yourself that you're stronger than this." Eugenia stood and pulled on her hand. "You must show the villagers you're fine and stop their speculation about you before it starts."

"Very well, Eugenia." Anthea stood.

"Excellent." Eugenia clasped Anthea's hand in her own. "Come along, then. We don't want to miss the train."

"Let me tell Mother—"

"Good-bye, Lady Fortesque," shouted Eugenia. "Thea and I are going for a walk."

Anthea shook her head. She didn't think this new Eugenia was very polite.

Eugenia chatted the entire way to the train station, for which Anthea was grateful. She was in no mood to chatter or entertain. The occasional "yes" or "no" sufficed. As Eugenia droned on, Anthea was happy to retreat into her thoughts. She wondered where Savernake was at this moment and if he was thinking of her. And she wondered how she could possibly marry the squire now. Duty was becoming too big a burden for her to shoulder.

"There's the station. Good. We haven't missed the train." Eugenia dragged her onto the platform, which was crowded with villagers. "I had forgotten today was market day in Oldsgate."

Anthea glanced around at the villagers. Many of them waved at her, but most were weighed down with the wares they were taking to sell at the market.

The deep whistle of the train sounded around the bend.

"Good. We don't have much longer to wait. Let's get closer so we can retrieve the package and leave this crush." Eugenia pulled her nearer to the edge.

Black smoke billowed into the sky as the train came into view. The crowd pressed forward. An elderly woman jostled Anthea's elbow. "Pardon me, miss," said the woman.

Anthea waved away the apology. Her lack of sleep was bringing on a headache. She wanted to go home.

"Don't you just love trains?" asked Eugenia. "There's always someone coming or going. Such excitement."

Anthea leaned forward to glimpse the slowing engine. The brakes of the iron behemoth screeched as the train slowed, and the train's whistle sounded. The noise was deafening. She placed her hands over her ears.

In that instant, she felt a shove. Her arms flew forward, trying in vain to catch hold of anything to keep her balance. She teetered forward, over the edge of the platform.

Anthea screamed as she fell into the billowing steam that rose from beneath the engine.

Savernake was out of breath by the time he reached Skettle Cottage. The same sense of urgency filled him as it had last night, but he dismissed it. What could happen to Anthea in this short a time? And after he warned her about Dougal, she would be safe.

Yet the sense of wrongness persisted.

He ran up to the door of the cottage and knocked. Lady Fortesque opened the door. She looked upset. "Mr. Savernake, thank the heavens you're here. You've got to go after Thea."

"She's not here?" Helplessness washed over him.

"Eugenia took her out." Panic sparked in Lady Fortesque's eyes. "Violet said something about Thea being in danger and dashed out after them. What is happening?"

"I don't have time to explain now. Forgive me. Where did they go?"

"Violet talked about the morning train."

He didn't wait another second. He dashed up the lane and turned toward the station. As he ran through the village proper, he ignored the curious glances of the townsfolk. Many people were out, and several vehicles crowded the road to the station. Glancing at the sky, he saw the smoke from the train rising just past the village. Ahead he saw Violet, but no sign of Anthea or Eugenia.

"Violet." He stopped beside the woman. "Have you seen Anthea?"

"No. She and Eugenia left the house before I could warn her. I don't trust Eugenia. She and Dougal—"

"I know. I have to get to Anthea."

"Eugenia mentioned the train."

He didn't wait to hear the rest. Weaving his way through the traffic, he entered the station. The platform was crowded. Where was Anthea? There. She was standing on the edge. The brakes on the engine screeched as the tons of iron slowed. Anthea lifted her hands to her ears. He was almost there.

As if in a dream, he watched Dougal step up behind her and shove her from the platform.

"No!" he screamed, but the sound was muted by the noise of the train. He saw Anthea fall. He pushed through the crowd, but knew he wouldn't get there in time. The train let out a shrill whistle and stopped.

Colin grabbed Dougal's collar and whirled him around. "You son of a bitch." He punched the larger man.

Dougal staggered back. Colin didn't wait to see if the man would return the attack. He peered at the wheels of the engine, but saw nothing. Steam billowed from beneath the engine, obscuring his view of the tracks. No trace of clothing, or blood, or anything that would tell him Anthea was trapped under the train.

As if it had a collective consciousness, the crowd seemed to realize something had happened and pressed forward to see.

The engineer jumped down from the still-hissing machine. "Where's the lady? Has anyone seen the lady? God, it tweren't my fault. You saw, I couldn't stop any faster."

The buzz of conversation built to a roar. Colin ignored it all. He jumped down from the platform and ran to the front of the train. A second blast of steam blinded his view. Cursing, he waited until it cleared. Nothing here either. He ran to the other side. A flash of blue from under the other platform caught his eye. Dropping to his knees, he saw her, knees pulled up to her chin, eyes shut tight.

"Anthea." He crawled to her and put his arms around her.

She opened one eye, then the other. With a cry, she grabbed onto his neck and started to sob.

"Shhh, you're safe now." He stroked her hair and kissed the top of her head as he cradled her in his arms. "Shhh."

He let her cry for a few moments until he heard the people coming toward them. "Are you hurt? Do you think you can move?"

She nodded.

He started to back away from her to give her more room.

"Don't leave me." She grabbed his arms.

"Never. Hold my hand; we'll climb out together." He grasped her hand and felt slickness in her palm. He turned her hand over. Her palm was bleeding. Fury swamped him as he saw her injury, but he kept his voice calm. "Easy now, careful. We're almost out."

They climbed from beneath the platform together. Anthea tried to stand, but cried out. Dirt streaked her face, and a bruise already formed on her cheekbone. Blood covered her hands, and her dress was torn in several places. He would kill Dougal when he saw him next.

"Miss, miss, are you all right?" The engineer rushed forward with the stationmaster.

"Lady Anthea," said the stationmaster, his eyes growing wide. "Are you hurt?"

"Of course she's hurt, you idiots," said Colin with a snarl. He helped her forward, but she cried out with the first step.

"I don't think I can walk," she said.

He swept her into his arms. She had lost a shoe, and blood matted her stockings as well.

Killing was too good for Dougal. He would have to torture the man first.

"Thea." Violet shouted from above them. She jumped from the platform and ran to them. She started to cry as well. "Oh, dear heaven."

"I'm fine," said Anthea in a voice ragged with sobs.

"You most certainly are not," said Colin. He carried her toward the station. The crowd parted for them.

Placing her on a bench, he turned to the stationmaster. "Where's Hobblesby?"

"The squire? He isn't here, sir."

"Not the squire. His son." Colin searched the area for the man.

"I saw Dougal running from here, dragging Miss Eugenia behind him," said an onlooker.

"Dougal?" asked Anthea.

"I forgot you don't know." Colin took her hands in his, mindful of her injuries. "He's the one who pushed you."

"But—" Fresh tears rose in her eyes.

"I'll explain everything later." Colin turned to the stationmaster. "Get the constable for me."

The man nodded and hurried off.

Anthea glanced around the waiting room. "I want to go home."

Colin saw the curious faces staring at them and nodded. "Does anyone have a carriage we can use?"

A villager stepped forward. "I've got me wagon outside."

He lifted her again and smiled into her gaze. "I think I've done this before."

To his relief, she smiled back at him through her tears.

"Lead the way." He followed the man to his vehicle.

The journey to the cottage took little time, but Colin checked on Anthea at every bump in the road. Violet sat beside her sister in the bed of the wagon. At the cottage he thanked the man, jumped down, and reached to help Anthea. Violet ran ahead to open the door. The wagon drove off.

He held her against him.

"I was afraid I'd never see you again." Anthea lifted her tear- and dirt-streaked face to him. She had never looked more beautiful.

"We have much to discuss."

She nodded.

"But first . . ." His voice broke. "God, I thought I had lost you." He kissed her.

She turned in his arms with a small cry and met his lips with hers. He savored her with a hunger fueled by the fear and relief that coursed through him. She was his, and he didn't care who witnessed it.

"Lady Anthea!"

Anthea tried to step back, but Colin held her to him. He wasn't afraid of that voice. With deliberate slowness, he turned to see the horrified expression of Mrs. Ulster.

Chapter 27

Lady Fortesque rushed forward to her daughter. Her expression transformed from surprise to horror as she took in Anthea's injuries. "Anthea. My sweet girl. What happened?"

"They were kissing," said Mrs. Ulster.

"Not now, Rowena," said Lady Fortesque in a scolding tone. "Can't you see my girl is hurt?"

"But she's to marry the squire. What will he say?"

"Nothing, if you don't open your mouth," said Colin. He scooped Anthea into his arms and started toward the cottage.

Mrs. Ulster opened and shut her mouth like a fish.

"Will you help, or will you stand there gaping like a fountain blowing water?" asked Violet. She gave the woman a sweet smile.

"I—I—I . . ." Mrs. Ulster's face reddened.

"That was wicked, Violet," said Anthea with a giggle.

"Now I know you will be fine, if you can enjoy the humor of the situation." He brushed her forehead with a kiss, not caring that Mrs. Ulster watched them. He entered the house without a backward glance at the woman.

Lady Fortesque clicked her tongue. "We'll speak about the two of you later. Right now I want to get

Anthea cleaned up. Will you take her to her room please, Mr. Savernake?"

"My pleasure." He climbed the stairs, followed by Anthea's mother and Violet. He placed Anthea on the bed.

"You may leave now, Mr. Savernake."

"Yes, Lady Fortesque." He gave her a quick bow, then winked at Anthea before he left the room. When he returned downstairs, he found Mrs. Ulster standing in the parlor with a scowl on her face. Iris sat on the settee with her arms folded across her chest. He gazed at Anthea's younger sister. They hadn't had many opportunities to speak.

"I don't believe I've ever been treated quite so rudely," said Mrs. Ulster. "I think I shall head straight to the Grange and inform the squire of the doings of his betrothed and her family."

"I suggest you hear what has happened before you run to the squire with your news, as it concerns you as well as Anthea," said Colin.

"Is this about Eugenia and Dougal?" asked Iris.

He glanced at her in surprise.

Iris shrugged. "Anyone who made careful observations would notice their interest in each other."

"There is nothing between my Eugenia and Dougal Hobblesby," said Mrs. Ulster. She lifted her nose and sniffed. "You are mistaken."

"She's not, but it doesn't matter. What matters is that your daughter tried to kill Anthea," said Colin.

Mrs. Ulster gasped. "I beg your pardon."

"Eugenia lured her to the train station where Dougal tried to shove her under the train." Colin's voice was cold.

"Preposterous." A speck of spittle flew as Mrs. Ulster

spoke. "You're trying to divert my attention from your outrageous behavior with Lady Anthea."

"Think what you will. The constable will be here soon, and I'll tell him what I saw at the station."

Mrs. Ulster clutched her reticule. "I won't stand here and listen to you malign my daughter. I'm going straight to the squire and tell him of your nefarious intentions."

Colin focused his unflinching gaze on her. "You do that. And be sure to tell him to wait for me as well. I'll be along shortly, as soon as I know Anthea will be fine."

"Humph." Mrs. Ulster tossed back her head and stormed from the room.

"She's not a good enemy to have," said Iris. "She's told stories about me more than once."

"You know about those?"

"I see she's told you as well." Iris smiled. "She's said nothing I couldn't refute in an instant if I chose to. She isn't very clever, you know."

He laughed. "Would you come with me? I could use an extra set of eyes."

"Will it help Anthea?"

"Absolutely."

"Then you may count on me. Anthea means more to me than even she knows."

"Can we leave now?"

Iris stood. "I'm assuming this task requires some urgency."

"I need to search Dougal's cottage before he tries to hide his activities." He glanced up the stairs.

"Anthea's in fine hands." Iris patted his arm as she followed his gaze upstairs. "Mother won't let anything happen to her. Let's go."

Her perception was as keen as he thought.

A few minutes later they were at the Grange, but they didn't enter the main house. They turned directly to the outer buildings and the cottage Dougal used as his own. Colin knocked, but no one answered. He pushed the door open.

"This is interesting," said Iris.

"What is?"

"The lace curtains."

"Why?"

Iris placed her hand on her hip. "Does Dougal strike you as a man who would have lace curtains in his home?"

"Evidence of a woman," said Colin, nodding. "I knew I wanted you along for this."

"What are we looking for?"

"Any of the things stolen from the Grange. Some will be long gone, but Dougal may have stashed some here." He told her of the missing items.

They started a methodical search of the house. As they searched, Colin told Iris of his suspicions regarding the thefts and Dougal.

"Hey, what are you doing here? This is Mr. Dougal's house."

Colin whirled around. Joe stood in the doorway, filling the entrance. The large man frowned.

Iris stepped in front of him. "We're looking for the things Mr. Dougal stole from his father."

Joe shook his head. "Mr. Dougal never stole nothing. He explained it to us at the start."

"What did he explain?" asked Colin.

"That he was taking those things to keep them safe. Besides, they were his, or would be when he inherited," said Joe. "But he didn't keep them here. Me and Bob helped him sometimes."

"Like with the chest of linens the other day," said Colin.

"Exactly. He said he didn't trust them new servants. He thought they might get greedy."

"You mean Fletcher and Pennyfeather," said Colin.

"Right. They're outsiders, you know. They don't love the Grange like Bob and I do."

"And you don't trust me," added Colin.

"Don't mean to insult you," said Joe. "Now, the young lady is Miss Anthea's sister. She's family."

"So you trust her."

"Of course. But I don't much like you poking about in Mr. Dougal's house." Joe pulled himself upright and took a step forward.

Colin readied himself for a fight, but Iris stepped up to Joe. "Can you tell us if Mr. Dougal has another house?"

Joe blinked and looked down at the young girl. "Sure. It's at the other end of the village. Right pretty, it is. Miss Eugenia calls it Robin Hood's Cottage."

Colin decided this was their best opportunity to leave. "Thank you for the information, Joe. I'll be sure to let the squire know how helpful you've been. I'm sure he'll even give you a reward."

The big man looked pleased. His cheeks turned pink, and a half smile lit on his face. "Don't know that I need a reward. Just happy to help."

Colin offered the man his hand. "No wonder the squire thinks so highly of you."

Joe shook Colin's hand, then stepped aside to let them pass. As they hurried up the road from the Grange, Joe waved to them.

"I thought he was going to strike you," said Iris.

"So did I," said Colin. "How did you know about the second house?"

"He wasn't keeping the stolen things at the Grange. Besides, Joe said he wasn't keeping them there, so he had to be keeping them somewhere."

"Remarkable." Colin couldn't help but admire the girl's logic. "Remind me never to do anything nefarious around you. So are you willing to come with me to Robin Hood's Cottage?"

Iris nodded. "I don't know what my family would say if they saw me scampering around the village. I don't even have a book with me."

Half running, half walking, they reached the cottage on the far side of the village in little time. It was hidden at the end of a covered lane. Colin recalled the day he saw Dougal at this same spot. They walked to the cottage.

"Do you think Eugenia or Dougal will be here?" asked Iris.

"If I know Dougal, he's probably concocting some story to explain away Anthea's injuries and my story, if I ever get the chance to tell it." He tried the door. It was locked.

"No one locks their doors in Middle Hutton," said Iris.

"They do if they're hiding stolen goods." Colin looked around. A window was open on the second floor.

"I can get through there." Iris's eyes gleamed. "I never thought burglary would be so entertaining."

"Why don't we try the back door first?" said Colin.

"Very well." Iris's shoulders dropped a little.

Colin chuckled. They hurried around to the back. The back door was fastened, but a key lay behind a flowerpot. He tried it in the lock. The door opened easily, and they entered the kitchen.

"We don't have much more time. Mrs. Ulster will have visited the squire already. You remember what we're looking for?" he asked.

"Yes. I'll try upstairs, shall I?" Iris dashed from the room.

Her enthusiasm was contagious. He turned to the cupboards. A glint of silver caught his eye as he opened the third one. He pulled out a large silver tray. If he wasn't mistaken, this was the one taken from the Grange.

Iris came back into the room. "Is this the bracelet?" She handed him a chain hung with diamonds.

"I never saw it, but I'd wager the squire will recognize it."

"There's a large wooden chest at the foot of the bed as well."

"No time to fetch someone to carry it now. Most of the other things will be long gone. These two items will just have to do." He pocketed the bracelet and tucked the tray under his arm. "Let's go see how Anthea's is faring and if she's up for making a visit."

Iris pulled back for a moment. "Are you going to marry Anthea?"

"If she'll have me."

"That's all I wanted to know." Iris smiled at him. "I like you. You don't make me nervous like other people. Let's go."

When they arrived at Skettle Cottage, Anthea was sitting in the parlor. She wore a clean dress, and her hand was bandaged. Her mother and Violet were beside her, trying in vain to calm her.

"Where have you been?" asked Anthea.

"Gathering evidence," said Colin. "You sound worried."

She waved a piece of paper in front of him. "Fletcher just brought this. It's from the squire. He wants to see me at once."

"Then let's go," said Colin. He grinned.

"You aren't taking this seriously," she said with a frown.

"More seriously than you know," he said with a wink.

"Really, Mr. Savernake, I'm not sure I approve of this behavior," said Lady Fortesque.

"Forgive me, my lady, but it shall all become clear soon. Allow me my mystery a little while longer." He bowed to her.

"What do you have under your arm?" asked Violet.

"A serving tray."

Anthea examined it. "Is it—"

"It is."

"Where did you find it?"

"All in good time." He knew he shouldn't feel so happy. The squire's world was about to come apart, but he couldn't help but smile when he looked at Anthea.

"I'm going with you," said Violet. She stood.

"I don't think—" said Lady Fortesque.

"Please, Mother. I can watch over Anthea and make sure nothing else befalls her."

"Very well," said Lady Fortesque with a sigh.

"And you, Lady Iris?" He held out his hand to her. "You were a great help to me. Would you like to watch the end?"

Iris smiled at him. "No. Too many people will be there. I've had my fun for the day, and I'm glad I could help Anthea. Violet will tell me all about it when she gets home. She's quite gifted with words."

"As you wish." He turned to the two women. "Shall we go?"

Chapter 28

Fletcher opened the front door for them, but Anthea hesitated. She wasn't eager to face the squire.

"Fletcher, take this for me," said Savernake, and he handed the butler the tray.

"You found it, sir. Congratulations."

Savernake nodded. "I hope you and Mrs. Penny-feather are ready to leave. My task here is done."

"Fletcher is leaving?" asked Anthea.

"Not just yet, Lady Anthea," said Fletcher.

"Where is the squire?" asked Savernake.

"In the parlor. But I feel I should tell you, Mr. Savernake, that everyone is there."

"Everyone?"

"Not Miss Jane and her husband. They are busy with the baby. But everyone else, yes, sir."

A wide grin covered his face. "Excellent."

Anthea shot him a glance. He was enjoying this. She was about to face her humiliation, the death of her dream to help her family, and he was enjoying himself.

She was not going inside. In the next moment, Violet and Colin surged forward and carried her with them.

As they entered the parlor, they nearly collided with Dougal. He looked intent upon leaving, but his eyes widened when he saw her. His skin lost its pallor, and he stared at her as if she were a ghost. Anthea could guess why.

"Going somewhere, Dougal?" asked Colin. "And I have such an interesting tale for you. You must hear it."

"I have no time to waste on your prattle." Dougal tried to push past him.

Colin shot his hands out and planted them against the larger man's chest, holding him back. "No, I insist you stay."

"You can't tell me what to do." Dougal's gaze narrowed.

"Sit down, boy," said Hobblesby.

"I have work to do," said Dougal.

"You will stay," said Colin.

"Enough, you two. I'll not have fisticuffs in my house." Hobblesby gave his son a chiding look.

With a sneer, Dougal backed away from Savernake. He crossed to the other side of the room near Eugenia.

Anthea entered farther into the room. She felt every gaze light on her. Holding her chin high, she tried to mask the pain she felt walking.

Her arms crossed, Mrs. Ulster stood triumphant beside the squire. Her smirk irritated Anthea.

"Mrs. Ulster has been telling some distressing things, Thea." The squire rose from his chair. "But before we talk about that, what happened to you?"

He took her bandaged hand and turned it over. Then he touched the bruise on her cheek.

"She was pushed under the morning train," said Savernake. His gazed fixed on Dougal.

"What?" Hobblesby turned Anthea's hand over. "How did that happen?"

"Why don't you ask Dougal?" said Savernake.

Dougal's face flamed red. Beside him Eugenia grew pale.

"Or perhaps we should just wait for the constable. He'll have to track us down, but I don't mind if he's a little more impatient than usual." Colin gave Dougal a superior smile.

"Constable? What are you talking about?" asked the squire. "I demand to know what in the blazes is happening."

"You mean Dougal didn't tell you?" Savernake clicked his tongue as he faced the squire's son again. "Shame on you."

Dougal took a step toward him. He balled a meaty fist. "Be quiet, you popinjay."

"Oh, no. It's too late for that." Colin eyed the bigger man without flinching. "I have no intention of remaining quiet."

Brody rose from his seat. "Father, I think you should listen to Savernake."

Mrs. Ulster shook her head. "No. They're trying to distract you from the issue here. I saw them kissing."

Hobblesby turned to Anthea. Sorrow filled his expression. "Is this true?"

Anthea hung her head, but before she could speak, Savernake answered, "Yes, I kissed her. Couldn't help myself. I was happy she was alive."

"You have feelings for Thea?"

"Most definitely," said Savernake.

"You see?" Mrs. Ulster raised her finger in the air to emphasize her victory.

Hobblesby rubbed his forehead. "I think I had better sit down. Maybe a brandy would help."

"Remember your gout," said Anthea without thinking.

"You lost the right to pretend to care for the squire when you kissed another man," said Eugenia.

Mrs. Ulster glanced at her daughter in surprise, as did Hobblesby.

Violet stepped forward. "Don't speak to my sister, you harridan. After what you did to her, you have no right to be in the same room with her."

"I didn't do anything," said Eugenia.

"The hell you didn't." Violet clenched her fists.

Brody grinned and applauded. "Brava."

"Violet." Anthea's eyes widened. "Your language."

"Sorry, Thea, but she makes me so mad. Imagine accusing you of impropriety after what she's done."

"Humph." Mrs. Ulster snorted. "My daughter is a gentlewoman. Your behavior has proven your lack of breeding. I wonder if your father was an earl at all."

Hobblesby turned to Mrs. Ulster. "That was uncalled for."

Mrs. Ulster shrugged. "I was merely making an observation."

"An ill-suited one." The squire frowned at her, then faced his son. "Let's try to make sense of all this. Tell me, boy. What is Savernake accusing you of?"

"I haven't any notion. I think he's trying to divert your attention from his own guilt."

"You lie, Dougal." Brody's voice was quiet.

Dougal whirled to his brother. "What would you know about anything, blind man?"

"I may be blind, but I can hear better than any of you. You should choose better places to hold your conferences, brother dear. A window carries sound quite well."

"I wouldn't be so eager to share your opinion. What would happen to you if Father were to die? You're nothing but a burden. You can't even walk without help. Where would you go then if you alienate me?"

"Considering he's going to marry me, I don't think it's as great a problem as you think," said Violet.

"Pardon?" Anthea stared at her sister.

"Marriage?" said Hobblesby.

"Well, I still have to convince him I don't care that he's blind, but after this display of brotherly affection, I don't doubt I shall. We can live with my family." Violet narrowed her gaze at Dougal.

Dougal laughed. "Some war hero you are, brother. Now you're dependant on little girls to rescue you."

Brody stood, and in a movement of remarkable grace, his fingers encircled Dougal's neck. Dougal was large, but as they stood side by side, all could see that Brody was no small man himself. "Never insult Lady Violet again. You've forgotten I've grown up, brother. I learned a few tricks in the army that I don't need my vision for. And I don't need daylight to find my way around, so you'd better pray you're a light sleeper."

He released his brother's neck. Dougal coughed and rubbed his throat.

"Enough," roared Hobblesby, jumping from his chair. "I won't consent to a melee." The room quieted as Hobblesby glared at each occupant. "Tell me what you know, Brody."

"I'd prefer to let Savernake lead this discussion. He knows more than I." Brody took his seat again.

Hobblesby let out a puff of air in exasperation. "Savernake?"

Colin smiled. This denouement was more enjoyable than he'd expected. "My pleasure. If I may begin at the beginning?"

"By all means." Hobblesby flopped into the armchair.

"First, let me say I am not Hobblesby's secretary."

"What?" Anthea looked at him.

He held up his hand. "I was sent here by Lord Stanhope to solve the petty thefts that plagued the squire."

"Good man, that Stanhope," said Hobblesby.

"You're not a secretary?" asked Anthea.

"No, my dear," said Hobblesby. "I'm sorry for the deception, but we felt he would have more success if no one knew why he was really here."

Colin raised an eyebrow. He remembered the squire objecting to the subterfuge. "The only one who saw through me was Brody. So I enlisted his help."

Dougal snorted. "How could a blind man help you?"

He gave the obtuse man a look of complete disgust. "By listening and taking advantage of the idiots who thought he could do nothing."

"Savernake, I won't have you speaking to my son this way," said Hobblesby.

"I have no argument with you, Hobblesby, but I won't tolerate any more noise from your son."

Hobblesby blinked several times.

"As I said, my task here was to discover who was stealing from the squire. This I have done."

"You have?" Hobblesby's eyebrows arched high.

Dougal took a step back.

Colin crossed to the bellpull and rang. Fletcher appeared a moment later. "Sir?"

"Bring me that tray, would you, Fletcher?"

"At once, sir." Fletcher disappeared and, a few moments later, returned with the tray.

Colin took the large silver salver from the butler and showed it to Dougal. "Do you want to tell your father where I found this?"

"How should I know?" said Dougal, but his voice wasn't steady.

"Because I found it in your house."

"One tray doesn't make him a thief. How do you know he didn't just borrow it?" asked Eugenia.

Colin nodded. "You're right, of course. One tray doesn't make a thief. So how about something else?" He reached into his pocket and pulled out the diamond bracelet.

Eugenia gasped.

Hobblesby stood. "That's my wife's bracelet. The one I wanted to give Thea on our wedding day."

"Care to explain how I found this, Doug, old chap? Care to tell everyone how it came from a lady's jewelry box in the house you have at the other side of the village? Do you care to tell everyone how you and Eugenia have been working together?"

"That's not true," said Mrs. Ulster. "My Eugenia—"

"Be quiet, Mother," said Eugenia.

"So much for breeding," muttered Violet under her breath.

Brody chuckled, then hid his smile behind his hand.

"You see, Dougal, Brody heard you." Colin crossed to them. "You and Eugenia. And Violet saw you kiss."

"No," cried Mrs. Ulster. Her hand covered her mouth in horror.

"Do you want to tell your father where you got the money for Robin Hood's Cottage? Or where you got that chest of linens that stands at the foot of the bed?" Colin leaned in as if taking Dougal into his confidence. "I spoke to Joe, you know."

"What of it?" said Dougal. "I took a few things. It's not as if I stole anything that shouldn't have been mine anyway. Or would be once Father dies."

"And that justifies stealing from your own father?" Colin wanted to push the man over the edge he teetered on.

Eugenia tugged on Dougal's arm. "Don't listen to him."

"You deceived your father, your sister, and your brother." Colin continued as if Eugenia had said nothing. "Do they deserve nothing?"

"Jane and Hubert have the mill. They're welcome to it," said Dougal.

"But you stole from the mill as well. Or have you forgotten the load of cloth? And what of Brody? Does he deserve nothing?"

"Nothing? Father bought him that fat commission in the army. Then the fool goes and gets himself blind. What a waste." Dougal didn't hide the contempt in his voice.

"You won't speak of your brother in that tone," said Hobblesby.

"Why? Because Brody can do no wrong?" Dougal stepped to his father. "He hasn't earned a penny for the Grange, and now there's no hope of him ever helping. I wasn't going to watch Father throw money away on a cripple when he wouldn't give me anything."

"So you admit stealing from your father?" Colin waited for the answer.

A long pause filled the room.

"What have you done, boy?" asked Hobblesby.

Dougal's gaze shot to his father. "I am not a boy. While you've been playing squire, I've been running the Grange. And what do I have to show for it? Nothing. You treat me like an incompetent fool. The only reason you can pretend you're some sort of important gentleman is because I work hard. Heatherstone Grange is successful because of me."

Silence settled over the room. Hobblesby's eyes bulged wide. Little color remained in his face.

Dougal glanced around the room and laughed. "You look shocked, but you know I speak the truth. I couldn't enjoy myself, because I had to keep the Grange running for *the squire.*" His voice dripped with resentment. He bowed to his father. "Well, *Squire*, how are you enjoying your reign now?"

"Stop this, Dougal." Hobblesby's voice was weak.

"I couldn't marry, because Father wouldn't let me. He claimed there wasn't a woman good enough for me. He never asked my opinion. But he found himself one, didn't he?" Dougal laughed. "I had to watch the old man make a fool of himself over Lady Anthea, the daughter of an earl. She'd bring him the class he lacked. He'd sire himself a new family, an aristocratic family. I never thought she'd be fool enough to accept him."

Dougal strode to Anthea. He gazed down at her in contempt. "It's your fault really. If you weren't so desperate to get Father's money, none of this would have happened. But I wasn't about to see my money go to some brat you whelped for my father."

"So you poisoned the tea." Colin brought the man's attention back to him and away from Anthea.

"Yes, I poisoned the tea. I knew no one would drink the stuff but her. But Father got sick instead." Dougal wiped his face. "For a moment I thought I had killed my father, and for a moment I was glad. I would have it all, and she'd get nothing."

"You hated me that much?" whispered Anthea.

"Yes," said Dougal with a hiss. "But even then I didn't

want to kill you. I just wanted to frighten you away. I thought if I could make you sick, you wouldn't marry Father." Dougal whirled around to his father. "And I didn't want to kill you either. God help me, I was hoping you could still love me somehow."

A sob broke from Dougal's chest. Eugenia hurried to his side and placed her arms around him.

"Eugenia, get away from him," said Mrs. Ulster.

"No, Mother. My place is beside him." Eugenia stroked Dougal's back.

"What are you saying?" asked Mrs. Ulster.

"Dougal and I were married several months ago. He is my husband."

Chapter 29

"What?" Hobblesby straightened and leaned forward out of his chair.

Mrs. Ulster blanched and sank onto the settee. Anthea fanned the woman with her hand. "I think Mrs. Ulster needs some smelling salts."

"Do you carry any?" asked Brody.

"No. None of us are the fainting type," answered Violet.

"Mrs. Pennythought should have something," said Hobblesby.

"I'll get her," said Colin. He ran from the room.

Mrs. Ulster let out a wail. "My baby, my poor, poor girl."

"Stop it, Mother," said Eugenia. "This isn't a tragedy."

Mrs. Ulster looked at her daughter and let out a fresh wail. "Married, and I didn't even get to plan her wedding."

"Tell me how this happened, boy—er, Dougal," said Hobblesby.

"What do you mean, 'how did this happen?'" Dougal sneered at his father. "We found a village where the reverend was more concerned with money than propriety, posted the banns, and got married."

Hobblesby slumped in his chair and dropped his

head into his hands. "Why didn't you tell me you wanted to marry the girl?"

Dougal laughed. "After the way you carried on about how superior we were to the Ulsters? What chance did we have of your approval? I hardly think you would have listened to my wedding plans when you were so busy with your own."

Anthea had stopped fanning as she listened to Dougal. Hobblesby looked so unhappy, so unsure of himself. Her heart went out to him. She knew her behavior hurt him, but this struck him deeper.

Colin returned with a small vial. "Found some." He opened the top and waved it under Mrs. Ulster's nose.

She coughed and pushed his arm with surprising strength for a woman on the verge of a faint. "Get that away from me. It smells awful."

"It's supposed to," said Violet.

Mrs. Ulster took the time to glare at Violet, then turned back to her daughter and started to cry again.

"What about the attacks on Anthea?" asked Colin.

Dougal's gazed narrowed. "I wasn't about to let her take what's mine."

"So you tried to kill her?" asked Hobblesby in shock.

Dougal turned to his father. "I suppose it's too late to ask you to believe me, but I never meant to kill her. I just wanted to frighten her, to make her leave."

"*We*, Dougal. I helped you." Eugenia held her head high. "The strychnine was my idea."

"O-o-o-h," wailed Mrs. Ulster anew.

"Shut up, Mother," said Eugenia. "After we discovered Anthea had seen Joe and Bob take the chest, I knew we had to act quickly. Dougal attacked her last night, but Savernake rescued her. We were desperate, so I lured her to the station this morning."

"And I pushed her in front of the train." Dougal's voice was emotionless.

Anthea shivered.

"Dear heaven," said Hobblesby in a whisper.

Eugenia crossed to Anthea. "You won't believe me, but I'm happy you aren't hurt."

"Not hurt?" Anger blazed in Colin's gaze. "Have you looked at her? Her hand is bandaged, bruises cover her, and she couldn't walk at first."

Eugenia hung her head. "We were fighting for our future . . ."

"I have plenty for everybody," said Hobblesby. "My money was to bring joy to my family, not pain, not anger."

Fletcher entered the room. "Pardon me, Squire. The constable is here."

Hobblesby glanced at Savernake. "Please. I don't know . . . I need time . . ."

Colin shook his head. "Bring him in, Fletcher."

"No-o-o. What of my Eugenia?" said Mrs. Ulster on a sob.

"She'll suffer the consequences of her choices as well," said Colin.

"No, wait," said Anthea. She looked at Colin, then at Hobblesby. "If I am the injured party here, perhaps I should decide."

Hobblesby looked up at her with hope.

Anthea turned toward Fletcher. "Ask the constable to please wait in the kitchen. Mrs. Pennyfeather can give him something to eat while he waits."

"As you wish, my lady." Fletcher bowed and retreated.

"You can't be thinking to let them go?" Incredulity rang in Colin's voice. "They tried to kill you."

"I know. But they didn't succeed."

"I can't believe this." Colin threw his hands in the air.

Anthea drew in a deep breath. "I need time to think."

"Thea," said Violet. "They hurt you. How can you think about forgiving them?"

With a sad laugh, Anthea shook her head. "I don't think I'm a good enough person to forgive them, but I understand them. I'm not so innocent myself."

"Aha," shouted Mrs. Ulster from the settee. "You see, I told you she was—"

"If you don't refrain from speaking, I shall ask Fletcher to toss you out my door, Mrs. Ulster," said Hobblesby.

Mrs. Ulster opened and closed her mouth like a fool grasping for words.

"I would like to talk with the squire alone, please," said Anthea.

Colin glared at Dougal. "Don't even think of leaving."

"I'm not going anywhere. This is *my* home." With his arm around Eugenia, Dougal walked from the room with as much dignity as he could muster.

Mrs. Ulster padded behind them. "Eugenia, Eugenia, dear, we must speak. There is so much you must tell me."

Brody stood. "Lady Violet, may I offer you a cup of tea?"

Hobblesby let out a bark. "Don't think I've forgotten she said you two would—" Hobblesby stopped speaking. "Oh, hell, go ahead. Get married. I don't know anything anyway."

"Don't worry, Father. I won't do anything without you." Brody bent over the squire and kissed his pate. Then he and Violet left the room.

"I'll be packing if you need me." Colin followed the others out.

Anthea waited until the door closed before she faced Hobblesby.

"Anthea, my dear. I can't begin to tell you how sorry—"

"No need. I don't blame you for anything."

"You should. Dougal . . . Dougal is . . ." Hobblesby turned to her. Tears glistened in his eyes.

"He's your son, and though he may not know it at the moment, you love him." Anthea took his hand. "Your children never did like me."

Hobblesby sighed. "I know, but I chose to ignore it. I thought they would grow accustomed to the idea with time, especially when Jane had her baby. Yet you never complained."

"I didn't feel I had the right." Anthea paused. "I never meant to hurt you."

The squire chuckled. "My dear, I may be an old man, but I'm not quite so foolish as people think I am. I knew you didn't love me any more than I loved you. We both had our reasons for this marriage."

She nodded.

"But under the circumstances, I feel I should release you from the betrothal. I need to pay more attention to the family I have rather than worry about starting a new one."

She swallowed past the lump in her throat.

"Your family . . ." Hobblesby paused.

"We've done all right until now," said Anthea. "We'll get along."

Hobblesby released her hand. "The constable is waiting."

"I don't want to cause any more damage to your family, but I'm not sure I can just let them walk away from this." Anthea glanced at her bandaged hand.

Her every breath brought her pain, and she knew her cheek was an unusual shade of green. She needed no more reminders of Dougal and Eugenia's duplicity.

"If I swear that he will make restitution for your pain . . ." Hobblesby's voice broke. Pressing his lips together, he waited for her response.

Anthea nodded. "It's enough for me. And if what Violet says is true, I may end up related to him."

"You are a good woman, Anthea. I would have been proud to have you for my wife."

She shook her head. "I'm not good. I'm entirely selfish."

Hobblesby rose. "I'll speak to the constable. And then I suppose I have a new daughter to become acquainted with. Gad, now that Ulster woman is related to me. Fit punishment for my pride, don't you think?"

The squire walked toward the door, his shoulders stooped. For the first time, he carried himself like an old man. Anthea knew he would carry this day as a burden for a long time, if not for the rest of his life.

He paused at the door. "Imagine. I almost married the daughter of an earl. I. William Hobblesby, farmer." He left the room.

Anthea brushed a tear away with the back of her hand. She wanted to go home. She didn't know what would happen next, but she wanted to go home and spend time with her family. Leaving the parlor, she closed the door behind her with a strange sense of finality.

Fletcher hurried toward her. "Lady Anthea. May I get you something?"

"No, thank you, Fletcher. I wish to go home."

"I'll send for the gig. You shouldn't walk all that way."

"Thank you. I'll wait out front."

Anthea sat on a stone bench by the front door while she waited for the vehicle. She heard the crunch of the gravel before she saw it. Looking up, she saw Colin driving. He reined in the horse and jumped out to help her.

Handing her onto the seat, he scrutinized her face. "You're crying?"

"Am I?" She dashed away the tears on her face.

"Did Hobblesby . . . Was he . . . ?"

"He was the perfect gentleman. I do regret how I've hurt him." Anthea let a tremulous smile touch her lips. "I think I just need to get home."

Colin climbed up and clicked his tongue. The gig rolled into motion.

"I saw Hobblesby speaking to the constable."

"Yes. The squire is explaining to the man that Dougal will be under his watch for the crimes. He still has enough influence in the village to arrange these things."

"You're letting him go?"

"Yes."

"How can you? The man tried to kill you." His words echoed with disbelief.

"I think Dougal really believes he didn't mean to harm me."

"What he believes is irrelevant." Colin halted the gig. "I'm going back there right now—"

She put her hand on his arm. "No, Colin. Please. There's been enough unpleasantness today. I don't want to hurt that family anymore."

"The man is guilty. So is his wife. How can you let them go?"

"It isn't that simple."

"Yes, it is."

"No. Don't you see, by penalizing Dougal, you're hurting the squire? He doesn't deserve any more pain."

"What of you? You're in pain as well."

"I'll heal."

"Forgive me if I don't agree with you." Colin clicked his tongue and lifted the reins. He stared at the road as the gig started forward.

She examined his profile. A muscle in his jaw twitched.

"You still plan to marry Hobblesby?"

She was taken aback. "No. We decided a marriage would be a mistake."

"So what will you do?"

She closed her eyes. *Love you.* "I don't know. I suppose I can look for a position as a governess or a companion. There must be someone who would like to hire the daughter of an earl." She gave him a weak smile.

"Marry me."

"Pardon?"

"Marry me. I can help your family."

Her heart hammered in her breast. "I don't even know what you do. I know you're not a secretary."

"I solve problems, and I'm very good at it. Marry me."

"Is this how you will solve my problem?"

"You're not a problem. I want to marry you." He laughed. "Can you imagine the look on my father's face when I tell him I'm to marry the daughter of an earl?"

She froze. "Why should that matter?"

"Because I shall enjoy rebuffing his efforts to ingratiate himself to you."

Skettle Cottage came into view. "When do you leave?" she asked without looking at him.

"As soon as possible. Today if I can." He stopped the gig. He climbed down and came to her side of the rig. "I'll come back in a week or two to speak with your mother and fetch you."

She accepted his help from the vehicle, then faced him. "There's no need for you to return."

"Yes, there is. If we're to marry."

"Precisely. I've already entered into one betrothal to a man who wanted to marry me to improve his status. I have no desire to do so again. Good day to you, Mr. Savernake." She turned toward the house before her tears betrayed her.

"Anthea?" As he ran after her, Lady Fortesque came out of the house.

"Oh, Mother," cried Anthea and flung herself in her mother's arms.

"Anthea," said Savernake.

"Make him go away, Mother." Anthea lifted her gaze to her mother. "Please."

"Go inside, Thea." After Anthea dashed inside, Lady Fortesque faced Savernake. "Mr. Savernake, my daughter needs her rest. Good day."

"But I—"

"Good day, Mr. Savernake." Lady Fortesque pivoted and left him gaping on the front steps.

Savernake ran his hand through his hair. What the hell just happened? She had spurned him because she was the daughter of an earl. Anger boiled within him—anger at Dougal, Hobblesby, his father. But mostly at Anthea.

Without a backward glance, he climbed into the gig and drove away. He had to leave this place before he lost any more of his sanity.

Chapter 30

Two weeks had passed since Colin had left, and she didn't think the hurt would ever go away. Oh, her bruises had healed, but she didn't know if her heart ever would. Anthea lay on her back in the field behind Skettle Cottage and stared into the blue sky. She wondered if he ever thought about her. God knew she thought about him all the time.

"Thea, you're not listening." Violet frowned at her sister. "You haven't heard a word I said."

"I'm sorry, Violet. I wasn't listening."

Violet let out a puff of air in exasperation. "I know that." She flopped onto the grass beside her sister.

"What were you telling me?"

"That we finished the book."

"Congratulations."

Violet paused. "Brody asked me to marry him today."

Anthea sat up. "Oh, Violet, how wonderful." She hugged her sister.

"You don't mind?"

"Why would I mind?"

"Well, he's the squire's son, and with everything that happened . . ."

Anthea shook her head. "I'm happy for you, especially with everything that's happened."

"We'll be living at the Grange for a while. Will you come to visit me?"

"They couldn't keep me away."

"Even though Dougal lives there as well?"

"Dougal has been working to fix Skettle Cottage so that we may have a comfortable winter. If I don't mind him here, why would he bother me at the Grange?"

Violet let out a pent-up breath. "That's a relief. I thought you'd be angry with me."

"How could I be angry that you're happy?" Anthea smiled at her sister. "Have you told Mother?"

Violet nodded. "She's pleased for me."

"She never was happy that I was marrying the squire," said Anthea.

"Oh, Thea, I'm—"

"Don't you dare say you're sorry. You were never happy either. As it turned out you both were right."

"I had hoped that handsome Mr. Savernake had fallen in love with you. He certainly acted that way."

Anthea said nothing. How could she when she wished the same thing?

At the end of the field, she saw Brody. "Looks like you have a visitor, Violet."

Violet looked over and smiled. Brody made his way forward with the aid of his cane. "Are you two here? Your mother said you were."

"We're here," said Violet.

"I love a bright day. I can almost see your beautiful faces," said Brody as he sat beside Violet. He turned to Anthea. "Lady Anthea, your mother sent me to fetch you. She needs you."

With a sigh, Anthea rose from the ground and headed for the cottage. As she came into view of the house, she stopped short. A magnificent carriage stood in the drive. Two horses pawed the ground. Who could the rig belong to? Certainly no one in Middle Hutton.

"Mother," she called as she entered the cottage.

Lady Fortesque hurried to meet her. Her mother's eyes were filled with tears.

"What's wrong?"

"Nothing, dear." Lady Fortesque wiped her eyes. "You have a visitor."

Anthea looked at her mother askance, but proceeded to the parlor. She stopped short in the doorway. Flowers of every hue filled the room. She spun around in astonishment. Blooms covered every available space, and some even stood on the floor.

"What is this?" she whispered.

"My weak attempt to apologize for how stupid I've been." Colin stepped forward from the corner of the room.

"Colin?" She took a step toward him, then hesitated. "Why are you here?"

He closed the gap between them. "To tell you how sorry I am. I should never have left without telling you how much I love you."

"You love me?"

"Yes." He kissed her. "I love you. I've fallen in love with the daughter of an earl."

She stared at him.

He took her hands. "And I would love her if she were a scullery maid or the queen herself."

She let out a little sob.

"I was an idiot. I thought you didn't want me because of my heritage."

"Never," she whispered.

"Hush." He placed his finger on her lips. "I know

that now. I knew that then, but I was too prideful to see. Iris helped me."

"Iris?"

"Violet's not the only writer in the family. Iris wrote me a scathing letter, calling me a coward and a dishonest cur for breaking my word."

"Your word?" The tears swimming in her eyes made her vision blurry.

"I told her I would marry you. Her letter made me realize just how cowardly I was. I was afraid you didn't think me good enough for you. You were right. I'm not good enough for you." He sank to one knee. "You are a far superior woman than I deserve."

She fell to her knees and cupped his face in her hands. The tears spilled over her lids now. "No."

He laughed and kissed away a drop, catching another on his thumb. "But you are. You've taught me things I should have learned years ago. You are my superior, and I want you by my side to teach me for my entire life.

"When I reached my resolve, I went to see my father. I wanted to throw my success in his face. But for the first time I didn't see him as the earl; I saw him as a man. An old man now, but nothing more than a man. As he waited for me to speak, I no longer had the urge to show him up. In fact, I even felt the stirrings of gratitude for him. He didn't have to take me in, but he did. He didn't have to educate me, but he did. I'm not saying I've forgiven him or his family, but I no longer felt the anger.

"You taught me this. Your love is so great you would have sacrificed your own happiness to help your family. I want my children to know such love. I want to know such love. Teach me to love."

"Oh, Colin." She kissed him then, and he responded with all the love he had proclaimed.

"You two can get up off the floor now."

They broke apart and looked toward the doorway. Iris stood there with a wide grin on her face, as did Violet, Brody, and Lady Fortesque and the twins.

Colin laughed. "So much for a private moment." He stood and helped Anthea to her feet.

"You said you wanted to know what family was like," said Iris.

"But I still have a question," said Anthea. "Whose carriage is outside?"

"Mine. I told you I wasn't a secretary. I have money. Lots of money. And I can think of no better way to spend it than on you and your family."

Anthea shook her head. "I think it will take some getting used to . . . having money again."

"Let me help you." Colin pulled out a long, flat box. He opened it. Her medallion lay on velvet, no longer tied to a ribbon, but hanging from a filigreed chain from which sparkled amethysts.

"You had my medallion?"

He glanced at her mother. "Fletcher found it the morning after your attack." As he leaned forward to fasten the chain around her neck, he whispered, "In my bed."

Heat blossomed in her cheeks.

"What did he say to you?" asked Iris.

"Only that I have a special license, and I don't want to wait to marry her." Colin turned to Violet and Brody. "You'll forgive us for beating you to the church?"

"Of course," said Brody.

"You're getting married, too?" Iris asked. She turned

to her mother. "Does this mean I'm next? Mother, I'm not ready."

Lady Fortesque laughed. "No rush, my dear. I'm not willing to lose all my girls at once."

"I'm never getting married," said Rose.

"Me, neither. Boys are too silly," said Daisy.

Colin crossed to Lady Fortesque. "I inherited a farm near Chester. It's more of an estate really. The house is rather large, and my work keeps me in London most of the time. I would like to offer it to you as your home. For you and the girls, and Brody and Violet as well if they wish."

"Oh, my," said Lady Fortesque.

"Anthea and I will visit often. I've discovered I like the country life." He returned to her side. "So what say you, Anthea? Will you marry me?"

Anthea smiled through her tears. "Yes."

A cheer rose from the onlookers.

"I expect it's unanimous," said Anthea.

"And now, children," said Lady Fortesque, "let's leave Mr. Savernake and Anthea alone."

"But, Mother, we want to watch them kiss again," said Rose.

"Now," said Lady Fortesque. She took both twins by the hand and pulled them away from the door.

"You know I can't see anything anyway," said Brody. "I don't see why I should have to leave."

Violet giggled and whispered something in his ear.

"On second thought, I have more important things waiting for me." He took Violet's arm, and they left.

"And I interrupted a good book because of this commotion." Iris smiled at them. "Does the new house have a library?"

"It does, but its collection has been woefully neglected. I'm afraid I'll need your help in filling its shelves," said Colin.

Iris grinned. "I knew I liked you." She disappeared from the doorway.

Colin turned Anthea toward him. "You forgive me?" asked Colin.

"I'm long past the forgiveness stage." She gazed up at him. The elation she felt threatened to burst from her. She didn't know whether to laugh or cry.

His arms slid round her and pulled her to him. Her upturned face waited for his kiss, and he didn't disappoint. His lips claimed hers. No fear of discovery came with this kiss, no lingering guilt spoiled the headiness that caroused in her body. She took what he offered and mirrored back every joyous emotion.

"I love you," he said a long moment later.

She didn't think she would ever tire of hearing those words. "Even if I am the daughter of an earl?"

"Then we are the perfect match, for I am the son of an earl."

Epilogue

London, three weeks later

"A letter has arrived for us," said Anthea.

"Another job?"

"No, it's addressed to both of us. From Lord Stanhope." She wrinkled her brow. "I thought he was dead."

"He is." Colin took the letter from her and broke open the seal. "Come sit beside me."

He opened the sheet as they settled on the settee together.

Dear Colin and Anthea,

"But I didn't know Lord Stanhope really. Why would he write to me?" asked Anthea.

If you are reading this, then my task is complete. Colin, as I watched you grow at your father's estate, I knew I wanted to help you in a way your father never would. When I met Lady Anthea, I had found my means. She is truly a gentlewoman, but with enough fire to stand up to any man, even you, Colin.

Colin laughed. "I never knew Stanhope had paid any attention to me."

"Or me."

Fletcher and Pennyfeather worked for me. I paid off the former housekeeper to make sure there would be a position for my spies. Their job was less to help you solve the squire's problem than to bring the two of you together so you might find each other. Since you're reading this, they succeeded. If I were alive, I'd give them the bonus they deserve. As it is, I left them plenty of money to enjoy themselves. I'm sure they're off somewhere enjoying another adventure by now.

As for the two of you, remember nothing is more valuable than the love you feel for each other. Not a label, not a title, not a name. Everybody has a name. Not everyone has love. Names are not important. It's the person who's important.

"Wise man," said Anthea.

"I wish I could have known him better."

Enjoy your lives, my young friends, and I hope you will never forget my small role in bringing about your happiness. May love be yours always.

Yours in eternity,

Lord Stanhope.

For a moment neither spoke.

"I can't believe a man would take the time to arrange such things." Colin looked at the sheet of paper.

"He must have been remarkable." Anthea wiped a tear from her cheek.

"He certainly had remarkable servants. Fletcher and Pennyfeather were almost too good to be true." Colin paused.

"And Fletcher has such a strange appearance . . ." Anthea looked at Colin. "You don't suppose they weren't real."

"As in not saying who they really are?"

She nodded.

"Quite possible, I would say. I think we may have found our next assignment."

In the next moment Colin's butler entered the room. "Pardon me, sir. This just arrived for you. It's marked urgent."

Colin handed Stanhope's letter to Anthea and broke open the seal on the newest missive. He scanned the contents. "I'm afraid Fletcher and Pennyfeather will have to wait. This is from the prime minister."

Anthea nodded as her husband moved to his desk and began taking notes. She folded Stanhope's letter and slipped it into her pocket. "Thank you, Lord Stanhope," she whispered. Then she moved to her husband's side. "Right, what do we need to do?"

ABOUT THE AUTHOR

Gabriella Anderson makes her home in Albuquerque, New Mexico, with her husband, three daughters, and assorted animals. When she's not writing romance, she volunteers at her daughters' school library, plays volleyball, and tries to avoid cooking and housekeeping. She holds a master's degree in teaching German and German literature, and she's even appeared on *Jeopardy!* and *The Family Feud*. Fluent in English, Hungarian, and German, as well as knowing Latin, Gabriella loves the way language works, especially when she can use it to put a story on paper.

You can reach her at P.O. Box 20958, Albuquerque, NM 87154-0958 or through her web site at www.gabianderson.com.